Anonymous

The Loyalist's Daughter

Or, tale of the revolution. A novel. Part 3

Anonymous

The Loyalist's Daughter
Or, tale of the revolution. A novel. Part 3

ISBN/EAN: 9783337051679

Printed in Europe, USA, Canada, Australia, Japan

Cover: Foto ©Andreas Hilbeck / pixelio.de

More available books at **www.hansebooks.com**

THE

LOYALIST'S DAUGHTER

A Novel

OR

TALE OF THE REVOLUTION

BY

A ROYALIST.

IN FOUR VOLUMES.

VOL. III.

LONDON:

ADAMS & FRANCIS, 59, FLEET STREET, E.C.

1867.

J. SWIFT, Regent Press, 55, King Street, Regent Street, W.

THE LOYALIST'S DAUGHTER.

CHAPTER XXXIII.

Yet was there light around her brow,
A holiness in those dark eyes,
Which show'd—though wandering earthward now,—
Her spirit's home was in the skies.—*Moore.*

Such was this daughter of the southern seas.—*Byron.*

THE action of our tale has necessarily been so closely compressed within such a very . short period—not more than about ten days—that we have so far been able to notice the most remarkable of the particulars crowded into each day as it passed. For the future, however, as the narrative extends over months and years, we must pass over with a general statement circumstances which do not immediately involve the persons in whom the reader is the most interested.

To the general reader, history divested of

ornament or fiction is a wearisome if not an
unwelcome thing. It becomes the more agreeable and entertaining the more deeply and the
more mysteriously we connect it with the adventures, the perils, the escapes, and the destiny
of the romantic beings whose fortunes it delights
us to follow and for the time to make our own.
While, therefore, the true history of real life
with which they are associated asserts its dignity
above the realms of fiction, our hero and heroine
and their intimate friends or foes have a more
constant claim on our attention ; and yet they
must not seduce us into that wild region of
imagination which lies beyond the precincts of
probability and truth.

The fugitive queen whom we left, after her
rough and boisterous voyage, on the 11th
December at Calais, had endured the most
heart-rending agonies and fears for the fate of
her royal husband, before any tidings of his real
situation reached her. One courier reported
that his Majesty had landed at Brest ; another
at Boulogne ; a third, that he had been arrested
in England ; a fourth kind comforter announced
for certain that the vessel in which the king was
embarked had foundered in a terrible storm,
that his Majesty with all on board had perished.

Scarcely had two days of anxious suspense
worn away, when Mary Beatrice, in the hope of
hearing something more certain, left Calais for
Boulogne, where, declining many honours,

she retired to a nunnery. Here the queen took up her retreat in weeping and woe, and would not be comforted in her affliction for her husband, whom she passionately loved. Even Louis XIV. declared he knew not what to think of the destiny of James. The pause of suspense was at length broken ; Sir Roger Strickland, the Vice-Admiral of England, arrived at Calais and made known there all which we have recorded in our last two chapters with immediate reference to James. Strickland was, among the faithless, faithful. Finding that Dartmouth would do nothing to redeem his first admission of the Dutch fleet, Sir Roger asked and obtained leave to retire from the fleet at Portsmouth, and immediately repaired in a little vessel to Calais. The painful intelligence he brought was, however, withheld from the queen by her nearest friends ; but in mercy to that suspense which is worse than the event of the calamity which we dread, a Benedictine monk, a Capuchin, also an officer who had just escaped, yielded to her affectionate importunity for intelligence.

" Sacred Majesty," replied they, in tones of deep sorrow, mingled with respect, "the king has been arrested."

The effect which these sad tidings produced on the queen exceeds description. " I will die with him," cried she, in the first terrible burst of her grief, " I will share his fate in the dark dungeon, or on the sad scaffold of his father.

The infant prince I will send to Paris. If there be a loyal heart that has not bowed down to the usurper to it I will appeal."

Her heart towards James was not more altered than her fortunes. He was in danger, and that was enough. Her faithful servants had the greatest trouble and evinced the greatest tact and address to dissuade her from her desperate project. They appealed to her understanding,—to her heart. They reminded her that her very attempt to rejoin him would only double the danger and aggravate the sorrows which she would alleviate. She could only defeat her own object, and involve both in miseries from which no power on earth could extricate either. But her settled grief was too deep in the heart to heed such remonstrance. She would not desist from her passionate purpose until Lady Strickland first suppliantly besought the queen, because she was a queen, but still more boldly appealed to her as a woman. " Your Majesty, madam," said the loyal governess, " would not surely bring upon your royal husband all those calamities which your heart desires to avert. You can render him no service but one."

" What is that?" meekly asked the poor queen.

" Simply, my beloved sovereign," said Lady Strickland, " to obey your loyal and loving husband ; to be implicitly guided by his last—his parting directions."

The queen could only murmur, " Strickland, you are right; I will be ruled by him."

To compose the queen, and to convey her beyond the possibility of returning to England, her attendants seconded Louis's arrangements for her advance to Paris. He had commanded that her royal progress should be attended by the same honours as if she had been a Queen of France. In the meantime a snow storm had covered the country, and shrouded whole villages in one vast white winding-sheet. The roads were filled up to the depth of several feet, leaving no trace of guidance or outline of the way, but throwing the snow veil over the plain and scanty woodlands, and confusing the whole landscape into one boundless field of dazzling white, only varied by the fantastic forms which the snow drifts assumed along the trackless, viewless waste. Hanging terraces, crowned by edifices of snow like white marble ; graceful slopes, enchanted grottoes. Beneath the gemmed canopy of apple trees, festooned in glowing tracery, the columned aisle, the side chapel, and even the altar draped in purest white, appeared to the eye of Fancy. Here were beautiful alcoves and mysterious labyrinths and swelling amphitheatres. The branches of such trees as appeared above the trackless wilderness were hung with wreaths, spangled with all the delicate rosy hues with which the noon-day sun began to tinge them in a silver filagree sparkling at the touch of light which trembled on each spray and shed a pleasing influence on every object. Nature's voice was still, but her handy work had left its most exquisite devices and fairest tracery, wrought in white garlands, which marked the queen's progress as a triumph celebrated by Nature. The snow storm had spread a mantle over the sad nakedness of the land through which she was to pass. Unsullied and spotless as that driven snow was her chastity, which, as a lily, among her other virtues, had bloomed amid the impurities of a dissolute court. This it was which supplied the freshness of her youth and brought to her countenance the maiden blush of the delicate rose. The love of God's beautiful works had never been defaced from her heart by artifice or crime. That rare charm, which, amid the wonders of the Creator, carries us out of ourselves and our sorrows to the true source of happiness and unfading delights, we may easily suppose, lightened her winter-day journey. These beauties so magnificently spread in her way by God, retarded not her progress. To the imagination of a child of Italy would they be as an illuminated MS. to divert her and invite her thoughts to outward things.

The King of France sent a band of pioneers to precede the Queen of England's carriages, to clear the road for her passage, and to mark out her way; making the rough places smooth and the crooked ways straight, and levelling all before her, so that she might be able to travel with the greatest convenience and the least fatigue. Her ladies felt and valued this gallant devotion of Louis to his royal visitor, and they were agreeably entertained at the novelty of the proceeding.

The Duke d'Aumont and a cavalcade of gentlemen escorted her Majesty from Boulogne, till within three leagues of Montreuil, where Mary Beatrice slept in a house of the King of France, on the night of the twentieth of December, and she arrived at Pois on the following Sunday. She there and then was apprised that Louis XIV. had assigned for her residence the stately palace of St. Germains. On her way through Beauvais, the bishop and all the principal people of the town came out to meet and welcome her. Indeed, similar honours had greeted her in all the places through which she passed. Here she heard that the king had left London. In the afternoon of December twenty-eighth the queen drew near St. Germains. Louis came in great pomp to meet and welcome her, with his son the Dauphin, Monsieur, his brother, all the princes of the blood, and the officers of his household; his cavalcade consisted of a hundred coaches-and-six. He awaited the approach of the fair fugitive at Chalon—a picturesque village on the banks of the Seine, below the heights of St. Germains-en-Laye.

At the appearance of the cortège, Louis, with

his son and brother, descended from his coach,
and advanced to greet the queen, having first
sent his officer of state to stop her carriage.
But to his surprise he found himself addressing
Lady Strickland as his royal sister of England.
When he discovered his mistake he transferred
his endearments from the governess to the
governed—the Prince of Wales. Lady Strickland and the nurse, with her royal charge,
alighted to pay their homage to his most
Christian Majesty. The queen in the meantime
alighting from her coach, was hastening to meet
him, when he advanced towards her with the
prince in his arms ; he had kissed, and greeted,
and tenderly embraced the royal infant, and had
made him a most gracious speech, prophetic of
his destinies as James III. of England, when
his attention was drawn to the queen.

"Never was there child of my own," cried
the Grand Monarch, "whom I so admired."
Again and again he lavished the most endearing
caresses upon the babe, and covered him with
kisses.

The king's manner and spirit were younger
than his age. The wonted haughtiness that sat
throned upon his brow was softened into smiles.
He still seemed to retain all the energy of
manhood, only strengthened by the even per-
manence of advanced age. He could not,
however, conceal from himself or his royal
visitor the fear, that the affairs of James were

irretrievable. He had not finished all his bright promises of protection, of nurture and aid to the unconscious babe whom he still held in his arms, when the queen stood before him in all the raptures of a grateful mother. She made the most grateful acknowledgments for the great monarch's sympathy and generosity, both for herself, the king, and the infant prince, who was now returned to his less august, but more skilful nurse.

"It is, indeed, Madame, but a melancholy pleasure you permit me to enjoy in rendering you this service under present circumstances ; but the time is at hand when my efforts to aid the king of England will, I trust, be as effectual as they are at this moment sincere," said the king. He presented the Dauphin and Monsieur to the queen in due form, then led her to her own coach, where he placed her at his right hand. The Dauphin and Monsieur sat opposite to their Majesties. In regal pomp the exiled queen was conducted by the Grand Monarque to the splendid palace of St. Germains, which was to be her future home. The Marchioness of Powis and the Signora Anna Vittoria Montecuculi, the Italian whom she loved, and in whose company she took delight, attended her.

"Sire," cried she, smiling through her tears, as the party ascended the lofty hill on which the château is seated, "here I shall meet my beloved consort again."

Anticipating her wishes, Louis led her at once by the hand to the apartment prepared in royal magnificence for the Prince of Wales. The nursery and suite, in fact, newly fitted up for this grand occasion, had been appropriated to the children of France. Here the king took leave of her Majesty. She had a moment for reflection. A vain vision of green and sunny sights passed before her eyes, while her spirit held communion with the deeper and darker thoughts of her own heart. From memory, the teeming treasure house of her pains and pleasures,—memory, whose office differs from the bright promises of hope,—memory, the mansion of reality—she drew things new and old : the memory of her joy was sorrow.

The clouded sky coming down in night over the château, the cheerless aspect of all outside, the bare and leafless trees, all bespoke the sad close of the year, and the dark evening of exile. At best, all, even the splendours of the palace at such a time, were darkly contrasted with the images of the far away land of her birth. The queen amid the borrowed splendours of a munificent benefactor was a way-worn and afflicted woman, really destitute of a country and a home.

The unquenchable spirit of the woman lighted up her eyes, which beamed through the big tears that came to her relief. Sorrow and regret had not yet profaned the fair beauty of her face y their furrows. The inward feeling of her heart, however, was that she was isolated, and, in the absence of her husband, as completely cut off from the world without as if the château had been a deserted island, and all around, whether animal or vegetable, as the waters of an illimitable sea.

The fond mother bent over her babe, now reposing beneath the richly spangled canopy studded with red and gold stars, which delighted his eye ; she thanked the King Eternal for His mercy and His love. In that little boy she saw through the vista of years the king of three crowns —the unbroken dynasty of the Stuarts ; but more dear to her heart there lay in health and safety her own dear son. To her he was truly the sweet young flower of promise and of prayer, growing out of the grave of her hopes,—that fertile grave which she had watered with her tears.

The apartments of the queen were only inferior to those of Versailles. Riches and art, and even genius, had combined to make this house of residence and its furniture as comfortable as they were sumptuous. Far less curious in such elegant specimens of the king's upholstery than her usurping successor, Mary was covetous of the beautiful cabinet and treasures which our fugitive had left behind : in her heart there was no room for such splendid toys, for them she had not a single thought.

After passing an hour with her ladies, whom she treated as sisters, talking of the past and the future, without much reference to the present, she retired to rest for the night.

Mary awoke the next morning to a sense of her royal benefactor's munificence, which had prepared for her a splendid palace and a royal household; but that liberality which is wedded to charity had not, as it appeared to Mary Beatrice, supplied her actual necessities. With this impression, she joined her ladies at breakfast, wishing humourously with them, that Louis had acted more like that Caliph, who threw large handfuls of money to his friends, saying, "These are my posterity." No dauphin, no child of France could at this crisis have been more welcome to the queen and her loyal ladies, than such golden descendants. Amid the regions of romance, valuable current coins are as thick as blackberries. A hundred gold pieces seem to grow on every branch of every tree. Every hero, or his loved one, as the case may demand, has a purse as full as his heart to fling to his gaoler or his deliverer. The queen, in her splendid reality, could not have been a heroine, for she had not the magic purses to fling at friend or foe.

That true greatness which never forsakes the high-minded and the noble, is ever serene and often sublime. Now clothed it was, in a vesture of amiable courtesy, and filled the little party with more mirth than apprehension. Each had some playful resource or lucrative invention.

Many and varied were the plans for meeting the unanticipated difficulty; but on one point all were unanimous,—that money was indispensable.

"At last," said the queen, "we shall be able without any difficulty to keep the oath of the Carthusians, which never suffers them to carry any money about with them."

Just as the assembly had come to the practical decision to throw their richest jewels into the royal treasury, and thus to realise the household exchequer, the rapid roll of wheels was heard; the next moment the ample doors flew open and Mrs. Plowden and her children were announced.

"God be thanked, here they are!" cried the queen, and embraced them as friends. As for Mary Plowden, she numbered her among her choicest Marys, and took her to her arms as her own sister. A faint blush overspread the face of the fair girl. To the rush of anxious questions poured out by the queen, Mr. Plowden's answers were regulated by his sense of delicacy, and his regard to the queen's feelings, which were terribly disappointed, evidently not by the arrival of the Plowdens, but by the absence of the king, for whose arrival she had mistaken their entrance.

After the first general greetings, inquiries and answers, falling down at the feet of her Majesty, who raised her affectionately to her arms, Mary

Plowden, as if unconscious of the presence of her whom she addressed, in an ecstasy of loyalty and joy, gave way to a flood of tears, exchanging mutual endearments and caresses with her beloved sovereign ; then looking inquiringly into her face, asked her, " Where is my brother, my friend, my dear comrade, whom I must ever recognise as my preserver and my guardian angel ?"

" He is not here, but is where duty calls him, and therefore happy," was the reply.

In London, the grand centre and attraction of intrigues, all the personages now assembled round the queen had met, and were by no means ignorant of the schemes of Lord Spenser. The attractive beauty of Mary Plowden, her brilliant prospects at court, and the great wealth to which she was to succeed at the death of her uncle, the minister of finance, pointed her out as a suitable, or, in other words, an affluent match to repair the wasted fortunes of Lord Sunderland's dissipated son, who at first flattered himself that he could negotiate an alliance so highly conducive to his interests, and so likely to restore him to society. His great chance, he thought, was to take advantage of the unsuspicious disposition of the queen and the unrestrained choice of the young lady. Late circumstances, however, had not only taught the noble profligate his incapacity for such an achievement, but practically convinced him that her friends deemed him altogether unworthy of her affections and her hand. Indeed, she had avoided him ; she loathed and rejected him with scorn ; yet his own self-love, or his innate sense of her noble bearing, would not suffer him to believe that the indignity put upon him, and the chastisement which he suffered at London Bridge, were inflicted by the fair hand which he sought.

In perfect justice to his character, to possess the lovely girl he had recourse to the unmanly stratagem of which the reader is already aware, and which was so signally defeated by the pro-digious prowess and valour of Cornet Strickland. At the touching recital of the agonizing fears and cruel perils which she had endured as a captive at the hands of the ruffian hirelings, the queen was deeply moved. Her sympathy was only exceeded by her indignation against the miscreant, who not only disgraced nobility, but dishonoured human nature. At the same time the queen was delighted with the exploits of her former page.

"That youth," cried she, with unwonted energy, " is every inch a Strickland, a worthy scion of a noble house,—as loyal," added she, looking at Lady Strickland (his aunt), "as he is brave, and as brave as he is faithful. His mission," continued her Majesty, anticipating the inquiry which Mary longed to make, "which deprives us of his attendance, I am sure justifies the confidence placed in his judgment, his tact, and his faithfulness, by his sovereign."

At this unreserved eulogium of her lover, Mary Plowden changed colour—turned pale. Again her cheek was flushed with a deeper tint than it usually wore; and in her eye, in all her features, the tender and hallowed nature of her love seemed to have stamped the beautiful impression of itself. In addition to what has already come before the reader, it appeared from what the fair maiden could recall, that so far as their disguises and her own hurried and confused observation could allow her to judge, that none of her captors corresponded with the proportions and height of Spenser; so it was not the instigator or the designer, but his bravoes, commanded by a Dutchman, who seized upon her horse and secured her to her saddle.

It was during her visit to Lady Winchelsea, that, taking a ride on her favourite jennet along the bridle-way of a secluded and sequestered wood in Kent, she was surprised and made prisoner in the absence of her groom, whom one of the villains, who lay in ambush for her, secured and bound to a tree.

The soldiers, with a mock courtesy, presented her with a paper, purporting to be a warrant from King William, as they called the Prince of Orange, in whose name they claimed her for his ward; in order to secure to the Crown the estates to which she was likely to succeed, or, in the event of her adherence to her royal exiled mistress to confiscate her property, and treat her as an outlaw. They fastened her to her saddle, demanding of her silence, as she valued her life. They assured her that their lord and employer—her true friend and future protector— would receive her in London, whither they were hastening. Nothing further, save the image of Strickland, could she distinctly recollect. The scene in the old church, and all which followed before her recovery, appeared to her but the vague dream of a dream.

Mrs. Plowden, glad to divert the queen's sad thoughts and inquiries from herself and the king, told all the rest. It further appeared that the family of the Plowdens, themselves, after their reunion, were the very first to relieve the anxiety of Lord and Lady Winchelsea, at whose mansion they rested before their embarkation for France. The groom had evidently been unhorsed, if not slain, for his riderless horse returned to the stables at the close of that dreadful day, which witnessed the victory of Strickland and the death of the wretches who sold themselves for money. The thoughts of her lover's bravery, and the assurance of free- dom and safety, spread a glow over Mary's cheek, sparkled in her eye, and thus told her joy at every allusion to the young soldier's bravery.

"But how did the groom escape?" asked the

queen, whose kindness descended to the most
humble of her servants.

Mrs. Plowden replied, " By his own imperfect
and incoherent account, explained by that of
the old widow, in whose cottage Lady Winchelsea, in her last search for Mary Plowden,
discovered him, her ladyship's most painful
alarms were aroused. The old woman had been
gathering dried sticks for her lonely hearth,
when to her horror she beheld the figure of a
man, booted and spurred, helplessly bound with
strong cords to a neighbouring tree. His faint
cry, for he was numbed with cold and half
famished, pierced the poor woman's heart; she
learnt from his exclamations that he was a
Catholic, and fear of the insurgents made her
hesitate about releasing him; at length she cut
the bonds with her bill, and gave the sufferer
refuge in her secluded cottage."

" She must have been a loyalist, if not a
Catholic," said the queen.

" No, may it please your Majesty. She had
lived under Oxendon, in principle a recusant
and a rebel. But she saw the poor man's
danger," said Mrs. Plowden; " saw in him a
fellow creature in deep distress, and forgot what
he was. She dressed his wounds, allowed him
to gain warmth upon her own bed, and actually
concealed him from a party of the insurgents,
who seemed to be seeking for him. She supplied him with food, and sheltered him till

Lord and Lady Winchelsea themselves found him, amid the solitude of the woods, in his place of refuge, and removed him into their household."

" It was noble in the poor widow," cried the ladies.

" But can a fanatic woman and a disloyal subject," asked her Majesty, "be capable of such generosity ?"

" Not only so," replied Mrs. Plowden, " but while two cavaliers, at least wavering loyalists, passed by on the other side, riding for their lives as recreant knights, the dear good creature risked her own safety and rescued the man from his dreadful fate."

" Had she not received some kindness at the hands of the king's troops ?" asked Lady Strickland.

" One of her sons, I believe, died by the hand of our young hero of the Guards who delivered my daughter," was Mrs. Plowden's quiet reply. " The poor woman's husband had been shot within these two months by a party of our corps, soon after the landing of William ; and two of her surviving sons, according to her statement to Lord Winchelsea, are probably at this very moment with the insurgents near Sittingbourne."

" I trust such generosity, wherever it may be found, will be rewarded," said the queen, feelingly ; " but we are running up an arrear of

c 2

obligation on all sides; when, however, we can attain the means of showing our gratitude, it shall not be wanting."

To escape from a conversation, in which, as the lover and the loved, she was the unavoidable subject, Miss Plowden had made her retreat unobserved by the party. Her maid attended her, and, true to her vocation, evinced as much curiosity to know as desire to communicate a hundred things which struggled for vent. She, too, had heard about the groom;—then her own adventures at Faversham. " A friend in need, Miss, is a friend in deed; but I'll tell you what it is, my dear young lady, a friend on each side is better still; then, when our enemies are too many for us, and when ' discretion is the better part of valour,'—"

" Yes; but, Kate," interrupted the lady, " silence is the better part of discretion."

" But, dear, dear Miss Mary, besought the maid, " let me speak, or, after all my eyes have seen and my ears heard, I shall die." She ran on, " Well, when I reached these sailor fellows, and made my duty to his sacred Majesty at Faversham, Ben Brown—oh! such a strong likely chap !—stood well with Whigs and Tories, with Protestants and Papists, as he said. This was how he did the agreeable to both, and got me out of the row."

To change the subject, and to comply with the rule of the court, Miss Plowden returned to

the queen, to crave leave of her Majesty to
dispense with her attendance for a short time.
Of all present perhaps she was the most thoughtful, and even dejected, not excepting the queen
and the oldest of her adherents.

Let not those who are middle-aged or old
speak lightly of the sorrows of youth. Let us
not suppose it can have but few griefs. The
troubles of young people are many and severe,
though transient. It is natural for us, experienced in human difficulties and weighed down
with many burdens and parental charges, to
compare our trials with those of our juniors.
Self-love, rather than philosophy, contrasts un-
favourably our hard lot with the flowery hours
of life's morning. Experience in the world
chills the heart, and deadens its most generous
sympathies, and narrows its purest affections.
Our growth in age too often ripens into selfishness. Hence it is that the old and the seasoned
think so little of the calamities of the young and
so feelingly of their own. Adversity wears
many shapes, and those ideal sufferings in which
it appears to the sensitive minds of youth, are
the most terrible of its forms, though unseen by
the cold eye of disenchanted old age.

The queen, though old in vicissitudes and
reverses, was still young in spirit and in her
converse with the young nobility, who ministered
to her pleasures or her wants. She perceived
that her favourite was unsettled and sorrowful;

she therefore was but too glad to accede to the
dear girl's request. "Mignonne Mary," said
she, "you must explore our new regions,
examine the richly furnished apartments of our
French palace." The queen delighted to give
any commission which could interest or amuse
the fair being, whose bright morning was already
obscured in the dark destiny of the royal family,
bade the young lady pass through the splendid
saloons, and make some observations on the
glittering ornaments—the tapestry—the carving,
pictures, &c., directing her attention particularly
to the exquisite taste and munificence which had
been so royally displayed in the elegant arrangement of her dressing-room and boudoir, but
especially her toilet table, and the splendid toilet
service that invited her acceptance. "Now I
think of it," said her Majesty, playfully, "there
is in the drawer of the table a casket of ebony
richly inlaid with gold and silver, of most curious
workmanship, which I am sure you will admire.
I rememember M. Tourolle, the upholsterer of
our royal benefactor, presented it to me, and of
which I have the key. It seemed to court our
acceptance and demand our thanks yesterday ;
but weightier matters left no room in our
thoughts for such a toy. Allez ! ma petite
Marie."

    In a moment Miss Plowden was fairly em-
barked on her voyage, and rejoined by her fille
de chambre, who tripped along in raptures at the

sumptuous splendour of the palace. She had for some time remained in silent admiration, but ventured at last, in her extravagant delight, to offer her opinion, and to compare all around her to the magnificence of Whitehall. " With your ladyship's pardon, Miss Mary, we might do very well here, if Master Strickland—I mean the young officer of the Life Guards—was here to ride out with you. Ah ! Miss, the country is like Richmond, or even more beautiful. Soldiers and sailors are the only men I have lately seen. When his Majesty comes over, Ben Brown said he'd like to be one of the crew."

" Hush ! Kate," cried the lady, as she preceded her attendant into the royal nursery and suite of apartments fitted up for the Prince of Wales. " Look here, Kate," pointing to the corner of a spacious and noble chamber, elaborately carved and gilded, curtained with crimson velvet, and furnished with rich couches and ottomans.

In this recess, to which the girl's eye was directed, stood the royal cot adorned with hangings of crimson and gold, depending from a canopy of the same materials. In this state cot lay the sleeping prince, in whom a thousand fears and hopes were centred. The unconscious object of all this pomp was watched by his lady nurses. As if by some irresistible impulse the girl, who had been left alone with the queen soon after the birth of this royal child, rushed to the cradle, and was about to smother him with kisses, when the nurse, shocked and alarmed, cried out, "Lady Strickland! Oh! my lady." These magic words were enough; the maid was scared from her affectionate purpose and desisted. The young lady exchanged glances with the now tranquil nurse, and smiling resumed her tour of the palace, until at length she found herself in the queen's private apartments. She was enchanted with the comforts, and the display of genius and of art. The result of wealth and the refinement of taste.

Charmed with everything around her, she felt a transport of gratitude and joy at the thought that her beloved mistress, though an exile, had not fallen from her high estate into poverty or contempt; forgetting, or rather not understanding, that the royal family of England were, in the midst of all this splendid dependence, simply indigent pensioners on the bounty of the King of France. Happy, thrice happy is it for woman in the day of her bitterest sorrows, that the narrow sphere of her own peculiar duties, her domestic concerns, and the many things about which she is cumbered and careful, the fair domain of her family endearments or recreations, her pressing household occupations, her ornaments, her needlework, her accomplishments, but, above all the rest, the imperative and hourly demands upon her exertions and her time occupy and absorb her.

Happy, truly happy for her is it, that these
engage her mind, absorb her being, and invite
her attention from the outside tempest, and the
storms of life, and the terrible assaults to which
the stronger sex is exposed, and which a man
sees and feels, which invade his repose, and call
him to the battle field of strife, of action, and of
mental conflict, with the errors, the passions,
and all the varied elements which oppose his
onward course.   Mary Plowden's distant future
had for a joyful moment ceased to intrude upon
the joyful present ; the delights of the queen's
pleasant palace of St. Germains was uppermost
in her thoughts.   Her only future on earth was
the prospect of meeting Strickland as devoted to
the king and as affectionate to herself as when
they both loved and lived together at Whitehall.
Her forgetfulness of the past, and momentary
disregard of the future, were the effect of this
one present and dearest dream.

In the young officer's active and glorious
career it is impossible, thought the fair girl, that
love should hold the supreme and undivided
empire it exercises on my existence, of which it
is at once the occupation, the necessity, and the
resource.   His whole soul and body, energy and
strength, must be in his labours and struggles
for the king.   The great business of his life in
Scotland can leave but little place for any one
created being.   His power over me is absolute ;
my power over him must be shared with a

thousand other mastering influences. And yet, were I the only object which could fill the heart, Robert were unworthy of my love. With these reflections she paced the ample apartments, but her reverie was soon broken by the exclamations of her attendant at the glowing decorations of solid gold, silver, rich designs, executed by the ablest hands in France; articles of vertu cast in marble, jasper, and porphyry, which shone in the queen's dressing-room, and adorned her toilet table, which reminded Mary Plowden of her commission, and from a drawer she drew the casket of rare richness and workmanship. The maid was in a flutter of delight, which winged her movements, and prompted her respectful offer to be the bearer of the beautiful souvenir of the gallant monarch. But Miss Plowden declined her service; the weight of the little shrine, however, was more than she had expected, so that she was compelled to accept the assistance she had at first declined. Returning to the saloon she gracefully and joyfully presented the object of admiration to the queen, whose secret thought, perhaps, was to turn it into money, and add the result to the general fund, of which, in the absence of Mary, much had been discussed. She applied the key which the grand upholsterer had placed in her hand the preceding evening. Her ladies crowded round her to inspect the royal gift; when lo! and behold! the lid flew open,—Mary Plowden's dark blue eyes, beaming beneath the long lashes, are fixed with an expression of watchful interest upon the queen's countenance, not on the casket. The queen raised her eyes in surprise, but could not raise her hand, which grasped the jewel within the cabinet; a sweet smile gleamed over her face, like a passing sunbeam upon delicate roses, and seemed to chequer the sad gloom of her existence.

The sense of present relief was evident in her face. "Here," said she, "is a treasure consigned to me; but it is a burden I cannot bear."

Her wise ladies answered her, "Cannot we share in the labour?"

"To each damsel separately," said the queen, "the weight is too much, but our united forces will be equal to the burden."

Miss Plowden, who was really the best judge of the weight, approached her Majesty, and, aided by Lady Almonde and Lady Powis, raised the secret deposit from its receptacle, in triumph. It was soon examined, balanced, and estimated. The result and reality were 6000 louis-d'ors.

With that kindness so peculiar to his character, Louis had designed this delicate surprise for the alleviation of the queen's distresses. This unexpected relief in their difficulties filled all present with that satisfaction which an unlooked for good fortune inspires. And here, at the close of this chapter of varieties, we must depart from the custom sanctioned by antiquity, and leave the heroine and her dearest friends and companions exempt from present peril, and extricated from every dreadful dilemma.

CHAPTER XXXIV.

Farewell, my home, my home no longer now,
Witness of many a calm and happy day ;
Farewell my home, where many a day has past
In joys whose loved remembrance long shall last.—*Southey.*

WE must now return to the king, and for a
brief space tarry with him, as with a heavy
heart and altered feelings he looks at everything through the dim sad light of his own
calamity. In this melancholy mood he spent
four days at Rochester. Here he received no
communication from William, but was visited
by many of his friends and adherents, who
brought him accounts of all that passed in the
metropolis, where his nephew had already begun
to exercise the sovereign authority.

Indeed, everything concurred to strengthen
the king's conviction, that the Prince of
Orange intended to assume the crown : and
when he compared the events of the last few
days with what he observed around him, he
was persuaded that his ambitious competitor
taking advantage of the religious and political
distractions, which he himself had fomented,

and which convulsed England, would rise to the throne by flinging himself with all the force of his powerful talents into the errors, the prejudices, and the passions of the people.

While egress from the house of his temporary residence towards the town was closed by the military posted at the front, the road from the garden to the river was left entirely unguarded. The very means of evasion thus afforded were an argument that he should *not* avail himself of the facility to withdraw from his kingdom. This inference was urged upon his Majesty forcibly by Lord Middleton in person, and by many of his most trusty servants, while others urged his flight.

Amidst the conflicting opinions, no wonder that the monarch's own resolutions were undecided ; but in his distress he repeated with the military the experiment which he had so unsuccessfully made with the aldermen, and with no better result. Still every hour the king received visits from his officers, who begged him to remain, and trust all to the fortunes of war, while others reasoned differently. The high-spirited Dundee, in the ardour of a dauntless soldier, endeavoured to revive the energy of his dejected Sovereign. "Rally your troops," cried he, "make your stand here. Summon your subjects to their allegiance."

Young O'Brian's eyes flashed fire, his nostrils dilated, his enthusiastic spirit could scarcely be

silenced. "Death or victory!" cried he ; " sure
there's not a drop of blood in our veins that we
would not shed for the Faith and for the King.
Down with the Dutch—let us drive them into
the sea. No sooner," cried the youth, looking
at the fiery viscount, " shall the royal banner be
unfurled in Scotland, than all Ireland will rise
up like one man. Oh ! for the word," cried he,
as his impatient zeal boiled over, and his hand
involuntarily grasped his sword.

Deep and heartfelt as his sorrow was for the
monarch, it was only when he thought of his
passive inactivity that our young Clare's anguish
burst its bounds. From very boyhood he had
loved and admired the king, whose manly courage
by land and sea, while Duke of York, had been
the theme of the sailor and the soldier. It was
not enough for the Irish soldier that the reverse
of fortune called up what many deemed the
noble spirit, whose courage was evinced by
resigned submission to the will of Heaven.
How cruel did the decree of Providence seem to
O'Brian ! not only that such a man should be
visited so heavily, but that his valour and decision of character, like his children, had forsaken
him when most he required their aid. Not only
so, but treachery, meanness, duplicity, and vice
prospered against him.

Clare was too young and too Irish to know
and feel that, after all, virtue has no grander attri-
bute than its powers of endurance. His mind was

deeply tinged with the tone of that faith which
has never died out, or even flickered in Ireland.
He had been taught that to sustain unmerited
afflictions with the noble dignity of a Christian
is the highest attainment of suffering humanity.
He could not, however, identify the destiny of
James in his adversity with that of the truly
good great man who bears it honourably, and
points the example of patience in suffering.

The young guardsman paced up and down the
hall with angry brow and rapid step, and in his
musings entered a little room which opened on
the lawn towards the river, and was used by the
king during his sojourn at Rochester, to receive
such of his trusty adherents and messengers as
came to him with intelligence or proffered advice.
Many a purpose had the distracted monarch
formed in that retired apartment, according to
the nature and extent of the reports to which he
there listened. They were as many, and as varied,
and as conflicting as Bossuet's " Variations,"
which came out in France about this time, the
last startling revelation always defacing the
impression of its predecessor. As young Clare
traversed the narrow space, urged to desperation
by his own deep sense of the necessity for exertion, he expected at every step to hear the
arrival of some officer, whom it was his business
to show into the king's presence. Surveying at
the same time all the dreary objects outside, he
saw the shadow of a man darkening the window,

and immediately a messenger from Turner, Bishop of Ely, was ushered into this little audience chamber, and announced as Mr. O'Brady. The fine old Irish, " O," had a charm the ear of the man who rejoiced in the same for princely prefix to his name. Clare claimed the honour of being a countryman of the new comer, though that gentleman was a friend and confidant of a Protestant prelate, for whom, after some friendly conversation with him, and an assurance that his mission was to remonstrate with the king, he gained access to his Majesty. Scarcely had O'Brady after his audience with James descended to the river, when it became Clare's duty to receive another visitor, a gentleman of grave and dignified manners, who introduced himself by the name of Belson, presenting at the same time his credentials from Lord Clarendon, and demanding admission to the king on a matter in which the highest interests, if not the life of the monarch might be deeply concerned; Clare apprised James of the important nature of the message, and of its bearer's urgent desire to see him without delay ; but soon returning, declared, with evident regret, that the king could not speak with Belson before the next morning, for that he was at supper at this time, and had many letters to write before he could retire to rest.

Belson shook his head, and said, with a sigh, " That will be too late—the morrow which never arrives ! "

VOL. III.   D

Belson was a good Catholic, and, even in the estimation of Protestants, a very discreet and honest man; one who never approved the injudicious and violent measures and counsels of Father Petre, as, in truth, did none of the sober Roman Catholics. The young Irish Catholic expressed deep sympathy in the sorrowful disappointment of Belson, who, in return, was right glad to impart to Clare such opinions as he felt at liberty to communicate.

To the Jesuit, Father Edward, brother of Lord Petre, both attributed much of the calamity which had overtaken James. His intrigues, his cabals, but, above all, his vaulting ambition which incurred the censure of his colleagues, induced the refusal of the Pope to make him a bishop or a cardinal.

"But," rejoined Clare, "the episcopal dignity is incompatible with the rules of his order."

"True," replied the other; "but the higher honour of cardinal has occasionally been conferred on members of the society. Innocent, however, was inexorable, and would not grant to James for his foolish friend either the mitre or the hat; and the unseemly promotion of the Jesuit by James to be a privy councillor, was hailed by his enemies as an event most favourable to their wishes. But by us Catholics, it was deplored as a common, even a national calamity, entailing on all the royal Stuarts an heritage of woe."

Clare's joyous, happy nature, the heirloom of his light-hearted father's house, led him to jest rather than to discuss questions. Clare's tongue and countenance wore no reserve or disguise. He was ready, dauntless, willing, active in mind and body, and even in his levity showed himself an observer, a ready contriver, with a sparkling wit which scorned imprisonment. His memory not yet overburdened, was retentive of everything he saw or heard. His confidence, his luck or his resources carried him over every obstacle,—more especially when he himself was not personally concerned, and when he had to manage the affairs of others; and under the gay garb of mirth and youth he had a secret supply of prudence. At the same time, to a severe observer he was not only rash and impetuous, but seemed to enjoy an indescribable pleasure and triumph in extricating himself from the scrapes and difficulties in which his own adventures involved him. He had been highly entertained by the importation of new fresh faces, and new thoughts which his Majesty had welcomed that evening; but with no visitor was he as much at home as he was with Belson. The king was naturally the theme of their conversation and regrets.

"He only insists in being Pope over the Church in Great Britain, and wishes all his subjects to bow to his own supremacy," said O'Brian.

"He never was right," added Belson, "since the loss of so much blood as these misfortunes have drawn from him."

"Sure 'tis only the bad dhrop that's escaped, and all the good remains," said O'Brian, "so that he will soon be as brave as he was before the puddle got into his royal veins."

"Who knows, after all," cried Belson, "whether there be not something in man's, or especially kings' nature,—some forewarning like the foreboding instinct of the creatures over which he is lord. As in birds and beasts there are sympathies with the elements which warn them of inclement weather, teaching them to fly for refuge, or even in birds of passage to take their flight from the land of coming storms, to some safer shore, so in man's nature, I think, there may be some mysterious influences of the finer elements, calling in a prophetic spirit and silently seeing some dreadful intimation of a coming trial or peril." "Or rather," rejoined the young man, "his Majesty's mind, from what I have observed, is tinged with a gloomy anticipation of his future, by the hues of outward signs and circumstances: little ominous clouds above him, figures in the fire, and trifling accidents, with which we can have no possible connexion."

"Whatever might have been the merits or demerits of the king," cried O'Brian, "the means employed by his ministers to effect their own personal objects were disgraceful; never, perhaps, was bribery practised with more glaring audacity, never did corruption display itself more glaringly in high places. The excited passions of the people were invoked by those whose duty it was to suppress them. The purchased influence of foreign courts and pensioned traitors; the miserable intrigues of men, who, in the character of patriots, became prosperous statesmen, because they had a dynasty to sell."

" Yet," retorted Belson, " that desire, which itself is an element to success, that never ceasing overmastering impulse to win the prize, hardens the heart against high feelings, which, along the even tenour of calm life, had triumphed over every selfish motive. In happier circumstances, men of truly noble and heavenly aspirations would have never stooped to acts which their calmer judgment would have scorned."

" The fact of the matter is," says O'Brian, " such a man as Halifax, for instance, is entrusted with secret negotiations, which, had he been only a third party and an uninterested observer, he would have condemned, being alike indignant with the tempter and the tempted. The rising pang of remorse is soothed by success, or lost in the victory of the man whom once it admonished to a better course."

Such was the nature of the dialogue between the young officer and the disappointed messenger, who early in the evening urged the necessity of his immediate return to London, and took his

departure, leaving our young friend only with
sad thoughts for his company, such as his conversation with Belson suggested. His destiny
seemed indissolubly associated with that of the
king. For a moment he felt that miserable
isolation of one who has no country, no field
for his enthusiasm, no legitimate and specific
object for his high daring. These reflections
and regrets, however, were soon broken by a
gentle tap at the door. Two seafaring men,
evidently prepared for rough weather, made
their appearance, and were at once, agreeably
to previous instructions, ushered by the guardsman into the royal presence. The king's natural
son, the Duke of Berwick, and Biddulph, one
of the grooms of the bedchamber, followed the
sailors without much ceremony, and were some
time closeted with the king and the sailors.
No sooner had all these departed from the house
in the direction of the river, than the Lords
Aylesbury, Litchfield, Middleton, and Dumbarton were conducted by O'Brian to the king,
who graciously released the young officer from
his post in the reception room, from which the
king had absented himself since the close of the
evening, and permitted him to join the distinguished party, who still consulted his wishes
and obeyed his commands.

" I was born free," cried his Majesty, " and
wish to continue so. I have often ventured my
life in defence of my country, and am not yet

too old to venture it again. Let me, therefore, withdraw while it is in my power. I shall still, my lords and noble adherents, be within call, whenever my deluded people shall open their eyes to their highest duty and their truest interest." He then handed a paper to Earl Middleton, on which was written more fully his sentiments and instructions ; and ordered him to publish it.

Soon after the king bade farewell to his faithful followers and retired to bed, leaving them all convinced that he was now fully confirmed in his original intention to follow his wife and son, and that nothing now could shake his resolution to take refuge in France.

About one o'clock on the morning of the 23rd, the king rose, and attended only by the Duke of Berwick, Mr. Biddulph and De Labadie, the husband of the Prince of Wales's nurse, left the house of his loyal host, Sir Richard Head, by a back stair and postern gate. It was not without a struggle on either side, that Sir Richard and the king met on that early morning for the last time ; and James took the hand of his generous host in both his own, while his frame trembled with agitation. Sir Richard's unblanched cheek, and clear steady eye, seemed to re-assure the monarch's courage, who after gazing on him steadfastly, with a look of gratitude blended with regret, said,—" I have experienced, my loyal friend, at your hands that affectionate, devoted, and delicate attention which the slander of my enemies cannot alienate or impair." Then drawing from his own finger a ring of emeralds, set round with diamonds, and placing it on that of Sir Richard, said, with deep feeling, "This is the only present an unfortunate king has to bestow; accept it as the gift of my heart. I shall never forget your courteous and respectful regard to the arrangements for my safety and comfort. In the very tide and whirl of the changes which have carried me to my capital, and driven me back again as rapidly upon Rochester; you are unchanged and undegenerated."

"Truly, my liege, the vicissitudes of life and fortune have never, never swept after each other in quicker succession than they have displayed themselves before us the last few days, like wave upon wave of the restless and turning tides of ocean. The recent pomp, the triumph, and the huzzas of welcome have only given place to the louder greetings for the invader to accept that monarch's throne. But the same honest hearts that were silent witnesses of your transient joy will ever sympathise in your sorrows, and minister to your wishes. Farewell, my liege."

The tumultuous feelings and overwhelming misfortunes, blighted hopes and strengthened fears, which distracted the monarch's mind, had one mercy for him—that stunning sense which

numbs the keen feelings so sensitively alive to
the first assaults of calamity. For a while his
unavoidable exertion, the expression of his
desires, the preparations for his flight, and the
conversation of his friends kept him awake to his
afflictions ; but now that all was settled, and
that he found himself out in the silent night, he
seemed almost unconscious of joy or sorrow.

Captain Macdonald joined the king in the
garden, who walked silently and mechanically
under his guidance to the place where Captain
Trevanion waited for him with a boat. These
two faithful officers, who were evidently the two
sailors who had had an interview with James
'the preceding evening, laboured to row his
Majesty and his comrades to the fishing smack
which had been hired for the voyage, and which
lay a little below Sheerness. The weather was
stormy, the wind and tide opposed their progress,
and after an ineffectual and dangerous attempt
to reach the boat engaged in their service, the
king and his party went on board the Eagle
fireship. The due respect and royal courtesy
with which the king was received by the ship's
company recalled his mind from its dull lethargy.
He was at home in a ship of war, and amid the
interest which he felt in the terrible works and
concealed combustible matter skilfully arranged
below, he almost forgot that he had not only
ceased to be admiral of the fleet, but that he had
abandoned the supreme command of that navy

which kept the world in awe—the bulwark of Great Britain.

" The next morning," says Lingard, " he proceeded to his own vessel. They were in all twenty men, well provided with weapons of defence."

As usual, James encountered very rough weather, many hardships, some dangers, and some diversion for his griefs. The voyage, we shall soon see, was not a mere blank in the royal existence; which, however, the squalls and hurricanes threatened fearfully. Heavy clouds were coming up on the rising wind, gloomy ministers of the storm charged with rain and sleet. James endeavoured to cast a last lingering look upon the coast receding from his view and from his rule ; but his sight could but dimly pierce through the gloom. The moon sailed out of a cloud ; his eye rested for a second on the land which he left behind,—again darkness passed over her face, James had seen the last of his beloved England.

The storm which had been long gathering, swept at last over the sea and sky ; more than black night brooded over the wintry waves ; the wind howled dismally, then raved madly around the little smack, and whistled and piped in the rigging. The very planks and ribs of the straining smack groaned and trembled, as if she were a living thing in agony. The battle between the winds and the waves was furious. The scene

that presented itself to the gaze of James,
seasoned sailor as he was, was appalling; it lay
between him and those most dear to his heart.
Poor James and his fortunes were indeed embarked on a sea of troubles and of danger.

His wife and his child were uppermost in his
thoughts—"Cæsar aut nullus" applied not to
him. To the view of all as they looked round
on deck, the scene was one that might well have
appalled even a stouter heart than that of James
at that hour. Even to the hardy mariners the
weather was dreadful and full of alarm. A
lowering and sullen sky, whose very aspect
seemed enough to quail the spirits by its por-
tentous and scowling features, frowned overhead,
and hung dismally as a sable canopy, mingling
the bottom of its funereal curtains with the
melancholy sea, which dashed in every direction
against the tempest-tost vessel. Indeed, so
threatening and ghastly was that night-flood
that surged against James and his comrades,
that the boldest could scarcely face with open
eyes the crested billows over which with the
speed of an arrow the straggling ship was carried—now rising with her head towards the sky,
now sinking into the abyss below. Those only
who have felt that downward plunge, with its
indescribable horrors, can form an idea of the
sinking of the heart as it goes down with the
vessel from the wall of waters to their very base.
At times the filling and rending sails could

scarcely drag the sorry bows of the boat over the watery hill which overhung them. Half buried and drenched with brine, staggering and unruly, she would burst away, catching in her topsail the powerful wind that without respite or lull hurled her about, up and down, and almost under the steeps : at one moment bending and bowing as if supplicating the storm, at another flung nearly on her keel, bounding like an en-larged stag, from the scud, shipping seas which flooded her deck. Great skill and watchfulness were required to make her answer to her helm, and to keep her from broaching to, under the successive and sometimes conflicting impulses on all sides which assailed her. Towards day break the wind freshened into a stiff but more steady gale from east north-east.

" God help me !" cried James to his comrades in danger. " It is a Protestant wind. The ele-ments in their course fight against us."

It was not till opposite the Downs in the open sea, that the gale having almost died away, the deck was safe for the short parade of the passengers. It was now time for the sun to rise, but he came not from his chamber of clouds; and no land could be sighted at either side of the Channel. The pelting hail-stone of the night had subsided into a drizzling rain. It was a dull chill morning, and the aspect of the scene was cheerless. The grey leaden atmosphere closed round the little vessel as an oppression which was palpable. Nothing caught the eye but the gloomy sky and the shadowy sea, which seemed mutually to darken each other, until they were blended into one black mass. The scene was in harmony with the king's mind. He paced the short deck supported by Berwick, who felt more tenderly for his royal father than his legitimate children, and thus spoke: "O that I could but avenge your wrongs, and punish those who have driven you to this."

"No, my son," retorted the king, "vengeance is not magnanimity; it is a noble thing to pardon when the passions rise up against an insult, like the waves of this troubled sea against our bark. Cowards have marched to the battle field and won victories; but a coward has never been known to pardon."

"May we not suppose, Sire," asked Berwick, meekly, "that crowned heads, and the rulers who hold the sacred right from the King of kings, may exercise a vengeance deputed to them from Heaven."

"The history of the royal prophet presents a very different example," answered James. "David was flying from his son as I am now flying from my daughter and son-in-law,—the son of my sister, your aunt. Well, despite of his son's rebellion, David loved him. The fugitive monarch bore all the signs of affectionate grief: his feet were bare, his head veiled, his garments rent,

while toiling up the Mount of Olives he wept
for that son who warred against him; he wept,
too, to think of bygone joys and a father's fondness; he wept to think of the vicissitudes
through which he was passing. His sad comrades in arms were touched by the silent sorrow
of their beloved prince. Look at the tree
assailed by a cloud of stones : on those who
throw them and wound it, it casts down its
choicest fruits or sweetest flowers. Let us in
like manner bless those who strike us, and pray
for those who have despitefully used us, and driven
us as outcasts from our country and exiles to a
foreign shore."

"Such is the spirit of the Gospel, my liege,"
said the son, " but that same Gospel commands
us to obey princes."

Here Biddulph joined the monarch and his
filial companion.

" The Gospel," broke in the gentleman of the
bedchamber, " enjoins obedience to those who
govern, whatever be the name they bear."

Labadie, who could not resist the opportunity
of putting in a word, asked his Majesty whether
Christian, in other words, Catholic subjects were
obliged to obey heathen or heretical kings.

"Yes, Christian morality," replied James,
" at Rome prescribed obedience to the senate
when the senate was charged with the Government of the Republic; in Greece, to the assembly of the people: in Turkey, to the Sultan.

If a government be equitable, and just, and
tolerant, what matters it to religion whether it
be of this or that form? Neither our blessed
Lord, nor His Apostles, nor the Church and
the Holy Fathers, ever sought to deprive the
subject of his liberties, nor the sovereign of his
legitimate sway."

" It is, on the contrary, may it please your
Majesty," said Biddulph, " daily reported
throughout the breadth and length of England
that Catholicism is hostile to the liberty of the
people, that its doctrines favour despotism."

" This assertion," cried James, with astonish-
ing energy, "is a calumny, an insult to the
religion of the Cross. When usurpation,
conquest, or due necessity have placed on the
people's neck the heavy yoke of servitude, Religion suggests to the suffering people, patience,
submission, and peace as the best remedy for
their evils. She lightens, but never imposes,
the yoke of tyranny. Much," says James,
" has been said about my notion of the divine
right of kings. God Himself certainly was
pleased to institute the magistracy, and to communicate to it a portion of His power, though
on rare occasions designated only to those whom
he thus commissioned. God Himself raised
Saul and David to the throne. There is not,
however, at present on earth a royal house
whose origin is not to be traced either to election
or conquest. Every government, then, is of

48   THE LOYALIST'S DAUGHTER.

divine institution, in this sense, that it is agreeable to the Almighty will that there should be
the governors and the governed. God," said
the king, solemnly, " will demand publicly of
kings and rulers an account of the human blood
and earthly riches which they have wasted;
from the people he will exact those loyal lives
that were destroyed by the dagger or the scaffold.
Then will the Omniscient disown the tyrant who,
under the garb of justice, has glutted his vengeance." Before he could say another word a
heavy sea struck the bow, and poured in a
cataract over him and his companions. " Luff!
luff!' cried his Majesty, " that's it." And the
smack turned up to the wind. Sheets of the
briny spray and foam flew over her. "Now!
Steady! Keep her there," said the king.

" There's a squall coming," cried O'Brian;
" hark! how it is already hissing."

Down went the peak, but too late; for the
wind catching the sail plunged the gunwale
under. The vessel reeled, staggered, but soon
righted; though not before her hold took in a
quantity of water.

" I'd take in two reefs," said the king, looking to this skipper, whose office he would not usurp.

" Not so, your Majesty, our case is too desperate," answered he. "If she can't rise to the
sea, she must now fill and go to the bottom,
with such a sea running and the wind consider-
ably veering round."

" You are right, captain," said the King; " it is no time to shorten sail."

" There it comes. Here it is, sir !" was the cry from a man on the look out. Like a cannon shot the wind struck the sail, and bent the mast like a fishing rod. She was to all but the most experienced sailor going down by the prow.

Neither by word or gesture did James show that he was flurried, or excited, or afraid ; yet no man was more conscious of the danger. The wind, still shifting to the westward, seemed to meet another current of air.

" The wind coming over the ocean will meet the land wind," cried James. Scarcely had he uttered the words, when a loud report was heard —the sail was reversed. The sprit which supported it snapped in two. In an instant the whole canvas fluttered down into the boat. Nothing but the foresail was left. Her course now altered, and she flew along like a horse with the bit in his mouth.

" That's because the spar snapped," cried one sailor.

" If the spar had stood," cried another, " she'd have gone down by the stern, as sure as my name's Ben Brown."

The voice immediately brought the Faversham sailor to the memory of the king, and he at once recognised Brown, and agreed with his opinion. All the anxiety of that miserable night was mercy when compared to what James now suffered in his dread of running into the Dutch men-of-war; for the Dutch fleet loomed through the darkness which was still upon the sea.

Control his fear as he would, still his impatience and dread of being driven into the jaws of his enemy, would break out in words of despair. " All these things are against me," he exclaimed.

Ben Brown, touching his hat to the captain, said, " Sir, let me set the mainsail on her end, and splice the sprit."

The captain assented. The sea was rolling heavily at the time ; every rope creaked, the frail boat strained and shivered at every bound. Just as the rigging was repaired, before the damaged canvas could be properly adjusted, a clap like that of thunder struck the vessel, and laid her nearly keel uppermost, answering to what sailors term a lurch. " A man overboard !" burst from many mouths. Ben Brown had been dashed from his dizzy footing, and was half-swimming, half-sinking, entangled in a portion of the rigging which had fallen with him. All beheld his body drifting astern.

The horror that succeeded baffles all description ; that sudden rushing to and fro, without a very definite object, which takes place when any sudden accident occurs by sea or land, embarrassed the crew and seemed to perplex the king.

CHAPTER XXXV.

O Lord! methought what pain it was to drown!
What dreadful noise of water in my ears
What sights of ugly death within mine eyes.
Methought I saw a thousand fearful wrecks,
A thousand men that fishes gnaw'd upon.—*Shakespeare.*

In this confusion, Labadie and Biddulph were the only persons who beheld young Clare tear off his over garments, and with one bound, crossing his legs and closing his feet, so as to cut the water, plunge into the sea; the act, indeed, was so sudden that the whole passed like the vision of a horrid dream before the eyes of the beholders. The king was the first to apprise the captain of young Clare's danger, who, in the quiet prompt way which ensures obedience, had the little stern boat lowered from its davits, and the refitted smack put about as quickly as he could. It was not from the tossing waves that Ben Brown had so much to fear, for he was an admirable swimmer; the portion of the severed rigging which entangled him was dragging him to the bottom. This was the dread which nerved the arm of our young Irishman as he buffeted the waves, and had stretched out already nearly half a mile from the smack.

E 2

The anxiety to rescue from a fearful fate the brave young man who had perilled his life for another thrilled through every heart on board. The little boat was like a cockleshell struggling with the waves.

" Give way there with a will ! " cried the mate to the four men whom he accompanied. " No mortal swimmer can hold out against such seas. By heavens ! " cried the mate, " he has reached Brown, who is clutching at him and pulling him down. Pull away, lads—pull ! " cried he again ; and bending their bodies nearly double with their steady stroke, they shot the punt ahead with an impetus which threatened to drive her through rather than over the waves.

The two men were now inseparable, for the sinking sailor had lost all sense but the instinct of self-preservation, and gave no chance to brave O'Brian to rescue him or save his own life. Though unable to turn his head round, still he was self-possessed ; he knew by the rattling sound of the row-locks that help was near, yet he felt that unless he stunned with a blow the drowning man, the chance of rescue was, indeed, hopeless to both of them ; so, gathering up his strength, he extricated himself from poor Brown, who once more rose to the top of the water and convulsively seized poor Clare. The sailor's last grasp seemed fatal to both lives, to the horror of the little crew in the boat, who could not possibly reach the drowning men till the direful

tragedy was complete : suddenly a third object
was seen ahead, scarcely above the wave, and
Lion, as quick as thought, was between the
men, and right under the breast of O'Brian,
whom he supported for a minute, enabling him
to strike out for the boat, into which he was in
a moment dragged in ; when Lion, once more
striking out with fresh vigour and spirit, was
in a few seconds close to the unconscious sailor,
but wary of his grasp. The poor fellow clung
with the tenacity of a limpet, and with all the
strength of life's last desperation to the rigging,
kept floating by a portion of wood to which it
was attached. The noble dog's effectual assistance was not a moment too soon. The powerful
animal, more destitute of fear than a man and
more sagacious in the water, bore his insensible
victim above the surge until the little boat was
lifted on its crest ; a few minutes served to get
both dog and man on board, when the animal
licked the face of brave Clare, then barked with
delight, and caressed Ben Brown, warming him,
and chafing his skin with his rough tongue.
In ten minutes later the whole party were
swinging from the davits. The smack again
put before the wind, which was now no longer
Protestant, but north-west.

Great was the gratitude of the sailors as they
received into the smack their rescued comrade,
and deep was the emotion of the king when he
recovered the preserver of his faithful follower,

to whom he extended his hand, which the
drenched and dripping guardsman pressed fer-
vently to his lips. With expressions of sensitive
compassion, the king said, mournfully: "But my
young friend, you are injured; your head bleeds."

"It is nothing," cried Clare, "but a scratch
by Ben Brown, whom for love I knocked down."
Then he carelessly wrung the brine from his
streaming hair. He patted Lion, who seemed
to claim his share of admiration and praise.

"Your own conscience and sense of this
noble deed will be a higher reward than majesty
has to bestow."

"It would," laughed the young guardsman,
"be difficult, sire, to say which in a romance
would be esteemed the real hero of the voyage:
Ben, who by repairing the rigging saved the
crew and passengers; I who vainly attempted
to rescue him; or the noble animal who preserved the lives of us both. In fact Lion is!"

Before he could utter another syllable, Lion,
hearing his name, dashed frantically about the
king, shaking his shaggy coat, from which the
spray flew up into his Majesty's face; then
springing up to him, and courting his royal
caresses, he flung the water with which he was
saturated all over the king; then crouched at
his feet, barking at him with delight, till
Biddulph exclaimed, "The king has yet a loyal,
if not a papist dog, to bark about him."

With a brief and courteous acknowledgment

of his Majesty's congratulations, Clare hastily let himself down into the cabin, or rather, into the hold, and in half an hour returned, having changed his dress, and taken a restorative, with the same light and cheerful countenance he always wore, and as if nothing more had occurred than a usual bath.

On Brown, however, the long immersion and the entanglement with the spar and torn canvas had produced a more serious effect; nor was it till he had been plunged in a hot bath and rolled up in warm blankets, that he slowly opened his eyes and faintly muttered " Grog!" Those who knew him best, and his love for the maid whom he followed, shook their sides with a burst of laughter, which was heard above the storm. " Do you mean Kate or Grog?" asked O'Brian, who had ascended in time to hear what was going on.

" Tell her to bring me the grog," groaned the shivering swain, if not the hero. The grog was supplied, and did its duty, though not ministered by the hand of Kate.

The ship had still a great deal of motion. The gale was spent ; but the sea called up by the violence of the wind had not yet subsided, and the waves rolled one after another, rising and falling again like the heaving breasts of men who are just desisting from conflict.

The rough weather, and the cold wintry showers had made the air so raw and the deck

so uncomfortable, that the king, highly diverted
and really in good spirits, followed the associates
of his voyage and went down in the little cabin,
where the brave Captain Trevanion had himself
made a wood fire, and was preparing something
hot and savoury for the refection of his Majesty
and his adherents.

Clare, who was still attending to Brown,
was suddenly astonished by a roar of laughter,
amid which to his delight he recognised the
mirth of the king, and rushed in to enjoy the
joke.   Sure enough he found his Majesty absolutely diverted from his excessive grief; not
only amused, but overpowered by irresistible
laughter.   More than ever was the Honourable
O'Brian impressed with the truth of his sprightly
father's doctrine, that in every real man, even in
the Saxon animal amid the darkest tragedy of real
life, there is a secret store of the comic, which
seems, perhaps, only the more ridiculous from
the close alliance there is between the tear of
grief and that of laughter.   Hard, indeed, and im-
penetrable must that bosom be which has no
little hatchway of fun or humour battened down,
it may be as a rule too deep and still for outward indication, yet susceptible of a certain
touch, and set in motion by the most simple
process; such as the accident which awoke the
mirth of King James in the midst of his miserable voyage, when he saw the brave Captain
Trevanion conquered by some eels which were

by no means reconciled to the operation of skinning them. They slipped through his fingers. When at length he managed to put them into the frying pan for dinner, they slipped soon out of the frying pan into the fire ; for in the frying pan there was a large hole which he had not previously discovered. The utmost ingenuity of the gallant officer was called into action, and the hole eventually stopped with a pitched rag. No sooner was the desperate escape of the eels thus prevented, than the captain proceeded with great composure to tie a tarred rag round an old cracked can, to make it hold hot water for the whisky punch they were preparing for the king. Here again the king's loud laugh burst out from under the pressure of mortal sorrow. All difficulties being at length mastered, the cuisine was accomplished. The royal party, less formal than classical in their attitudes, but still with deference to Majesty, made a serious attack upon the good things which the faithful Achates had prepared, "et socios partitur in omnes." O'Brian, however, positively but courteously declined the eel which was allotted to his share.

" There is one for each of us, young gentleman ; and I am sure your swim must have given you an appetite for the largest," said the captain and the cook.

"I never eat fish but on a fast day," answered the cornet.

"Well, but we have nothing better to offer you."

"I have another reason for abstaining particularly from eels," said the young man gravely.

"Pray, what is it, young Sir?" asked the king.

"Since your Majesty condescends to ask, I must answer," said the young man, with a profound reverence, at the same time helping himself to a piece of bacon, and arranging the materials for some punch, he said, with an expression of melancholy, "During my residence at Christ Church I joined an Oxford party, who visited the sister University, Cambridge, and on our return we explored the Cathedral of Ely, and supped at the "Lamb." Among the luxuries of the city we had oceans of fat eels, but I could never taste an eel since, for scarcely had we finished, when a minor canon joined us, and affected us much by his account of the scene of suffering and distress to which he, good man, had ministered in the Fens. The young widow of Ely and her drowned husband are still but too fresh in my memory. One foggy morning, when the viewless waste between Ely and a little village called Coveney was shrouded in one chaotic mass of gloom, the wife, who had scarcely passed the honeymoon, missed her husband, with whom she had not yet learnt to live on the best of terms. Nothing was heard of him for a fortnight. The wife, of course, was in deep distress ; so much so, that when his body was at last found in a dyke near Coveney, from which he had often supplied his fair bride with eels, no one liked to break the news to her, especially as the finding the body was accompanied by what her neighbours thought would shock her dreadfully : namely, that when the poor fellow was pulled out of the fen ditch a great number of eels fell on the grass from his body; the fact of the matter is," said the speaker, "that he was full of them. At last a friend undertook to break the intelligence and receive the widow's instructions. This he did, not omitting delicately to mention the eels. The story told, 'tis herself, he asked, 'What are your wishes ? for,' says he, 'with the rest of your friends, I am anxious to obey your orders.' The sorrowing widow removed her handkerchief from her eyes, and murmured out, ' Send home the eels, and set him again ! I am very fond of eels.'"

The inimitable way in which our Clare, whose face was a tragedy, told the story, filled the whole party with sympathy for the poor widow up to the very last sentence, when a roar of laughter, of which the most grave were ashamed, shook the glasses off the temporary table.

No sooner had this subsided, than the king, desirous to escape the charge of levity, accounted for the immoderate laugh which escaped him at the hissing of the fat eels grilling in the fire, by saying, "Among the many and popular plots hatched by the Duke of Shaftesbury and the exclusionists, for prolonging my banishment from my brother's court, when Duke of York, involving the duchess, there was one which ascribed to Madame de Mazarine and to us a contrivance to poison the king, my brother. The object of the plot was to bring a great army from Flanders and France to place me on my brother's throne ; a great many Parliament men were to be boiled alive to make a Sainte Ampoule, or oil, to anoint me and all my successors at their coronations. The rich savoury smell of the eels, the fumes of the rashers of bacon, which filled the hold with their fragrance, the simmering and hissing of the gravy, bore a chorus which sang in my ear the song of the Parliament men, undergoing the necessary decoction for the villanous unction." The monarch was going on to prove how this tale had been seriously deposed on oath before two secretaries of state, when he was abruptly cut short by the cry on board : "A ship ahead—ahoy !" The vessel was bearing down upon the sorry smack from the north-east. James's party, however, had no glass. As she neared them, therefore, they could not tell whether the vessel was an enemy or not. She had hoisted the English colours, but still continued to bear down upon the smack. Trevanion, not feeling secure, made the most of his battered sails, and put his craft right before the wind.

" I think our little guns will soon send her a splice of our mind," cried O'Brian ; " We are her match if it comes to fighting hand in hand."

The king was thoughtful; " She is an English yacht," cried he.

The weather, which had proved hazy all day, now cleared up, and fully revealed the craft, which to the thorough-bred seamen, familiar with the build and slight varieties in the rigging, appeared to be no other than the frigate of Lord Dumblain, son of Earl Danby. She was commanded by her noble owner, who claimed her as his own independent vessel, in which he crossed and re-crossed the sea with various despatches and resolutions between England and Holland, and promoted the object of William. She was doubtless still charged with intelligence to secure the throne which he had usurped.

No sooner had the master of the smack made out the frigate to his satisfaction, and directed the king's attention to the Union Jack, which was waving aloft in defiance of some formidable foe, than his Majesty declared, that of late men sailed under such false colours, that the most skilful sailors were often puzzled how to trim their sails quick enough for the protestant whirlwind, and the political hurricane. Such mariners as my Lord Dumblain, will go to

bed an Englishman to-night at Dover, and rise
out at sea a Dutchman, under Dutch colours
next morning.

"Or, may it please your Majesty," said the
Captain, "under any ensign by which he would
try to mislead those who are too well experienced
in his manœuvres to be deceived by any colours
which he may display. The best ruse, however,
was that carried out by Captain Gray, who, though
unconscious of the royal charge of the queen
and the prince, deceived the worst designs of
these double-faced Anglo-Dutchmen. The despatches given up by Gray to the Dutch commander, have baffled and confounded all the
traitors at the Hague. They are still on a
wrong scent, and therefore no counter-plot can
imperil us with the Dutch men-of-war, which
are by this time off the Downs. They are
more perplexed by the schemes of our men, than
the thunder of our cannon. Had Dartmouth
been as faithful as Strickland, your fleet had this
hour been the bulwark of your throne."

The king was much affected, but assured
all present that through the assistance of the
King of the French, and the co-operation of
the Irish, he should soon recover his dominions.
The king's voyage was not a mere blank in his
existence ; for it gave him a fresh interest in
life and recalled his thoughts from himself, and
carried them on to the queen and the prince.
Still the exertion which he had made to cheer

his comrades in adversity was too much for him, and once more he relapsed into his former gloomy state—paced up and down the little deck with hurried uneven step—until worn out with fatigue, he took advantage of the calm and went down to rest, and was soon asleep. It was the sleep of weariness, not of peace ; his mind was agitated, even during slumber with many of the exciting subjects and circumstances which had occupied his waking thoughts and were the theme of his conversation. Still he awoke not, until aroused from his heavy slumbers by the grating of the fishing-smack against the shores of Ambleteuse, near Boulogne, on the early morning of Christmas-day. The first struggling contest between light and darkness was a very dreary time ; the December air was cold—the want of real refreshing rest was by all severely felt. Stupor usurped the place of sleep, and was heavy on their eyes. The relaxed nerves and careworn spirit of James presaged the misfortunes which they had no strength to bear, but which were happily after all but the prophecy of a mournful heart, unsolaced by the solemn blessing of the midnight mass for which he had devoutly sighed, but sighed in vain.

The king sent his son Berwick forward to prepare the queen for his arrival at St. Germains towards the close of the following day with the rest of his party.

Passing along the picturesque banks of the
Seine, below the heights of St. Germains they
were soon on the verge of the circle of mountains
that surround the plains of Paris. A region of
royal magnificence was spread before them, associated with the influences of the capital.

Down to the period of the Bourbons, who
were indeed kings, and had left the indelible
history of moral, as well as physical power,
expressive of their dynasty of five hundred
years—monuments which seemed to connect
their past with the present, and point to their
future rule.

Nearly every step of the amphitheatre of hills
to the west of Paris is a history. Palaces,
pavilions, forests, parks, aqueducts, gardens, or
chases bear witness to the splendours of fallen
greatness.

A carriage-drive or terrace, of a mile in length,
of striking magnificence, overlooks the river at an
elevation of several hundred feet above it. The
palace itself, a quaint old building, the architecture of which is something in the style of that
of Elizabeth of England, has now long been
abandoned as a royal abode. Its last royal
occupant seems to have been our unfortunate
monarch, who approached it to join his queen
on the 28th of December, 1688. It is
said to have been deserted by its royal pro-
prietors because it commands a distant view of
the beautiful, but sombre, spire of St. Denis,

whose walls overshadowed the vaults of the
Bourbons, as the solemn and silent monitor of
their mortality.

An aqueduct, almost worthy of the Romans,
gave an imposing idea of the scale on which
these royal works were carried out. It might be
seen at the distance of a league—a vast succession of arches, displaying a broader range of
masonry than is generally to be seen in Europe.

The winter evening, however, had set in too
heavily to reveal much more than a very dim and
indistinct outline of their future residence to the
travellers.

After the long and weary toil of travelling
a hazardous and distressing journey, about six
o'clock James and his devoted followers were
entering the grand château or palace, into which
the queen had only passed the day before.

Her Majesty and her ladies had disposed of
the casket with its valuable contents, mentioned
in a former chapter, and had just taken her
place on the royal couch prepared for her, when
Louis and his courtiers filled the chamber where
her Majesty, Mary Beatrice, received them. It
was while sitting near the queen that Louis
heard that the king of England was already
within the château, and he hastened to welcome
his unfortunate cousin. They met in the hall
of guards. James entered at one door as Louis
advanced to meet him by the other. With slow.
and faltering step, overpowered at the munificent.

hospitality of Louis, the King of England bowed
so deeply, that he seemed to be throwing himself at the feet of his royal kinsman, when Louis
caught him in his arms and embraced him cor-
dially, or, as the news letter from Versailles, in
Lingard's appendix, says : "Ils se sont em-
brassés à quatre ou cinq reprises, toujours égale-
ment baissés, et cela à duré près d'un pater
noster, sans qu'on ait entendu ce qu'ils se sont
dits dans ces embrassements. Incontinent le
roi l'a mené dans la chambre de la reine, lui
donnant la droite sur lui. Sa Majesté l'a pre-
senté en même temps à la reine en lui disant,
Madame, voila un gentilhomme de votre con-
noissance, que je vous amène."

Mary Beatrice uttered a cry of welcome, and
wept for joy. The ceremonious French courtiers
were astonished by James's passionate demonstra-
tion of affection for his wife before them all.

The château assigned for the residence of the
exiled King and Queen of England was one of
the most beautiful and healthy of all the palaces
of France. There was scarcely a room in it, or
an object in the neighbourhood, which was not
endeared to James by many tender associations.
Here, though a fugitive with the queen his
mother, he had passed the days of his boyhood
and early youth ; here, after a quarter of a century, he found himself an exile once more, and
the only survivor of his comrades in adversity.
Mother, brothers, sisters, all were dead ; but

though dead, still spoke mournfully and affectionately from their graves, and his sad spirit held communion with theirs.

But the children whom God had given him, who not only owed him their being, but the very power of wounding him, had betrayed and forsaken him. The son of his beloved sister, the cruel husband of his false and unnatural daughter, had driven him from his throne, and involved all who were most dear to him (on this side heaven) in his fate. The cloud which long, long ago passed over the morning of his days, now seemed to be darker than ever, charged with a thousand vicissitudes and sorrows, and now shrouding the evening of his life in a retrospect of melancholy. The dark tragedy of his father's death would involuntarily arise to his memory and his heart, and inscribe there in letters of blood a fearful dream of the future.

The shrubs and fountains, the pleasure-grounds and the well-remembered scenes through which in youth he loved to stray, where with his brothers and sisters he was wont to play, all called up the past—all were calling " James." But the James whom they invoked was absent.

If there was much to cheer, there was, indeed, much, very much, to make him sad.

It was truly a happy evening, that which the re-united king and queen passed in the palace of St. Germains, for there is nothing which so pleasantly heightens the zest of joy as the calm

remembrance of pain—nothing makes the sense
of safety so glad as dangers past. Tears flow
from joy and sorrow. They now flowed from
both, and like kindred drops were mingled into
one stream. The queen divided the griefs of
her husband and doubled his happiness ;· but
still both were mournful. Their reunion in
France was in reality separation from England :
banishment from their realms, the loss of their
throne. No wonder, therefore, that their hour
of bliss was tinged with melancholy.

To God and themselves their own deep, secret,
mutual woes, and trembling hopes were known.
Their hearts' fond treasure, the little prince,
was the first dear object of their wishes and
desires. It was, therefore, a relief to both to
hear, just after the first gush of affection and
raptures of such a meeting, the friendly voice of
Louis inviting James to the royal apartments of
the Prince of Wales. On his way to his second
treasure, James followed Louis through all the
glowing splendours of the gorgeous saloons and
withdrawing-rooms. The two monarchs, in their
progress to the grand nursery, passed through
the courtiers of France and the adherents of
James. On both the royal cousins bestowed
those looks and words, and graceful condescen-
sion which became each : which none but kings
can pay, and none but courtiers know how to
receive and acknowledge. As there was no
parade or display affected in the politeness of

the kings, so their respective addresses put all present in good humour with themselves; and yet the courtesy of England was put to the test by France and the formality of the period. At length, to relieve the king from the embarrassment of his position, and the courtiers from that restraint which they could not but feel in the presence of the Grand Monarque, Louis said, directing his looks more particularly to the King of England and his followers,

"I will show you a real treasure, on our way to the one you value most of all;" and approaching gracefully a small panel covered with two richly-carved and gilded doors, he opened them, and drawing aside a silk curtain, displayed to the view of all near him an inner frame, containing a Madonna exquisitely painted.

"That," said the Grand Monarque, "is an undoubted Corregio, and one of the most perfect pictures that master ever painted. See the bend of that head; so full of grief and resignation; look at the beauty of the colouring, too; that tear upon the heavenly cheek; the faint pink tinging the nostril, partaking of the blue of the drapery. The hands crossed on the breast. Every point so correct—all so graceful and so full of contour."

With her head still bent, and her eyes now bending upon the ground, there was one beholder. She took a few steps apart from the rest, then turned again, and raising her eyes between

irresolute conduct and apprehension, as if she
wished, but feared to speak. The King of
England spoke to her with gaiety and cheerfulness, for he had known her almost as his own
daughter. Whether it was the roseate tint of
warm blood rushing from the heart, or the
bright glow of the lights reflected from the
damask curtains on her cheek, history declareth
not; but she felt there was crimson rising to
her face; on some light excuse, therefore, she
left the room, and in her retreat was startled to
find herself in an ante-chamber through which
the monarchs were passing to the royal babe's
apartments. They discovered the poor young
lady with a handkerchief in her hands, wiping
away those tears which she could not restrain.
She fixed her eyes anxiously on the king,
apparently struggling to speak; words, however,
at that trying moment, failed her; the sorrowful
glance of the King of England met hers. Calm,
dignified, and almost affectionate, it was; and
suddenly turning a look full of paternal regard
on the fair girl, who but too evidently desired to
say something to him, which her tongue refused
to speak, he extended his hand to her, and
motioned her to approach; then, agreeably to the
custom of the time and place, he kissed her on
both cheeks, and spoke of her father and mother.
There was in her manner something affecting
which she could not conceal. The same drops
which flow from sorrow, seem also to have their

source in joy ; and the King of England knew not to which of those feelings to ascribe those of Mary Plowden. But taking her trembling hand in his, he asked her whether her grief was for the destiny in which his fortunes had involved her, or for gladness at the reunion of the royal family.

" For neither, my liege," said the unsophisticated girl plaintively. " Why then, since you are one of us, how can you thus grieve ?" said the king. " But Robert," said Mary, " when shall I see Robert, my early friend—my brother —my deliverer ?"

" He is gone to second loyal hearts in Scotland, and will accompany me probably to Ireland on his return," answered the king almost sternly.

She coloured deeply. The king, with his royal conductor passed on, and so absorbed was he in his own domestic affairs and public interests, that there was no room in his thoughts or his heart for the little affair of Mary's love and fear for him whom the king had banished from her presence.

In the first burst of her grief, Mary forgot her heart's treasured consolations, which reason and religion had garnered up in her days of tranquillity. The stores which she had gathered were not equal to her regrets. She could only think of Robert and his absence—her former happiness and the sad separation from him she loved.

CHAPTER XXXVI.

O call not to my mind what you have done!
It sets a debt of that account before me,
Which shows me poor and bankrupt even in hopes!—
Congreve.

NOTWITHSTANDING all the proofs of friendship
which the great King of France so hospitably
evinced for the English royal party, on whom
he conferred the richest gifts of munificence, and
that noble sympathy which alike did honour to
his head and heart, it was too plain, that even
his influence and support could not restore the
exiled monarch's crowns.

Their reign in England was at an end. If,
amid the Highlands of Scotland, there still
beamed a gleam of hope, it was fitful and uncertain; and though Ireland was still faithful,
the Stuarts were pensioners on French bounty;
yet everything which charity could suggest or
courtesy accomplish was done to alleviate the
dependence of the fallen family, and to recon-
cile them to their position. The French state
officers and dependents were quickly superseded
by the noble English, Scotch, and Irish emigrants. Among these the members of the

queen's household were most distinguished for
their fidelity and loyal devotion. Nearly all
the adherents who followed their Majesties
had applied to the Prince of Orange for pass-
ports to France. William granted the passes,
but outlawed all that availed themselves of
them, and confiscated their property — members of the Church of England, as well as
servants, and even menial servants; even the
queen's old coachman, who had formerly served
Oliver Cromwell in that capacity, was at St.
Germains, reinstated in his office, and there
died at an advanced age.

Those ladies of the bedchamber who were
compelled to remain in England with their
husbands and families, like Lady Arabella Went-
worth, Mrs. Dawson, and others, defended the
queen's character in England with great zeal.

It was only a few days after the reunion which
we have described, and on the evening of the
same day on which the first court was held by
the exiled king and queen at St. Germains, that
the queen sat in her own apartment, surrounded
by her ladies, her beautiful large dark eyes were
tearful, her complexion beautifully clear and
somewhat pale. Her sensitive mind apparently
received but little pleasure from the splendour
with which the generosity of Louis surrounded
her. She evidently felt at her secret heart that
the splendid sorrow to which herself and her
unhappy lord were reduced as a degradation.

Many a little incident, piece of furniture, or memorial of other days, served to remind her of the height from which she had really fallen.

Her chamber was hung with a superb set of tapestry from the designs of Le Brun, and the upholsterer had, with artistic regard to pictorial effect, chosen the alcove, which, according to the domestic arrangement of France, is the recess in which the bed is canopied and secluded, as the fittest place for the scene represented,— the tent of Darius.

"I cannot," cried the queen, plaintively, to those around her, "repose myself on my bed without having the pathetic history of that unfortunate family, and the king himself, all throwing themselves at the feet of Alexander, always before my eyes. Am I not," cried she, "sensible enough of my calamities, without the picture of them constantly before me?"

Mary Plowden silently listened to this involuntary burst of the queen's complaint, and resolved instantly to have, if possible, the tableau of the royal suppliants removed, and replaced with another piece representing a triumph, a welcome to former glories, and reinstatement. Had Mary's happiness been less identical than it was with that of the queen's, she must have felt for her anguish; for the young lady herself, in virtue of her well-known place in the queen's regard, was honoured in a similar manner. The alcove, which was decorated and dedicated to her slumbers, had also a history, which brought before her, in one glance, a romance and a tragedy, which, if depicted in a book, could only rise before her line upon line, here a little and there a little; but which in her tableau brought at once into her presence a world of love, of crime, of mortal passion.

Miss Plowden was on her way to the vice-chamberlain, to seek his interference with Louis for the immediate removal of the offensive tapestry, when she met Clare, to whom she had been introduced as to an acquaintance of Robert Strickland, and a young gentleman of great merits and loyal principles. His appearance said he was but a mere boy. His manner, too, though perfectly courteous in the presence of the young lady, was at first diffident and embarrassed. In such cases, particularly with a young Irish-man, the young English lady has a decided advantage.

Mary was still hesitating outside the door, when Clare in his passage to his own apartment met her.

She endeavoured to drag him into a conversation for a few minutes, and make him more at home. She talked like a connoisseur on all the subjects in which she was told he was versed; she called his attention to fine pictures, cabinets, china, and other articles of vertu, with which the apartment in which they met was decorated. One thing led to another, so that she adroitly glided into the matter of the tapestry, which grieved the eye of her Majesty, and the fair girl's own wish to have it changed for something more cheerful.

"Is it your wish, fair lady, that the picture should be removed at once, unknown to our poor queen ?"

"Certainly," replied the damsel.

"Trust it to me, and it shall be done," said the cornet, and immediately repaired to a French officer still in the household, well-known to Lauzun, whom Clare had met at Whitehall. It was the same household officer who had super-intended the putting it up, equally regardless of expense and the queen's feelings. It was at once removed ; but no sooner had the queen heard of the step which her favourite lady had ventured to take, than she mildly chided her, and regretted that in a moment of unreserve she had com-plained of a beautiful design, which was intended for her pleasure. The young lady excused her-self by the acknowledgment that her sympathies for her Majesty were called into action by the images which stood out dismally before her own eyes, in her own alcove, and which disturbed her dreams.

"Easy is my bed," said the fair maiden, "it is easy ; but it is not to sleep that I incline, for the scene which is spread before me is ever impressed on my imagination, on it my eye rests, and through it sees the original. My thoughts trace the calamity of life, I know," said the maiden, "and evoke the same sufferings,—levelling misfortunes awake the same feelings in the breast of us all, young and old."

"But, surely, you can sleep in peace and honour?" said the queen.

"Yes, madame, but the picture assumes a life and a meaning which transports me to the times and the persons whom it portrays."

In reply to the queen's desire, Miss Plowden reluctantly described the figures on her tapestry.

"It is," said the blushing girl, timidly, for she was in the presence, not only of the queen, but many of the court ladies, "it is the history of Fair Rosamond—of love and crime. She is sitting with her maidens binding up flowers. A cavalier is gazing on her from the background, and evidently exciting greater interest than the flowers. In the second compartment the maiden is seated apart from her companions, the flowers scattered and neglected by her side. The colour glows richly on her cheek; there is a smile upon her lips. The third, a cavalier, is kneeling at her feet, while the downcast eye and yielding hand betrays that his suit is granted almost before it is asked. Fourth, a banquetting-room—the cavalier and the maiden are seen beneath a royal canopy. The gems are bright in Rosamond's braided hair; her neck and arms are laden with orient pearls; but her cheek is

paler than its wont, and the soft blue eyes have
a look of care far different from that they wore
when heeding how best the primrose and the
violet might consort together.   This was followed
by the parting of the frail one and her royal
lover—she may not accompany him—his face is
averted.   Fifthly, she kneels a penitent at the
foot of the crucifix, her long fair hair is unbound,
and the sackcloth robe is girded by a cord round
her slender shape, her hands clasped, her eyes
bathed in tears.   Sixthly, a different lady sits
beneath the royal canopy ; she is alone—the
diadem is on her cold and haughty brow—there
is no pity in her stern cold face, and the smile
on her lips bodes death.   Before her stands the
lovely culprit, whose fatal beauty, and, still more,
her fatal love, are to be so dearly requited.
The mouth is yet red with the blow inflicted by
the vindictive queen, but her eye, though sad, is
resolved.   The dark cup is in her hand—she
turns aside from the dagger, too cruel for her
gentle grasp.   Seventhly, a little chapel, where
the mourners are ranged torch in hand, and
before the altar the robed priests are chanting
the service for a departed soul.   An old man
stands near.   His face is buried in his cloak ;
and in the midst, laid upon an open bier, is the
' Fair Rosamond.'   King Henry, kneeling by
the coffin, bends in speechless despair over the
victim of his love."

She had scarcely finished this description,

when Clare entered the apartment, and presented
on one knee a note from Lauzun, who begged
to wait on her Majesty at her convenience. The
young officer was gracefully retreating with the
queen's answer, when she motioned him to delay.
She was already aware of his success in removing
the Greek representation from her alcove, and
affected stern displeasure at such a bold undertaking without her sanction.

The youth pleaded that his motives were his
only apology, then slightly colouring, as he
glanced at Miss Plowden, he added that he was
sorry to have exceeded his duty, but that he was
under the impression that it was her Majesty's
pleasure that the solemn tableau of ancient
history should give place to something more
sprightly. Severe and sudden as had been the
changes of her voice and manner through this
short interview, there was a playful smile which
broke through the unusual harshness of the
queen's countenance. Mary Plowden kept her
eyes fixed on the ground, then raising her head
declared that she, not Mr. Clare, was the culprit
in consulting the queen's, or rather her own
wishes.

"I see through it all, ma mignonne," said
the queen, "the gay young Irishman is claiming
the privilege of a—friend." The pause which
preceded the tardy word brought a slight blush
into the maiden's cheek.

Strickland had told Clare she was beautiful,

but thought he, as he now beheld her, " she is
perfectly charming." His large speaking eyes
and flushed cheek confessed unconsciously the
claim, and while they did so, the queen gravely
said : " We impose upon you, young sir, as a
penalty for your temerity, the task of imparting
our wishes to the officers with whom you have
such influence in our court, to change the tapes-
tried scenes in the alcove of the ante-chamber
opening into our own royal sleeping apartment."

More than once during this interview he felt
that he was outstaying the ordinary limits of the
time allotted to a formal commission, and retired
as soon as he could, with a deep obeisance,
assuring her Majesty that her commands should
be executed without delay. Her Majesty's ladies
seemed anxious to turn the queen's thoughts
from the immediate embarrassment of her position in a palace which she could not really call
her own. And they chatted pleasantly on the
decorations of ancient and modern tapestry,
which afforded such employment for the noble
ladies in their solitude, and in the absence of
their lords. Lady Powis entered into a minute
detail of the elaborate execution of most skilful
designs and pictorial combinations. The devices, worked with needle and threads of various
colours, on a texture of silk and cloth known in
eastern countries from very remote ages. The
queen was observing that the tapestry of Bayeux
was much celebrated for its beauty ; that it was

said to have been made by the Duchess Matilda for Notre Dame, of Bayeux. Even before her the Duchess Gounor had presented magnificent tapestry hangings to Notre Dame, of Rouen. The art had also received great importance in the reign of James I. ; she was also proceeding to speak of some of the paintings of Italy, to which it had been compared, when the Dauphin was announced. He was soon seated on a fauteuil, in her presence, but of course lower than the one on which she sat. Through him the dauphiness pleaded illness as an excuse for not accompanying him.

"For my own part," said the queen, addressing him, "I am only denying myself the happiness of a visit to Versailles, to pay my compliments to the king and dauphiness, till we can procure a dress suitable for the occasion." She was but too well aware that her toilette, and the mode then prevailing, were no slight achievements.

After some days the dress was accomplished, and she prepared for her visit to the French court. Her ladies, and particularly Miss Plowden, were consulted upon the momentous undertaking. It was what is now called a "success," and won the approbation of the most fastidious of the ladies of the French court.

"When the Queen of England," says Madame de Sévigné, as quoted by Miss Strickland, "went to visit the dauphiness she was dressed to perfection. She wore a robe of black velvet over an elegant petticoat ; her hair was beautifully arranged ; her figure resembles that of the Princess de Conti, and is very majestic."

Louis conducted her to the apartment of the dauphiness, who came to the door to receive her.

"I thought, madame," said the queen, " I should have found you in bed."

"Madame," replied the dauphiness, "I was resolved to rise, that I might properly receive the honour done me by your Majesty."

Louis XIV. withdrew, because the mighty laws of court etiquette forbade his daughter-in-law to sit in an arm-chair in his presence.

The sham invalid held a crowded court in her bedchamber on this grand occasion.

When Louis returned to the apartment after the queen had taken her leave, he suggested, in language far too plain to be pleasant, that the Queen of England was what a queen ought to be,—in short, every inch a sovereign,—the very model of royal dignity and graceful bearing. This declaration had been made by the great master of fashion. The Grand Monarque had spoken it. From his decision there was no appeal. The grandest duchess in France was now ready to kiss the hem of Mary's robe, if not, indeed, to emulate her in dress.

The interest of our narrative will not carry us through the terrible formalities of the court of France, which two successive Spanish queens had rendered almost as solemn as they were absurd. Circumstances suggested to the master mind of England's fallen queen the policy of propitiating these ladies, even of incomparably lower birth than herself. To the general reader it is well known that Maintenon was not only the wife of the French king's bosom, but his counsellor and confidential friend in state affairs. It is true she was but Scarron's widow, to whom public opinion denied the title of queen. Yet she wore the fleur-de-lis and ermined mantle which none but the true wife of the King of France was permitted to assume.

The first time Madame de Maintenon paid a visit to Mary Beatrice at St. Germains, the latter regretted the few moments she had kept Madame waiting, for she had lost by the delay so many minutes of her conversation. The king, whom it delighted the Grand Monarque to honour, was lightly esteemed by the French nobility, because he could recount all that was passing in England without emotion. He was considered brave and good, but inferior in manner and intellect to his queen.

The dauphiness, as we have seen, feigned sickness, fearing that in the event of her visit to her Britannic Majesty, the envied fauteuil would not be accorded her, after the laws of her august father-in-law. Monsieur, the king's brother, also threw himself into a huff, and was sullen and sulky withal, because the queen had not kissed him. The appellate jurisdiction of the great king, with the consent of our queen, decided the matter according to the etiquette of France, which altereth not. The Britannic queen therefore kissed Monsieur, who, gratified by the honour, dispensed with the fauteuil, to which he had so lately and so ardently aspired, and desisted from further complaint to the king, his brother.

The poor sailor king was weary of the pains and penalties of French royalty, and heartily sick of the frivolous toys and trifles of the full-grown children of France, sought relief from it in the presence of his queen, and some of her most select maidens, amongst whom, and who sat by her side, was Mary Plowden. She was venturing a witty censure on the French, who so ceremoniously exchanged kisses.

" Very true," added the queen. " Though I saluted Monsieur, I know it is not the custom in England, for me to kiss any man."

" Except me," cried the king, exerting himself to repel the charge of dullness brought against him, at the same time affectionately kissing her Majesty. " But when we are in France, we must do as they do in France," cried he, playfully, forcing himself from his mood. But I must be avenged of your love passage with Monsieur, and repaid for it, too ; and that on the fair damsel, who laughs at court etiquette. Suiting the amiable action to the

word, he stole a kiss, the threatened kiss,—
imprinting his lips on the blushing cheek of
Miss Plowden, whose confusion and surprise,
nay, resentment, electrified the whole party,
including the queen, with merriment, which
burst the bounds of French court decorum.

" Be not displeased," said the kind-hearted
offender ; " even on the throne of Great Britain
the monarch has the privilege of kissing the
ladies presented to him."

" Not of my rank," was Mary's dignified reply.

" Your rank in England is among us little
inferior to a duchess of France. Now, my dear
young lady, all the duchesses of France are
demanding of me what you resent with scorn."

To draw the attention from Mary Plowden to
herself the queen observed in her own placid
manner :

" Nevertheless, we will concede all that we
can by graceful courtesy to conciliate the
goodwill of each princess who courts our acquaintance ; but I fear the French ladies will
never attach themselves to onr interests, or
pardon our aggression on their province," said
the queen.

" Were the misfortunes of the English royal
family greater than our queen's beauty, the
jealousy of haughty damsels would be less," said
Lady Powis, glancing from Mary Beatrice to the
king.

" The queen of England," said the favourite

countess of Almonde, " is not as jealous of Miss
Plowden as poor Madame Maintenon is of her
Britannic Majesty."

The queen graciously smiled, and expressed
her surprise that such a brief sojourn near the
royal father who had adopted her, could inspire
such a deplorable feeling. Even at this stage
of the conversation, which had certainly wandered beyond the prescribed limits of the court
canon, Miss Plowden could not conceal her cha-
grin. She spoke inaudibly to the queen, who
immediately changed a word and a look with the
king. His first feeling was evidently anger at
himself, for suffering himself, in the presence of
the queen, to salute the gentle girl, who seemed
to resent what was intended as playful courtesy;
just as if, in his advanced age, he had been
guilty of some silly flight of romance.

" If Robert Strickland were here," said Lady
Strickland, who at that moment had joined the
party, " I am sure he would feel no pain, but
pleasure, at the gracious and affable attention
of his Majesty."

Miss Plowden blushed crimson. But the
proposal of the queen amazed all present, and
even diverted the shy maiden from her grievance.

" In the absence of Cornet Strickland," said
the queen, " let Mr. Clare appear before us,
and if it be his Majesty's pleasure, pronounce
his untutored opinion on the royal etiquette and
privilege question."

The young Irishman, who had been up to the moment engaged in conversation with a group of noble French gentlemen on the subject of the *Irish enterprise* and the preparations for it, which were going on under their directions, on being summoned, suddenly turned to follow the messenger, under the impression, doubtless, that the king had some weighty military instruction to impart. His approach to the royal presence for an instant interrupted the discussion of the committee who were debating the despotism of beauty, and whether his Majesty had done more than exercise the royal rule rightly to all.

After some formal commands addressed to the guardsman, the king, as if he had forgotten something, motioned him, while hesitating whether to advance or recede, to come nearer, and actually submitted the important question to the opinion of the youth. Partly abashed by the extraordinary words, partly admonished by the tone of the royal speaker, the youth was for a moment silent.

" My liege," said he, at length, " we must appeal to the fair ladies." The ladies, especially Lady Strickland, took occasion to remark, that Shakespeare and the dramatists of Elizabeth's era, whose works even O'Brian evidently then held in admiration, were by no means free from levity ; " but his female characters," said she, " usually command respect, and even love ; and if the intellectual giants of that day sometimes condescended to the distaff, they never forgot to wield the club with unrivalled power in defence of the dignity, the honour, and the virtues of our sex."

The queen pressed the gay Irishman for a candid opinion of his own, such as he would give unrestrained by the presence of the royal party.

After a minute's reflection, he said, " It is not my mother's son that can be silent ; but 'tis not in such circumstances, that I am an adept," said the youth. " The *Irish* ladies of the highest society, as well as the merry girl on the mountain side, are never prudish ; armed in the armour of faith, they throw the shield of virtue between their virgin purity and its peril. They may transgress conventional laws, but in the majesty of their chastity they are secure and unassailable. They freely and unreservedly mix with their countrymen, unsuspicious as children, and safe in their innocence."

" But," chimed in the ladies, " we want a rule for the Saxon."

" There are those present to whom it would be presumption in a mere Irish boy to give judgment," said Clare.

" Not at the command of the king," said Miss Plowden, timidly.

" It is my command, sir," said his Majesty.

" My notion is, then," said Clare, " that since the ladies are warm admirers of the great dramatist, and since his verdict is impartial, we may be influenced by it. Indeed, an it please your Majesties, it is the very excellentest notion I wot of, and sprightly withal, as the poet hath it," continued he, attempting the style of Shakespeare, "and sheweth what modesty maketh noble ladies deny; while it keepeth the gallant at arm's length; still," added he, with a gravity and knowledge on such a delicate subject, for which few ever gave him credit, "the universal publicity of the custom of kissing was the very best security for its innocence; and though in England it is now considered, to say the least of it, as a personal endearment warranted by natural affinity, or some other close connection, it was one hundred and fifty years ago nothing more than a general ceremony, as it appears now to be in France. In Shakespeare's play of Henry VIII., at the Cardinal's banquet the king says to Anne Boleyn—

'Sweet heart,
'T were unmannerly to take you out and not to kiss you.' "

Lady Strickland, seeing an expression of disapprobation on the countenance of the queen, took up the subject good naturedly, and declared that even in her day this ceremony was performed at the opening of some dances. "It was," added that noble lady, "gravely and profoundly noted down as a part of the figure. In a black letter dialogue between Custom and Verity, concerning the use and abuse of dancing

and minstrelsy, Custom puts this question to
Verity :

> 'What foot would dance,
> If that when dance is done,
> He may not have at ladies' lips
> That which in dance he won?'"

Scarcely was the last line recited, when the
vice-chamberlain announced the arrival of his
grace, the Duke, and his desire for the promised
audience.

This distinguished and romantic nobleman was
no other than Lauzun, whom, at the request of
Mary Beatrice, Louis had not only pardoned for
all past offences, and presumption in loving and
wedding the royal lady whom it delighted to
accept him, but elevated him to the rank of
duke; and King James, in acknowledgment of
other services which we have narrated, in con-
ducting the escape of the queen and the prince,
had invested him on the eve of his expedition
to Ireland with the Order of the Garter in the
Church of Notre Dame.

The king at once withdrew to receive the
French nobleman in person. At the same time
the whole party dispersed, some to prepare for
the reception of the brilliant assembly, who were
to offer their congratulations on James's projected
expedition to Ireland and to wish him farewell,
others to pass a few hours of affectionate intercourse with the dear relations from whom this
Irish adventure was so soon to separate them.

On the evening of this day, at the close of February, 1689, the grand saloons of the royal palace of St. Germains were filled with a brilliant assemblage to compliment king James on the energetic preparations and bright anticipations of his triumphs in Ireland. The men were in larger proportion than the gentler sex. There was a world of courtesy, and plenty of all those elegant civilities, which is the small change of society ; less scandal and more small talk than might be expected where state affairs and intrigues, which affected not only the three crowns of Great Britain, but half the thrones of Europe. Shadowy visions of the immediate restoration of James flitted across the eyes of the most youthful and inexperienced of the company, while clouds of ill-forebodings on the countenances of the seniors, were but ill concealed by the playful ripples on the surface, and by the practised laugh. Not even the Frenchmen were indifferent to public opinion, which all dreaded as much as they affected to despise it.

The one feeling which perhaps prevails in the hereditary aristocracy, who are exalted so high above the vulgar herd, that they see not and hear not the under current of the human tide— a belief that society of their own exclusive and elevated rank and station is the faithful and infallible exponent of a nation's wishes or a country's voice. The pointed sarcasm, or the

elegant epigram of a high-born wit, launched at
a cabinet minister, is often more dreaded by him
at whom it is aimed, than the popular tumult, or
the national discontent, which at the period of
our tale agitated Great Britain to its very centre.

The belief of James, and perhaps, of many of
his friends was, that the masses act, but never
think : the highest rank only, thought many of
that day, set the rest of the machine in motion ;
but there were several springs of action below
and out of sight. This belief in the intellectual
influence from above, made spies, and doubtless,
even at St. Germains, on this very evening, there
were more than one who could communicate the
doings and the sayings of the court of St.
Germains to that of St. James's.

It was not long before Lauzun entered
conscious of his new dignity ; wearing the collar
and jewel of the order, which he had so lately
received, and which became him well. They
were richly ornamented with diamonds, the same
that had belonged to Charles I., which had
been preserved by honest Walton, and returned
to Charles II.

Advancing at once towards the queen, he
kissed her gloved hand with all that gallant
bearing, yet profound deference, for which, as a
polished courtier, he had been remarkable from
the very dawn of his lofty aspirations.

Notwithstanding the nearness to her person,
in the scenes of humility and danger through

which he had recently conducted her, under his immediate protection, amid the darkness of the night, through perils by land and by sea, there was nothing in his approach, as he knelt before her, which to the eye of the keenest observer, betrayed that the slightest intimacy existed between them. His homage was respectful—her acceptance of it dignified and majestic.

He did not say many words to the queen, but with a tact and a delicacy more intuitive, perhaps, than acquired, he, respectfully yielding his place to others, withdrew, mingled freely with the crowd, and soon made a deep obeisance, but with less ceremony to the king, who retired with him and discussed the real object of their meeting. Lauzun afterwards introduced the most distinguished of the hundred noble French volunteers, who had under him placed their services at the command of James, in his Irish expedition.

"My own immediate force," said the monarch in a cheerful tone, which might be heard by nearly all present, "consists of two thousand of English and Scotch emigrants. I am, I must confess," says the unwise king, most injudiciously, but enthusiastically, "unwilling to employ foreign troops, or even to owe to them my reinstatement on the throne. I will," burst out he, "recover my own dominions with my own subjects, or perish in the attempt." But even in the course of the evening, he was like many a lofty and reluctant spirit, forced to bend to circumstances and friendly reasoning.

"The Grand Monarque has authorised me," said Lauzun, "to assure you that his vessels of war and troops are at this moment in readiness for Ireland. Already his Majesty has provided and shipped off for your campaign equipages, camp beds, and toilet furniture of a magnificent description, and all the necessaries and comforts befitting a monarch of three kingdoms."

"I have also the supply of four hundred thousand crowns, a loan from my royal brother of France," said James.

Louis had indeed done much, and promised more, to encourage the royal adventurer, and to what monarch on earth could another in his calamity less painfully incur arrears of obligation than to that sovereign whose mighty influence and character had been so long and so often acknowledged by all the powers of Europe? His fame and fortune equalled that of the greatest of the Cæsars.

Eight or nine times since the sun of that monarch rose had the Papal chair received a new occupant. The fourth emperor, since the birth of the same auspicious day, bore sway over Germany. Four Czars had held sway over their vast territory, the precarious tenure of their absolute rule. In England, besides Cromwell, four Sovereigns had borne the crown which sat so loosely on the head of the exiled King

James, ere the glorious sun of Louis XIV., though waxing faint and dim, went down in night for ever.

James had much confidence in the will and the power of this august Sovereign, and in the strength of his Irish viceroy, Tyrconnel.

" Am I not still," cried the king, " the undisputed Sovereign of Ireland ?" Having uttered these words audibly, he again spoke privately and earnestly for some time with Lauzun.

In the mean time, in this assemblage, where there were the representatives of four nations, all interested in one and the same cause ; the wonderful changes which had passed over the face of Europe during the reign of Louis the Great, became the theme of conversation. At length Lauzun, with his usual urbanity, which bordered on benevolence, reminded the monarch that duty imperatively called him away to complete the arrangements for their departure for Ireland.

He accordingly, accompanied by the Duke of Berwick, the Earls of Powis, Dumbarton and Melfort, Thomas Stuart, and the Honourable O'Brian Clare left the saloon. One by one the rest of the company retired ; but before the last guest of the evening had taken his departure, the queen's old coachman, bursting through all restraint and jostling violently against more than one officer of the household, made good his way right into the presence of the king and queen, who sat in close and tender conversation about their approaching separation.

Strange and somewhat grotesque as the old man's appearance was at such a moment, and so far out of his province; the venerable character of the veteran charioteer; the long and varied services which he had endured, secured him a condescending—almost a cordial reception.

" Oh Lord! Oh Lord!" cried he, wringing his hands with the gestures of wild and violent grief. " All is lost!—he's drowned;—and he so young, so handsome; so fine and clever!"

" What has happened?" asked the queen, calmly. " Who is lost? Who is drowned?"

" We are disappointed—undone," cried the old man. Oh, my Heavens!—mercy on us. Oh my! Oh my!"

" Whom do you mean, old John? Speak plainly," said the commanding voice of the king; affecting before the queen, less than he really felt. " What is all this about?"

" 'Tis the page, the young officer I should have said, your most sacred Majesty, that took charge of the baggage and all the beautiful things for the wars in Ireland," cried old John.

" Once for all, sir, speak out boldly like a man, and say what's happened," again exclaimed the king.

" His corpse, and a fine corpse it must be, is not yet found," said the old man, quite incapable of collecting his ideas. " Oh! oh! like Pharaoh and his horsemen and chariots, he is at the bottom of the sea. And he such a whip—such a young gent for four-in-hand? Oh dear! Oh dear! the beautiful young man!"

The queen almost fainting with terror at some new disaster of which she could form no very distinct notion, in her own soothing manner, though with difficulty, learnt from the venerable domestic what already was but too evident to the king—the ominous catastrophe that had just befallen the king's favourite page, who was drowned at Pont de Cé. The vessel in which he had embarked with his Majesty's luggage was lost, freighted richly as it was with the costly presents bestowed by Louis XIV.

This sad circumstance spread an ill-boding gloom over St. Germains, and filled the domestics with grief.

The king and queen now alone with their more immediate attendants, Lady Almonde, Miss Plowden, also young Clare, who was the constant bearer of messages between the king and his officers engaged with the troops, seemed deeply affected at the tidings of John, which were perfectly intelligible to their minds.

The royal husband and wife sat silently gazing on each other for several minutes, sorrow and dismay depicted in their faces; nor were they conscious of the lapse of time, when the door, through which the old coachman had retreated, opening again, presented a Scotch officer in complete Highland regimentals to their view. It was Colonel Gordon, whom we introduced to the reader on the Mall, in company with the king, the day before his Majesty's last departure from London. This was a loyal officer, faithful and true, from whom are descended more than one valiant officer of much the same rank in the army; brave, good men of our own day, who have never lost the faith, or fallen from their first estate.

CHAPTER XXXVII.

War suspends the rules of moral obligation. . . . . Civil wars strike deepest of all into the manners of the people. They vitiate their politics; they corrupt their morals; they pervert even the natural taste and relish of equity and justice.—*Burke.*

COLONEL GORDON was a man of sound solid Scotch sense, acute perception, deep thought, indefatigable application to whatever he undertook ; of few but significant words, deep devotion to the church and to his king.

"May it please your Majesty," said he at once, " I am charged with dispatches from my noble relation, your very good servant, the Duke of Gordon, and am desired to state his inability to defend Edinburgh Castle, and hold out against the forces which the Dutchman is mustering from all quarters, without, my liege, you can co-operate with us in sending a reinforcement. Mackay is flaunting the Dutch colours almost in our eyes—even on our native hills : we must soon . come down upon him in some Highland pass and cut his rebel rascals to pieces, or Scotland is lost. The brave General Dundee is a host in himself; but should he fall,

H 2

Edinburgh falls with him. In your favourite
officer of the guards, young Strickland, he finds
a youth after his own heart. His deep sense of
duty and his prudence can scarcely restrain his
loyal indignation at the insolence of Mackay's
cornets and ensigns. He declares he will wrest
from them the Dutch standard, or die in the
attempt."

Mary Plowden turned deadly pale, and would
have fallen; but the queen, who sat near her,
and who alone observed the shock which the
poor girl had received, supported her as if she
had been her own daughter, and with her
habitual tact and affectionate manner, endeavoured to impart to the maiden a courage and
a comfort which her own heart was far from
feeling.

" Be seated, my Marie," softly whispered the
queen.

The young lady sat down, and soon recovered
herself, and evinced no further emotion. By
the time the queen raised her head from the fond
object of her royal attention, Colonel Gordon
was gone.

It was now the season of the Carnival, and
never did the feast of reason and the flow of soul
sparkle more brilliantly; and never did the fountains of Versailles play more pleasantly; and
never had the vast palace or sumptuous gardens
presented a gayer aspect than they now displayed
in honour of the exiled king, whom the munificent

monarch of France so royally entertained. In the evening the two Sovereigns, after a long and earnest conference in private, made their appearance before a brilliant circle of lords and ladies.

"I hope," said Louis, in his noblest and most winning manner, "that we are about to part never to meet again in this world. That is the best wish that I can form for you. But if any evil chance should force you to return, be assured that you will find me to the last such as you have found me hitherto."

Soon after Louis paid in return a farewell visit to St. Germains. At the moment of the parting embrace, he said, with his most amiable smile, "We have forgotten one thing, a cuirass for yourself. You shall have mine."

The cuirass was brought, and suggested to the wits of the Court ingenious allusions to the Vulcanian panoply which Achilles lent to his feebler friend.

The next day witnessed the separation of Mary Beatrice and her husband. Their parting scene was sad indeed. Adversity had been busy in the royal family since their flight from Whitehall. The queen often stole away to weep.

" Her voice was ever soft,
    Gentle and low, an excellent thing in a woman ;"

But now plaintive in earnest entreaty with the king to avoid all unnecessary danger, it was toned to supplication.

"I am so painfully inured to affliction," she

would say to her maidens, " that grief seems my
very aliment. It is, I suppose, so good for me,
that God will not let me live without it." The
royal pair sate together in their mute anguish,
each being afraid to address the other, lest the
answer should be " Farewell !" Overcome with
agitation the king burst into tears. Mary's tears
had long been flowing ; but when she saw her
husband weep, she threw herself into his arms
with a shriek of thrilling agony, which her resolution could not stifle. She clung to the king's
bosom with the energy of a tender lover ; while
 he from whom she was to be once more torn,
endeavoured to soothe her by every fond and
hopeful expression which he had the heart to
utter.

" Shall I go with you ?—May I go with you,
James ?" she sobbed convulsively. " I cannot
leave my king, my dearest 'husband," she cried,
and she twined her arms round him. Then, as
if recovering from a delirium of woe, suddenly
disengaging herself, she exclaimed, " Go ! go
where honour calls you ; and may God and the
Saints protect you !"

He kissed her cheek and rushed away. The
officers of his staff approached and conducted
him to his coach, into which the Duke of
Berwick assisted him, then took his place by
the side of his unhappy father, in whose ears
the last parting words of Louis sounded painfully. They rapidly dashed away across the

faubourgs of Paris, attended by the earls Powis,
Dumbarton, Melfort, Thomas Stuart riding at
one side of the carriage, the place assigned to
young O'Brian at the other side being, to the
the surprise of all, unoccupied. Where was he ?
Candour, honour, and truth demand the answer,
which, for the sake of the Irishman, we would
gladly withhold. He was in good time punc-
tually repairing to his post, when, by accident,
he met Miss Plowden hastening to the queen,
who had summoned the poor damsel to her
presence. An open letter was in her hand, but
her perusal of it seemed to afford no relief to her
uneasiness, for it was moistened with her tears.
It was from her fond, loving, and beloved
Robert Strickland. It had convinced her that
however he might desire to conceal from her his
real hardships and dreary prospect of a long and
perilous absence, he was, in truth, in daily
expectation of a severely contested battle in the
Highlands ; that, should he survive the struggle
and retain his liberty, his destiny would be
Ireland. Between their first hasty greetings
and their final farewell, they mutually and almost
involuntarily entered into a rapid conversation on
the Irish expedition, now so interesting to both of
them. Minute after minute flew, but the
speakers took no note of time. Before, however, she could speak a word on the subject
nearest her heart, she rapidly changed colour.
The delicate tinge of the early rose, banished

the pale hue which again gave way to a brighter glow. O'Brian was sorrowfully persuaded that it was not fatigue or bodily illness which chased away the bloom from the maiden's beautiful complexion. Even before offering the services which she was so glad to accept, with reference to her dear friend and early comrade, Strickland, there appeared on her brow such an anxious and plaintive expression, as diverted for the moment the soldier's thoughts from every other subject, excepting the doubts as to what sad intelligence from Scotland could possibly have given rise to such a change. The placid brow—the fearless eye of conscious innocence—the lips which but yesterday seemed ready to speak in candour and in confidence the dictates of her heart, assumed at first an air of cool reserve which gave him pain ; and he asked himself if, in seeking her confidence, he had intruded into the sanctuary of her affections, or trespassed on the pure and undivided treasure of a heart dedicated to another. She could not throw off the deep dejection she felt, and he could not understand it. It might be that the fate of the page, whose dead body had just been recovered from the gloomy waters, had tinged her mind with melancholy and gloomy forebodings of the event which awaited her lover as well as her king.

To a spirit of that romantic adventure which pervaded his mind and urged him into action, the sight of the young, amiable, and beautiful

Saxon in sorrow, which had no visible cause, filled him with tender concern for her happiness. Of the king's departure he seemed unconscious ; he felt as if there was no one near him but the object of his interest—the idol of another's heart. She regretted that her own personal influence detained him. Her eyes encountered his gaze, then bent upon the ground, while a deep blush showed how much she felt that she had attracted his attention by her outward expression of her inward solicitude for Strickland. The Irish youth blushed as deeply as the maiden herself, and looked rather than spoke farewell.

Mary rose from the seat on which she had rested, and recollecting herself, hastened to the queen.

O'Brian had never fallen into love, and only felt that he had carried away with him, from the spot where they parted, a mysterious indescribable feeling, as delightful as it was forbidden.

His new train of musing was pursuing the subject which occupied it thus unaccountably, when the manly yet musical voice of Lauzun spoke a word in his ear which startled him. " What, Cornet, have our preparations for the journey so much fatigued you, that you sleep upon your feet ?"

" Now may heaven, St. Patrick, and all the saints forbid !" said the Irishman, " if there be action or duty in the wind."

" I am only waiting," added Lauzun, " to

receive the commands of Her Majesty ; but your place, I thought, was in the king's escort."

Unconscious of the time that had elapsed, young O'Brian was startled, as if out of his sleep. The terrible breach of duty flashed to his disturbed mind. He felt that each moment was worth a lifetime. He dashed away like lightning, mounted his charger, now impatient of delay, and was instantly at full speed on the high road, and fell into his place before the royal party reached Orleans.

The king and his immediate attendants, including our young friend O'Brian, embarked early in March for Ireland. It was a morning true to the varieties of the fitful season. Now dark clouds rested in huge ledges on the waters, the thick chilly atmosphere closing dismally around the vessel. The shore at one moment lost in the mist, when nothing caught the eye but the gloomy sky and the still darker sea, which mingled together. Soon the scene was changed, and with it the spirits of the brave company. The gusty piping of the wind, however, with the mournful cadence of the waves, broke and plashed against the shore their farewell. The sky, which a moment before had been as black as ink, was lighted up by a sudden burst of the emerging sun, and became a vast expanse of blue, which, when mirrored in the water, was as bright, and as transient too, as the hopes which sustained the passengers. The

waves danced merrily in the March morning
sunshine ; the threatening clouds had given way
to the burst of the golden sun, which bathed
the heavens and the sea in its genial light. In
less than half an hour the white sails were bending gracefully to the breeze ; the water rustled
at her prow, and the lofty vessel stood out to
sea. As she rounded the point outside the
harbour, a cheer—the best which Frenchmen had
the skill or the lungs to put up—broke from the
assembled groups on the shore, and was answered by a stunning return from the ship—a
cheer which none but Englishmen can tune and
vociferate.

The hearts of the king and his adherents beat
high with hope once more ; a joyous feeling rose
in every breast, and the exhilarating influence of
the bracing sea breeze gladdened all on board.

A thrill of ecstacy ran through the pulse of
O'Brian, when he thought of the victory the
king's army was to win in the land of his birth.
Already he was transported to the hills and
valleys of Erin ; he longed to repose on her
green banks, beneath her changeful skies. His
memory carried him back, and his hopes carried
him forward ; and among the youthful comrades
of his voyage, he beguiled the time with song or
story—now telling of the ancient greatness of
his country, and the deathless faith which it had
retained through all centuries of religious oppression and trial—now venturing an enthusiastic

hope of her coming prosperity. Every early aspiration which had stirred his heart or evoked his energy was revived within him, and found utterance. The youth was the life of the party around him, and seemed to impart to others the patriotism which inspired his own feelings.

All were determined to enjoy the general sunshine and prospering gale, whatever were the troubles which awaited them, or the dangers to which the chances of war must so soon expose them. They felt no present anxiety, or cared to avert the event of war ; but that cheerful conversation and joyful recollections of the past, without reference to the evils of to-morrow, would, when regulated by Christian principles, prepare them for the worst which could befal them.

The Duke of Berwick felt a great interest in the observations of the different speakers, who freely conversed together. But his Grace quietly dissented from O'Brian, and some senior Irishmen on the same side, drawing a contrast between England and Ireland, unfavourable to the latter.

His Majesty hearing the Duke's voice, was attracted to the scene of the friendly discussion, and at once gave it as his opinion, that though Ireland, as the Island of Saints and the land of the loyal, was the brightest gem of the ocean, England is the glory of all lands in her natural advantages and national character. Then pointing in the direction of that part of the

channel which interposes between England and
France, towards the coast of Devonshire, James
exclaimed, " There is nothing in Ireland equal
to the woods which sweep down the sides of
those hills, till they almost bend their branches
into the sea."

When some one respectfully reminded him
that, so far as romantic scenery went—the lofty
mountain and the dismal pass—enchanting lakes
and verdant landscapes certainly crowned Ireland
as the queen of beauty—as superior to England
as the emerald was to the cornelian. " She
is," cried O'Brian, " a flower whose life is
beauty, and whose breath is fragrance."

An officer standing near the enthusiastic
Irishman, retorted, that in the north they were
likely to see enough of her in her naked deformity,
where her breath was redolent of gunpowder.

Captain Stuart, of the life guards, observed
that he had visited many and distant countries,
had mingled, when abroad, with the natives
of those countries, had learned something of
their manners and their language, so that he
enjoyed at once the advantage of their society
and the real happiness of comparing each
company with that of North Britain ; and the
result of his experience was that, next to Scotland, England was in all respects the finest
country under the sun.

" Probably," said his Majesty, after more
reflection than he usually bestowed upon a

subject involving no real matter of fact, "the chief difference between England and every other land, is the delightful aspect of contentment growing out of cheerful industry and actual exertion ; happy qualities in themselves, but still more happy in their results. The neatness of the rural cottages, however lowly ; the care daily bestowed upon them to keep them as clean inside as they are pleasant outside ; the labour to adorn with flowery shrubs or simple plants their little garden, so as to give a grace to the humblest dwelling, evince habitual care and national taste." ·

"Not to mention these fine intellectual gifts, honourable ambition, and insular pride," said a French noble.

"It is only in Ireland," said O'Brian, "if I may be so bold, that there is a supreme genius which surmounts all difficulties. Where will you find a man like Viceroy Tyrconnell? And some of the most enlightened men of England have lived much in Ireland. Englishmen are so steeped in business, so solid, and so matter-of-fact, that they live in the eternal shop ; they think shop, and speak shop."

"I'm sorry," said the king, regretfully, "Mr. O'Brian, that a young gentleman with all your enlightenment should thus express the vulgar prejudice against the Saxon."

"Pardon me, my liege," said the youth ; "I would not speak in an ungenerous tone of the

sister isle, much less in the presence of my
sovereign and his English subjects. I only intended to contrast the characters of the two
nations ; the careless sprightly gaiety of the
one, with the sober gravity of the other. It's
the bright sunny scene which speaks that sweet
calm of unclouded existence. But lest my allusion to England be odious, I would only contrast
all her boasted advantages with those of any
catholic country under heaven. Take France,
for instance, and see which in everyday life, to
the wayfaring man and the peasant, affords
brighter promises, and directs him most elo-
quently along his pilgrimage to heaven.

"As the weary, wayworn travellers refresh their
thirsty lips at some welcome roadside well, and
feel grateful to the charity that carved the little
fountain in the rock, and placed there the drink-
ing shell; so the poor laborious catholic has
ever and anon, visibly before his eyes, some dear
memorial of the faith—some material evidence
of the old, old religion. Images of Him whom
they adore, and of His mother and their mother,
to whom they pay their devotions as the mother
of God ; revered representations of Calvary
and the crucifix. In short, the wayfaring man,
at each stage of his journey, has representations
of the saints and martyrs who went before him ;
they are associated with the holiest and happiest
recollections, which can cheer, sustain, guide,
and arm him along his rugged path to the city

of God, the residence of those whom it delights
their country to honour. In these statues, enshrined and preserved throughout ages, the passenger reads the complete volume of sacred history, which, to the unlearned, is the gospel itself.
It elevates the faithful to a sense of his true
dignity ; it identifies him with the saints themselves. It is a comfort in his sorrow—an
example of patience which makes him thankful
for his afflictions. Besides, such stations tax
the selfishness of the rich by the sacrifices which
they demand. They appeal from the fathers
of the church to the human heart, to which
they hourly bring home the consolations of
religion.

"In my walks," says the zealous advocate
for the emblems of what he deemed the only
true faith, "I have been struck with the devotions of the rustic labourer or peasant, signing
himself with the sign of the cross, or, as we say
in Ireland, blessing himself, as he passes by the
cross or the crucifix, or before the image of the
Madonna offering up a ' Hail Mary,—' "

How far the young Catholic might have gone
on in this strain we know not had he not been
interrupted by a Protestant loyalist, who declared
that there was no scriptural origin for such a
system. "Without offence," said he, "I must
remind the young gentleman who has mono-
polised so much of the discussion that the in-
vocation of saints, as well as the veneration of

images is a deceit inspired by the spirit of delusion, a fond conceit without any warranty of scripture."

King James, whose theological knowledge was only exceeded by his desire to display it, replied that his Protestant friend had only re-echoed the declaration of the heretics of the last century.

" With great submission to your Majesty's authority," retorted the other, " even Vigilantius, as early as the fourth century, declared against the doctrine which Mr. O'Brian advocates."

" If, then," answered the Irishman, " he had been vigilant enough to have lived in the second, or even the first century of the Christian religion, he was a right down heretic, and I would have told him so to his face."

Perceiving that the conversation was taking a course which none of the company had antici-pated, James, with more tact than he generally evinced, turned the subject gracefully to the habits of Catholic sailors; their votive offerings and peculiar devotion to the Blessed Virgin; the mutiny which the mass, celebrated by Admiral Strickland, excited ; the false charge of popery brought against Pepys, whom he always associated most honourably with the navy ; with other similar matters not more interesting to the reader than they were to the monarch's more reluctant hearers. From such topics he glided almost imperceptibly into the naval history of the

country, particularly during his own command of
the fleet. In his own desultory way he assured
all who were about him, that nothing was more
hereditary than the mystery of ship-building; that
for several generations it had been preserved in
the same family. He told the company, that
when cannon were first introduced into ships,
about the end of the fifteenth century, they were
mounted over the gunwales; but portholes were
invented by a French builder about the year
1500. " Of all the monarchs of England," said
he, "I admire Henry VIII. as a promoter of
the British navy. He guarded the Channel with
his own fleet, maintained at his own expense."

At the request of the ship's officers, who
highly appreciated the king's naval experience
and profound knowledge of shipping, his Majesty
gave a brief sketch of what they desired.

" The naval history of Great Britain is," said
he, " divisible into three periods : First, its in-
fancy from Alfred to Henry VIII. when ships
were at best but mere tubs."

These dates accord with the song to the
mariners—

> " That guard our native seas,
> Whose flag has braved a thousand years
> The battle and the breeze."

Secondly and thirdly its youth and manhood
from Henry VIII. " Ships in their earlier history," he continued, " were regarded chiefly as
useful bridges across the Channel, fields of battle,

or sources of revenue. The first fleet that ever left the English coast on a foreign expedition was that of Richard the First, for the Holy Land. The first naval battle between France and England was fought and won by John, with a fleet of 500 vessels. But," adds the King, with enthusiasm, " it was the ' Sovereign of the Seas,' built in 1637, which astonished the whole Christian world. But what is worth our special notice is the extraordinary fact, that besides her tonnage, just so many tons in burden as there had been years since our Saviour's incarnation, namely 1637, and not one pound under or over ; a most happy omen !" exclaimed the monarch, " which, though it was not at first projected or intended, is now, by true computation, found so to happen. She hath three flush decks " (he went on, apparently reading from his note book), " and a forecastle, an half-deck, a quarter-deck, and round-house. Besides many other ports, she hath thirteen or fourteen ports more within board, for murdering pieces, besides a great many loopholes out of the cabins for musket-shot. She carrieth, moreover, ten pieces of chase ordnance in her right forward, and ten right aft. She carrieth eleven anchors, one weighing 4,400 lbs. The master builder of this ship is young Master Peter Pett ; this family have been in this trade upwards of 200 years. This grand vessel was at first only designed for splendour and magnificence ; but being made a subject of complaint in the reign of my martyred father, she was, to meet the requirements of the time, taken a deck lower. She then," cried he, " became one of the best men-of-war in the world, and so formidable to her enemies, that none of the most daring among them would willingly lie by her side. She had been in almost all the engagements of her time; and in the last fight between the English and the French, encountering the ' Wonder of the World,' she so warmly plied the French admiral, that she forced him out of his three-decked wooden cabin ; then chasing the ' Royal Sun ' also before her, forced her to fly for shelter among the rocks, where she became a prey to lesser vessels."

The ship which James seemed so anxious to describe, was set on fire at Chatham, by negligence, and was devoured by that element which she had so often employed for the destruction of others. From her obituary, written two years after the event, it would appear that she only survived the date of James's expedition to Ireland, six years.

Several days were thus beguiled of their weary sameness, by anecdotes and varied discourses in no way necessary to our story. It was about midnight, succeeding the fifth day, that James was deep in the history of the De Courcys, when the royal passenger hailed the sight of land.

At length, while the grey light of the breaking day was shedding a cold gleam across the green water, as the waves resounded along the shore, the lazy mists rolled heavily away, and disclosed, a few miles to the leeward, the high bluff of old Kinsale, whose lofty crest appeared above the summit a hundred feet from the waters which laved its base. Between the coves which dipped into the tide beneath, peered out here and there the hut of a fisherman, who was already in his swift hooker, tacking about in different directions. The bay presented an animated scene. The wind died away, and the tide rose with the sun.

James landed in the harbour on the afternoon of the 12th of March, and was received by the Roman Catholic population with acclamations which might be heard for miles. The few Protestants also who remained in that part of the country greeted him in all sincerity; for though an enemy to their religion, he was not an enemy to their nation, and they might reasonably hope that the worst king would show somewhat more respect for law and property than had been shown by the Merry Boys and Rapparees. The Vicar of Kinsale was among those who went to pay their duty; he was presented by the Bishop of Chester, and was not ungraciously received by the king.

Nearly a year had elapsed since the government of the country had been given in charge to Tyrconnel, to raise the Irish to a decided supe-

riority over the English interest, so that Ireland
might be in a position to offer a secure asylum
to James and his friends, if, by any subsequent
revolution, he should be driven from the English
throne ; but this Lord Deputy had a further and
more national object in view—to render his
native country independent of England if James
should die without male issue, and the Prince
and Princess of Orange should inherit the
crown. Louis XIV. gave strong assurances of
his support to Tyrconnel. On the arrival of
James, his viceroy had mustered an army of
40,000 men, but they were alike destitute of
weapons and military discipline.

A day was spent at Kinsale in putting the
arms and ammunition out of reach of danger.
Horses sufficient to carry the royal party were
with difficulty procured ; but, on the 14th of
March, James proceeded to Cork.

The city at this period extended over about
one-tenth part of the space which it now covers,
and was intersected by muddy streams, which
have long since been concealed by arches and
buildings. A desolate marsh, in which the
sportsman who pursued the water-fowl sank
deep in water and mire at every step, is now
covered by the stately buildings of the great
commercial societies. There was then but one
street in which two-wheeled carriages could pass
each other. James was here received with
military honours by Macarthy.

While the king and his party were engaged in procuring carriages and horses for their own use, and to transport the money which had been brought from France, from Kinsale to Cork, Tyrconnel arrived from Dublin and brought fresh hope to the little party. James proceeded to Dublin as rapidly as he could, and entered the city on the 24th of March. The city was at that time in extent and population the second in the British Isles. It contained between six and seven thousand houses, and thirty thousand inhabitants. Of the many elegant and stately public buildings which now grace both sides of the Liffey, not one then existed. The college lay quite out of the city, and the present principal streets were then open meadows. Most of the houses were built of timber, and have long given place to more substantial edifices. The castle was almost uninhabitable.

Every exertion had been made to give an air of triumph and festivity on the occasion to the district which the king had to traverse. The streets, generally deep in mud, were strewn with gravel; boughs and flowers were scattered over the path; tapestry and arras were displayed from the windows of the rich; while the poor supplied the place of the rich stuffs by blankets and coverlids. In one place was stationed a troop of friars with a cross; in another, a company of forty girls dressed in white and carrying nosegays. Pipers and

harpers played, " The King shall enjoy his
own again." The Lord Deputy carried the
sword of state before his master. The judges,
the heralds, the lord mayor and aldermen,
appeared in all the pomp of office. Soldiers
were drawn up on both sides to keep the way
clear. A procession of twenty coaches, belonging to public functionaries, was mustered.
Before the castle gate the king was met by
the Host, under a canopy borne by four bishops
of the church. At the sight he fell on his
knees and passed some time in devotion ; he
then rose, and was conducted to his palace,
once — such are the vicissitudes of human
things—the riding-house of Henry Cromwell.
A Te Deum was performed in honour of his
Majesty's arrival. The next morning he held
a Privy Council ; discharged Chief Justice
Keating from any further attendance at the
board ; ordered Avaux and Bishop Cartwright
to be sworn in ; and issued a proclamation
convoking a parliament to meet at Dublin the
seventh of May.

At this time the parliament of Ireland, as
well as that of England, was the supreme court,
convened by the sovereign's writ. The laws
were made by the Houses of Lords and Commons,
and when sanctioned by the supreme Ruler of
Great Britain and Ireland they passed the seal
of England, became the law of the land.

James opened his parliament with such declarations of religious liberty to all persuasions, as gave general satisfaction. Thousands assembled around the king's palace. Many and motley were the groups and knots which might be seen talking with all that enthusiastic eagerness which the engrossing events of the day suggested. From the frieze coat and brogues to the full costume and military uniform of the highest ranks, there were all sorts of dresses, representing every social circle of the capital. There was the plain garb of the Irish squire, contrasted with the brilliant attire of the officers of the Viceroy's staff. There were present on that memorable occasion persons of every age. The animated spirits of the varied assembly, seemed to be free from political acrimony, judging from the peals of hearty laughter that burst forth here and there. We may easily believe that the destinies of Ireland, or the result of the coming struggle between two rival sovereigns of hostile creeds and conflicting politics, were not the subjects which engrossed the thoughts of the light-hearted crowds.

In the meantime, James was distracted by the conflicting opinions of his Irish advisers.

" Reflect," said Tyrconnel to his Majesty, " that the government of Ireland is a difficulty and a science ; you can do nothing even with the army, till you find out their way. The most intelligent men, fresh from England, cannot manage their militia. The Irish character is a

study.   They must have your royal praise,
before they earn glory.   They must have our
confidence.   They will fight for their religion
and for old Ireland; but we must dissociate the
cause from the cause of England.   I have
known Ireland for a long time, and I know well
the spirit by which my countrymen are actuated.
They never fight so well as abroad, partly
because they are under no regular discipline,
and partly because they have nothing of value
to fight for at home.

The peasantry constitute the greater part of
your Irish army, and their reverence for high
birth is almost religious.   They will fight up to
their knees in blood for any leader in whose
descent and daring they can confide.

" I am resolved to lead them in person,"
said the king.

" Then, my liege, let me implore your Majesty, for the sake of your realms—for the sake
of your son, the Prince of Wales; but above all,
for the sake of the queen—take care of yourself," said Tyrconnel.

" I have a distinct duty to perform, and I shall
suffer no domestic or selfish consideration to
shake my determination," replied the King.

Of James's residence in the Irish capital,
which he made his head-quarters for some
months, there is little to relate worth notice
which history has not recorded.

We do not, in this place, tax the reader's

patience with a transcript of the names of those whose conflicting counsels, and various opinions and measures, were proposed and rejected— accepted or declined.

The freedom of debate allowed too much latitude for any very decided line of action or decision of conduct. Enough it is to say, that some there were, and these the greater number, who advised a speedy attack on the enemy in his own position; others, and perhaps the most judicious, thought it was safer to resist every effort of the Orangemen to force them to a battle, even should they feign a retreat. Nor must it be forgotten that there were others of unsuspected integrity who suggested a third course—which has ever been the statesman's favourite number—as wiser than the others, but it was alien to the mind of James—it was to make a fresh selection of officers, and to entrust them with some discretionary power. On hearing such a proposal his gracious Majesty could only exclaim, "Sancta Maria!" being the nearest approach to an adjuration which he had, of late at least, permitted himself to make, and was apparently about to utter something rash, when Tyrconnel with great adroitness prevented him.

The despatches the king received at this time from Dundee and Balcarres, did not conduce materially to any very satisfactory line of action on the part of the king. They urged him to come to Scotland, and lead his native chiefs and highland clans to victory. "The pibroch," said Dundee, in his despatch, "will awake once more the sleeping echoes of the mountain rock, and make itself heard above the roaring river and the thundering cataract. Trust not too much to the Sassenach who still lingers with you. Let the Saxon banners float over the standard of the traitors! Repair to the Highlands and meet your chiefs; we are eager for your presence; and the clansmen are gathered on the mountains, which are tinted with the many-coloured tartans. Hosts of shepherds and highland peasants," continued the Scotch patriots, "would, as if by magic, at sight of their king, be transformed into warriors, with their implements of husbandry turned into swords, and flock to your banner. Only let it wave over the mountain tops, and the victory is certain."

The king at this interval was also entreated by a strong party of relenting and penitent rebels to resume his throne in England; "they being now brought to a better mind, came without an hour's delay," they said, "to return to their duty and their king."

Even the far-seeing, clear-headed Danby, and the political speculator Halifax, assured Sir John Reresby that King James might be reinstated in less than four months if he would only dismiss his priests.

"Some of the authors of the revolution," says

Miss Strickland, in her own inimitable manner, "began to make overtures to their old master, in the same spirit which sometimes leads gamblers on the turf to hedge their bets when they see cause to suspect that they have ventured their money on a wrong horse."

No sooner had the excitement of events a little subsided, than the most honourable and worthy of the English clergy, on closer acquaintance with the new sovereigns, discovered much that was unsatisfactory. The supreme head of the established church was now a Calvinist, or, rather, a fanatic, whose creed was the single dogma of predestination. Indeed, some even asserted that William had never been baptised. As for Mary, though she had not outwardly ridden over her father, she had crushed his heart in her triumphant ascent to the throne. Long prayers and four sermons a day scarcely atoned, in the estimation of the people, for her unnatural conduct and cruelty. The high church had no sympathy with a crowned dissenter, and had already resolved to sacrifice their bishoprics and their benefices to their conscience, rather than take oaths of allegiance which suited the ultra-protestant faction.

The native Irish had not even outwardly submitted to the Orange dynasty; so that James had, before his departure from Dublin, as much to encourage, as he had to distract and perplex his deliberations.

CHAPTER XXXVIII.

To them that list the world's gay showes I leave,
And to great ones such follies doe forgive,
Which oft through pride doe their owne peril weave,
And, through ambition, down themselves doe drive
To sad decay, that might contented live.—*Spenser.*

WE must now beg leave to go back a little in point of time, changing the scene from Ireland to Scotland ; and, in order to bring every character in our story to the same point, must turn for a while to an interesting gentleman, of whom we have seen nothing since the day of the king's final departure from Whitehall for France. ·

Cornet Strickland, who has so far distinguished himself as the hero of our tale, on the day after James's expulsion from Whitehall for ever, and that on which the Prince of Orange arrived at St. James's, with misgivings in his mind and tender recollections of the girl whom he loved, sorrowfully associated with the scenes from which both were now severed, and also severed from each other, was prepared to set out on his journey to Scotland. Having adjusted his route according to the directions which he had received, he

was seeing that his horse was properly equipped
for such a journey—for he always personally
examined the shoes and everything belonging
to his steed, on which so much depended—to be
sure that all was in good order, when a letter,
marked "private and confidential," was placed
in his hands.   It was from Viscount Dundee.

The great object of the bold viscount had been
to oppose the Dutch, but every opportunity of
displaying his military courage and skill had
been denied him when James fled from Whitehall and Feversham had disbanded the army.
Dundee felt that his Scottish regiments were
left in the midst of a hostile nation without
promises and without pay.   He is said to have
wept with indignation and grief.   No sooner,
however, had James returned to his capital, than
Dundee repaired instantly from Walford, where
he lay with his Scottish troops, to London.
There he met his friend Balcarres, who had just
arrived from Edinburgh : a man remarkable for
his handsome person, and only less distinguished
for erudition and accomplishments, than his
amiable descendant, the present noble head of
the family of the Lindsays.

It will be remembered that Dundee and
Balcarres, when walking up and down on the
Mall with James, accepted from his Majesty
a commission to manage the affairs of Scotland.
Lord Balcarres undertook the civil, and Lord
Dundee the military business, and both sincerely

disclaimed all thought of making their peace with the Prince of Orange. Both Dundee and Balcarres, however, swelled the crowd which thronged to greet the Protestant deliverer, and were graciously received. Both had served him on the Continent, professed respect for William, but would not concur in deposing James. Without an escort of cavalry, Dundee's journey through Berwickshire and the Lothians, where he was hated and feared, would have been perilous. He had, therefore, to obtain the protection of William, which made delay unavoidable. The letter was accordingly written in confidence to Strickland, to inform him that some time must elapse before the earl and viscount could meet him at Edinburgh, but that he must hold himself in readiness in the north of England for any duty, during the interval, to which he might be called. Than this arrangement, nothing could be more grateful to the young guardsman; for it would give him an opportunity of paying a long projected and much desired visit to Sizergh Castle, in Westmorland, where his uncle, Sir Thomas, had often asked him to spend his earliest leave of absence with him.

This fine old residence lay most pleasantly in the way, requiring only a little détour, which would afford an agreeable variety to the long dull roads which, at the date of our story, were in many parts only passable to horsemen. A

less valiant traveller might well have hesitated
in setting out in such weather. Difficulty, however, was a stimulant to Strickland's spirit.
His hardy, determined nature, with such a
prospect of scenery and adventure before him,
actually revelled in the thought of difficulties to
be overcome. To him obstacles, under such
circumstances, were pleasures. He who had
never suffered himself to be overcome by a
mortal combatant, would not be beaten by the
enemy that raged in the tempest and the storm.
Though relays of horses in the present state of
the country and the roads, would ordinarily have
been refused to anything less than bribery or
force, yet through the loyal districts, which the
report of James's last day in London had not
reached, the appearance of the young officer,
and his commanding manner, silenced all
opposition. Still the words, " in the name of
the king," were an order which none were
prepared to resist. So he dashed along by
short rapid stages.

For some time his local acquaintance with the
country enabled him to proceed on his road
rapidly, though he occasionally diverged two or
three miles from the direct way, to avoid disloyal or disaffected villages. But at the best,
the roads, or rather bridle-paths, were so rough
and so complicated in some places, and so
uncertain and impracticable in others, for quick
travelling especially, that on the third day, in

spite of the spur, and though he only delayed to
bait his horse once at a small hamlet, which he
passed on the morning of that day, it was
nightfall before he reached an eminence on the
borders of Shropshire, from which the Welsh
mountains would have been visible in broad
daylight, but from which the country all round
seemed lost in that hour of twilight between
day and night; neither star nor earthly direction could he see to guide him on his way.

Under the influence of undefinable apprehension, young Strickland, now struck his spurs
into his jaded steed, and, while forcing him
down the steep descent at a fearful pace, which
threatened to break his horse's knees and his
own neck, his eye was caught by a light from
a house in a hamlet called Edgeton, and to
which he urged his stumbling horse. At length
he gained a narrow street, through which his
tired horse paced slowly and reluctantly; it
seemed almost deserted and desolate, except
where the latticed window of the little inn, called
the Plowden Arms, showed a glaring light, and
several voices were heard in rude revelry.
Before the door of this inn the jaded nag, by
the instinct which attracts a hackney towards
accommodation for man and beast, made a
sudden pause; and so expressive of his will,
that the rider thought it better to dismount than
to keep his seat under the circumstances. The
name of the inn, now seen by the light, filled

him with a sort of mystic surprise, and awoke tender memories. His first wish was to relieve his anxiety, by inquiring the situation of the place in which he now found himself, and of the state of the country, when he was surprised to hear, bursting from the tap-room of a house with such a loyal title, a ribald song in ridicule of the loyalists and their dissolute courses; neither did the Plowdens nor the Stricklands escape the lash of the scurrilous satirist.

Already the influence of the revolution, Strickland felt, must have reached the place. Both at the hamlet and the inn it had grieved his heart to hear poured forth, in the very house which exhibited on its signboard the armorial bearings of one of the most loyal families in England a doggerel song, as disloyal as it was slanderous. To chastise such insolence was the impulse of his feelings; but to attempt such a rash act at such a moment, in a strange country, his better judgment forbade. While he was hesitating whether he would enter, or urge his reluctant steed further, Strickland was more surprised than pleased to find that mine host, with much shrewdness and curiosity in his countenance, though without actual rudeness, accosted him with many inquiries with reference to his journey and destination. He had many reasons for wishing to avoid answers to such impertinent questions; for he found that he might be mistaken for a disguised Jesuit or young seminary

K 2

priest, travelling upon a mission to convert England, and to banish the northern heresy. At the same time it was difficult to shake off the interested host, who seemed determined to remain by the side of the horseman until he could elicit the desired information.

"These are times which crave careful riding, sir. The night is setting in, and there is no other hostel for many miles. Had you not better rest your jaded steed here and take shelter for the night? If you proceed, sir, twenty chances to one, unless you keep your horse awake with the spur and raise the curb rein, he will kiss the ground, and you will measure your length with it," said the host.

"I am willing to purchase or to hire a fresh horse," said the cornet, impatiently.

"Sir," answered the host, "there is much business on the road, and we have no fresh horses in the stable."

"I am pressed and must go on at any rate," replied the traveller; and as he was vainly, to the amusement of the landlord and one or two others who had now come to the door, attempting to move on the sorry steed, the rapid trot of horses was heard.

The tone of the landlord became more courteous, for he knew not whether the approaching horsemen might not be connected with the traveller. He thought it better, therefore, to keep a civil tongue in his head for the present, and invited the stranger into the house; but before Strickland had taken many steps in the direction, and while he was delivering up his worn out steed to a stable boy, his ears were greeted by the elegant words of a loquacious Protestant.

"I take it on my damnation," says the zealous Catholic-hater, "that I could with half an eye detect the marks of the beast on every Plowden betwixt seventeen and seventy as plainly as if Old Nick had marked them with his blackest ink, or as if they had crossed themselves in the blood of the saints, in ashes or in holy water. Since we shall now have a Protestant king, who has never been branded with the sign of the cross, or been regenerated by water, or governed by priestcraft, who cannot very well uphold papishers, prelacy, or a mumbled mass: why, damn my eyes! the cause must not stand still for lack of evidence. There is a priest up at the great house still."

"You might keep your oaths to yourself," cried another, "they may give offence to the God-fearing, and choke the seed which is about to sprout and quicken around thee; and at any rate it is a waste to throw them away before your oaths are required in courts."

The first speaker, "I am only keeping my tongue in practice. But you never, in my most unguarded moment, heard me swear by the saints, or the ancient superstition, by St.

Anthony, or St. Michael, or by the mass, or any of 'the abominations of desolation,' or the objects of idolatry. I only garnish my words with oaths in season, in the cause of the Protestant king and the Protestant faith."

Sick at heart, and disgusted at the undisguised brutality of fellows who feared not God, nor really regarded Protestant nor Papist, beyond the interest of the moment, Strickland was reluctantly entering the inn, when he heard the following alarming conversation, of which he himself seemed the object.

" Who is that young officer ? for such I am sure he is," said the slow, soft accents of the more precise and gentle of the party, " Methinks I have seen him somewhere before ; he is not from these parts."

" A stranger," said the other, " a stranger, never saw him before."

" He is a well-looking gentleman, and he has a purse and a heart large enough to pay for your civility," added the soft gentle voice,—the well-known voice of Horseman, for it was no other, which Strickland now began to recognise.

This speech concluded the dialogue, which Strickland thought himself justified in over-hearing. Scarcely had it ceased, when Horse-man secretly gave him a sign to avoid the house.

Just at the moment, when, to get out of the hamlet unobserved, seemed to Strickland the

wisest plan, the troop of horse came up in a
hard trot, and demanded admission and immediate attendance. That well-known voice of
authority, which silenced the pot-valiant party
within, was familiar to Strickland.

"Oh! Mr.—Colonel Plowden I mean," cried
the youth; "how unexpected and welcome
this meeting is! While I thought you were
in France, and I alone in a hostile district, here
you are! I congratulate you on your promotion."

A few words mutually spoken and answered,
relieved the cornet and rejoiced the Colonel of
the Life Guards. Such was now his rank.

The loud talkers skulked away out by the
back door. Harry waited on his master, and
washed his charger's mouth. The men who
escorted the Colonel, also refreshed their horses,
and, by permission of the Colonel, a bumper a-
piece to the health of King James, in which the
now obsequious landlord devoutly and conspicuously joined, was quaffed in great haste.

The horses of the troop were brought forth,
and officers and men mounted in order to depart
in company. The Colonel's private led horse
pranced gaily under the Cornet, and raised him
from a painful sense of weakness to a conscious
feeling of power, which can only be enjoyed by
an accomplished horseman on a noble steed.
The host and hostess with courteous homage
saw the horsemen depart, handing the privates
the stirrup cup, which passed rapidly from mouth

to mouth, and was again and again replenished, and proffered to Horseman, but which he declined. Soon the horses, refreshed with water, were in full trot.

" Your acquaintance with the country seems to give you confidence that we are not deviating from the right road," said Strickland.

" What road ?" asked the Colonel, greatly amused.

" The road," said Strickland, " that will take me to Sizergh, in Westmorland."

" That's rather a long ride at a stretch," observed the Colonel, playfully. " I ought to know this road reasonably well," he continued, dryly, " for I have known it long, and not above a mile further there is a mansion of an old acquaintance, I may perhaps call him an old friend of mine. I almost think he would give us a night's lodging. How much time have you to spare ?" asked the Colonel. " I am aware that your movements must be regulated by the plans and orders of Dundee."

" I intend," said Strickland, " to pass at least a fortnight at Sizergh, if Sir Thomas has not departed for St. Germains. But where may the residence be of which you speak ?"

" You will soon see. Do you see the Welsh hills, over which the moon is beginning to shed a pale light ? Well, just under those hills is the mansion, and the owner's hospitality extends to some of his guests for weeks ; perhaps he may entertain us these Christmas holidays, and, if so, with him we can spend them peaceably and cheerfully. The place, if you are a true lover of scenery, will delight you. Its sublime and picturesque beauty, the swelling and heaving of the distant hills, the mountain, the forest, the glades and dales, green fields and rippling streams that murmur through the meads—all diversified and contrasted—tend to produce effects the most novel and enchanting. The proprietor has a daughter, whom you might think interesting and attractive were she at home. I'll lay a wager of the best horse in the regiment, that she would rivet you to the spot to the last moment you will have in England."

Strickland, we may imagine, blushed while he said, tremulously, " Colonel, you know me better than to suppose it possible that any girl on earth could for a moment divide the sovereignty of my heart with our dearest Mary. Remember the old church."

" I will stick to my bet," cried the Colonel, earnestly. And as he said so, they entered the approach to the mansion, of a mile in extent; not artificially prolonged by device of winding sweep and turning, but in reality proceeding the nearest way to the house, for the advantage of a good view of the Welsh mountains. Nor was the house, standing out in the clear bright moonlight, unworthy of its proud position. It might originally have been an abbey, so Gothic

was the architecture, embellished with some of
the decorations of the latter part of the sixteenth
century. The roof consisted of a succession of
tall gables, in which by the light of the moon it
appeared to Strickland some saints were enshrined in stone. Spacious and imposing as
this great mass of building appeared at first
sight, it might from its general aspect have been
only a portion of a still greater whole.

The features of the mansion from within were
not less diversified than the outside. Many
apartments looked as if they had been built with
long intervals between them ; and one wing really
looked, with its quaint windows and small narrow
portal, as if it might have been built early in
the fourteenth century. The whole edifice wore,
however, the aspect of nobility and good taste.
It was—to use the words of the owner—the
"ramshackled" abode of his ancestors.

There were objects rare and curious enough
within the walls to linger over; but even if we
might take such a liberty with our reader, our
duty would not permit the domestic dalliance :
still we must for a brief space conduct him with
the two gentlemen who, towards the close of
1688, entered through the great hall, of which
Strickland particularly noticed the well-monialled
and transformed square bay windows, and in the
recesses deer-skins spread out for carpets, with
halberts and ancient crossbows here and there
filling up the corners. The lower rooms were

at the date of our tale wainscoted with black
oak, and many articles of the furniture were as
old as the mansion itself, and of that stately
solid kind which befitted the dignified style in
which the grandeur of our ancestors rejoiced.
While the young guest was equally gratified by
the hospitality and domestic comfort of the noble
old house, he seemed astonished to find the
servants of every department anticipating every
wish and executing every order of the Colonel's.

In a spacious apartment, with two bay windows on one side, and a fire-place—ah! such a
fire-place, on the other. There, in a venerable
arm-chair, the senior of every piece of furniture
in the whole room, the brave English colonel
sat, the cornet reposing in an easy and less an-
tique seat. After the fatigues of a hard ride,
and a little skirmish on the part of the Colonel,
the two gallant soldiers thoroughly enjoyed their
substantial and inviting supper, and, according to
the fashion of the time, neither, despised—nor,
like men of our own day, affected to despise—a
social and congenial glass of wine on that night.
The motto of the two officers was, not knowing
what troubles a day might bring forth, " dum
vivimus vivamus." As the claret passed rapidly
from one to the other, while olives, sliced hart's
tongues, caviare, and other innocent provoca-
tives, recommended some favourite old port to
their taste. Robert Strickland, who well knew
the sober, though soldierlike habits of the

Colonel, did not think it necessary to put a check on his own enjoyment of the evening, but indulged the hope that every moment as it progressed, something might occur to introduce him to the owner of the mansion, and the dispenser of such hospitality; but he waited in vain.

The conversation was animated and mutually interesting to the two gentlemen, amid which the elder asked merrily, " Shall I present you a brimmer to the health of the lady you wot of— the eldest daughter of an ancient house."

Strickland turned red; whether from the immediate influence of the wine, or some stronger and deeper feelings, faithful history does not say; then turning to the social speaker, said, " Such a question might be answered by a man of wit and pleasure about town, Colonel Plowden, such as my Lord Spenser, satisfactorily enough, but a true hearted cavalier and an honourable soldier divides not the empire of his heart with rival loves.   Let the gaudy gallant still hovering about court play his little game ; for Robert Strickland, the sister of his childhood, the companion of his youth, the sharer of his early joys and recent sorrows, is all in all.   When you introduce me to the host, and when I see his fair daughter, you may be certain I will say and do anything which courtesy may demand, but with reference to the lady, at any rate, nothing more."

"I take you at your word," said the elder

soldier, adding, only : " We shall be early
stirrers to-morrow morning. I propose, if you
young gentlemen are so disposed, that we do
go to bed."

Strickland being as yet, at any rate, no seasoned vessel, and not much of a boon companion over his cups, right gladly seconded
and carried the motion, and moved after the
open-hearted colonel towards the broad staircase, just as the wintry night wind's increasing
blasts made the old casements rattle, and the
last log of the wood-fed fire gave its last crack,
and the tapers began to fail, and the sleepy
eyelids longed to fall over the weary eyes. They
commenced the ascent up the ample stairs,
and soon found themselves amidst an endless
series of portraits, from the time of the bluff
tyrant Hal to James II. Stiff ladies and gentlemen in doublets and ruffs, others with cuirasses
and long flowing hair, black dresses, and love-
locks, bespeaking the well-known cavalier principles of the house in the times of the great
Rebellion ; and ever and anon gentlemen in long
three-quarter frames, with many a square yard
of pink or blue velvet for their coats, cuffs
turned up to their elbows, waistcoats big enough
to make surtouts for any of us poor, tame, de-
generate, indoor moderns. There was a portrait
with the forefinger and thumb of one hand on the
pummel of the sword, the other gently placed on
some gilded table. There was another of a

gallant gentleman, remarkable for his beautiful complexion and handsome face, turned not disdainfully aside, but apparently courting with graceful pride some comely dame with a green négligé, or habited as a shepherdess. Scandal said the portrait was that of Anne Countess of Sunderland, second daughter of the Earl of Bristol; according to Evelyn an admirable person, and no less a favourite with the muse than the gentleman. Such a correct likeness of the Colonel was the portrait of the gentleman thus glancing towards the countess, that the youth observed it; and in an instant it flashed across his mind that the living original was his host—that he was the guest of Colonel Plowden at Plowden, the lord of the mansion where they both were located. He stammered confusedly an apology for the very disrespectful manner he had spoken of the Lord Spenser, Lady Sunderland's eldest son; but more painfully, and yet absurdly embarrassed was he at his obstinate refusal to drink the health of his host's daughter, who, after all, was no other than his own beloved, Mary Plowden. Of course, "une affaire de gallanterie" was kept snug; but unfortunately the name of Henry Sydney was, in the mind of Strickland, associated with the lady in green; and this, too, before she had become a widow.

Aroused by the romantic and extraordinary discovery, Strickland evinced such an interest in the birthplace of his young playfellow, that he induced his friend, whom we may now call the host, to mount the staircase leading to a spacious drawing-room. But here no personages more ancient than the great-great-grandfathers and grandmothers of the possessor of that day exhibited themselves in canvas on the walls. Among these stood out conspicuously in a good light, the full length portrait of Francis Plowden, to whom Queen Elizabeth offered the dignity of the Chancellorship, on condition of his abjuring the Catholic faith ; a proposal which, in the spirit of all the Plowdens, he rejected. There was also a portrait known to the children as the "Red Man."

No rustling of stiff silks was heard along the corridors, no women's voices, save those of the old housekeeper and three maidservants, resound through the now almost deserted mansion. The ear, however, of Strickland's fancy, drank in the sweet echoes of the past—the loved accents of his Mary, who had often laughed and prattled in childish play, long, long ago, amid the rooms of Plowden. At length they reached the yellow room into which the hospitable Colonel ushered his guest, wishing him that rest which the many fatigues of the day demanded. It was a capital place for a man to take up his quarters, either for exercise or repose. There was very pretty sleeping in that vast bed, where some three or four might comfortably snore side by side, and yet be under the pleasing delusion that each enjoyed a separate

couch ; but it was somewhat sad to dwell there
alone. But the room had been recently occupied, and was well-aired; besides, it was the
chief place of honour. The young traveller's
taper, though it burnt brightly, only illumined
the centre of the middle space, while all the
distant recesses were obscured in visible darkness—a very region of ghosts and superstition.
In the panel over the fire-place was a looking-
glass—then quite the correct thing—all cut in
facettes and diamonds at the sides, and adorned
with bouquets of flowers tied by true lovers' knots
towards the middle. It struck Strickland that
it might have been a bridal gift to some fair
daughter of Plowden in the time of the late
king, for it gloried in what appeared to be a
frame of gold, tarnished, as if its glories were
already departing. At each side of the roomy
fire-place were portraits of the Plowdens, four
brothers, ecclesiastics of no early period, for they
appeared to be the works of Sir Peter Lely.
Extending from the pictures, along the wains-
cote were bookshelves, which were but scantily
supplied; but among other works were seen
those of St. Francis of Sales, St. Augustine,
Thomas Aquinas, Bossuet's sermons, Dryden's
works, and Whycherly's poems. Here and
there on the walls might be seen some celebrated
pictures of Cupids and their beautiful mamma.
Famous landscapes there were, too, of Plowden
and its park and ample gardens, terraces, and

lawns; of its solemn woods and wooded hills; its fertile vales; its noble avenue of limes, that led down to the ancient gates on the main road, and its magnificent though now leafless oaks; belts of beeches circling round the gardens, and shutting them out from the rest of the estate; the lofty, mountains of North Wales mingling their heads with the sky in the background. The mere outlines of such a panorama made our hero anxious to explore the country round, and ascend the sublime heights, once the fortress of the ancient faith in Britain.

The first streaks of daylight, beaming through the east window into his bedroom, found him rising from his lofty couch.

The important and urgent business which recalled the colonel to his ancestral halls, left but little time to talk over the breakfast table, during which it was announced that a gentleman from Shrewsbury desired instant admission to Colonel Plowden.

"It's only Wrightwell, the notary, before whom I am to execute a deed of conveyance of this estate to two Protestants, whom I can trust, to preserve it from the clutches of that mongrel Dutch dog, the usurper," said the colonel in a low tone to his guest, who only observed—

"I was under the impression the property had already been secured, before you left London on your way to join Mrs. Plowden at the seaside, to see her embark for France.

" Obstacles were then thrown in the
way of these measures, so considerately
projected for the security of my estates by
Master Wrightwell. To defeat my object
was the work of Cheat-the-Gallows, Maysfiend and Co., clerks of Old Nick, of whom
even his sable Majesty is ashamed. By
badgering, bribery, perjury and protected insolence, they out-Heroded Herod, and disgraced
even the foul spirit to whom they sold themselves. All the satirists ever wrote of the
corruptest limbs of the law might have passed
as an eulogy on the foul nest of hell-birds, who
hatched treason, and stung all who admitted
them to their confidence. They merit, I grieve
to say, the worst that can be said even of
lawyers, — the necessary evils and infernal
evidence of man's curse and fall.

" Witnesses, supposed to be indifferent persons. were seduced into perjury by the snares of
Cheat-the-Gallows, condemned beforehand to a
species of moral pillory by Maysfiend, with his
sleek face masked in a practised smile, through
which the fiend peeped out, and in some unguarded moment wrote "villain" on his Satanic
brow. This fellow smiled and smiled, and was a
devil, who pelted his victims with all the foul jests
the fox wit of a heartless ruffian can suggest.
Like foul toads they croaked on the edge of the
slimy slough into which they would frighten
their victims. Cheat-the-Gallows was the tool

of Maysfiend, who made him do the dirty work which could not be concealed. Mischief for its own sake was the element in which Cheat-the-Gallows lived, and had his being. Mischief for filthy lucre's sake was the essence of Maysfiend. In ordinary cases it had been observed that their cunning wove round them a net which they intended for others, but which at last entangled themselves. One villain was necessary to another, and the safety, if not the lives, of both the villains, depended on the third. But however fine one thread might be drawn across another, or whatever poor fly might enter their web, there might be a possibility of escape for the prey, unless Popery and Royalty were caught in the meshes. To them the toils are fatal. The honest Protestants, to whom the estates of Plowden and Aston were conveyed, it would appear, were declared malignants, Papists, and Rebels. They had once harboured a priest, twice protected a nun, and worse than all, declared that James was the lawful king, and were, therefore, incapable of holding the property.

"The very delight which Cheat-the-Gallows feels in practising his art, renders it a necessity of his nature. Maysfiend believes that the object to be attained would richly pay him for his labour in transferring the property from the rightful owner to a wealthy client of his own, who was ready to swear allegiance to William, or anything else, for the sake of the property to

be obtained by such Protestant claims as his
client had to prefer."

We must not here take any note of the political intrigues and technical points of the law,
which deprived Catholic loyalists of their hereditary estates. It will be enough to say that
Colonel Plowden was the only person who stood
between William or his minion, and the possession of the noble estates of Plowden and
Aston. There was only one way by which the
estates could be preserved to any member of the
family.

Unwilling to expose to the matter-of-fact man
of business the nature and extent of his own
private feelings and affairs, which he could with
great comfort communicate to our young hero,
the Colonel had, while this conversation was
passing, sent Master Wrightwell out of the way,
on a visitation to the different farms, in company
with the resident steward and auditor, to ascer-
tain the inclinations of the tenants and the state
of their farms ; and whether it might be ad-
visable to convey any portion to a Protestant
situated on the largest holding, just outside the
belt of trees. The result of his observations
would materially assist them in drawing out the
necessary instrument.

" Were any legal provision made which could
secure my estates to my family and my children, among whom I include you, in whom we
all feel such a deep interest, both on your own

account and that of her whom we love," continued the Colonel, turning with paternal warmth towards Robert Strickland, " I should be resigned to any penalty which the invader could impose upon myself."

Before our hero could make a suitable acknowledgment or reply, the notary re-entered the room, exclaiming, " Satan blows the breeze that blows good to no man, Colonel, and the Protestant wind has already blighted our prospect of any safe conveyance of estates to men who may retain them for themselves in perpetuity, or, to faithful tenants from whom the tyranny of the Orange-man may be able to wrest them."

After a brief discussion on the subject of addressing a spirited memorial and plain statement of the case to William, to be presented by the notary himself, Colonel Plowden suggested that his honest advocate should lose no time.

" As soon as you can reach London," says he, " you may obtain an audience."

" Nothing more easy than access to the presence of William of Orange. But kings are not fond of giving hopes, unless to gain some great object ; they leave the disposal of hopes to their ministers. Unless there were actual certainty in the case, they are wise enough to keep civil, silent tongues in their heads," said Wrightwell. " His High Mightiness, colonel, will send me back again with about as much in-

sight into his intentions, as if I made a visit
to the King of the Cannibal Islands, and consulted his carnivorous Majesty as to the particular flavour of Papist pie or a raw bishop.
He would signify his pleasure through some
English traitor or Dutch intruder as early as
possible."

Inability to arrive at any practical result, induced the faithful notary and his client to abandon
the proposed transfer of the estates.

" I would," said the good notary, " make it
my earliest business, good sir, to collect your
rents, and settle such affairs as are still in your
power this very day."

" Then," replied the hospitable colonel, " you
will join us at dinner."

It was in vain that the notary pleaded his
many engagements ; the host would take no excuse.

The two officers repaired to the hunting-field
where, for the last time, perhaps, in England,
they thoroughly enjoyed the sport, and were
only outwitted just under the foot of the
nearest Welsh mountain ; and when they
met at dinner, the varied fortunes of the chase,
the checks, the bursts, the falls, and the cunning
run of the old fox, left, it appears, but little
room for more serious conversation. The
evening passed pleasantly in that light and
joyous conversation which taxes not the
intellect, but invigorates the mind. The

three gentlemen talked of everything but that which concerned the business of each or all of them. The Plowden hounds—their meet at the village of Lydbury—the game fox, which after crossing and re-crossing the river along the valley Horderley, wound his way cunningly backwards and forwards, through flood and field skirting Kempton, then away to Basford, where, after a short check, the hounds turned him, and ran him along Myndtown Slopes to the foot of the Longmynd, where, after a run of six hours and thirty miles, he took earth, leaving the hounds at fault only two hundred yards behind him; nor were they called away till the moon appeared over the hill of Hucklemynd. The artful dodges and baffling cunning of old Reynard afforded conversation for the evening, and were pleasantly compared by the dinner party to the subtle game and foxy tricks of an attorney, whose countenance is a lie. The notary, who gave every man honestly his due, denied that the face of Cheat-the-Gallows was guilty of a mask; for, says he, the creature has the physiognomy of the serpent, as cunning and treacherous as it is destitute of all power but that of mischief; and though the studied smile of Maysfiend may assume a better cast, yet to the physiognomist the distortion will be apparent.

CHAPTER XXXIX.

Though few the days, the happy evenings few,
So warm with heart, so rich with mind they flew,
That my full soul forgot its wish to roam,
And rested there, as in a dream of home.—*Moore.*

THE morrow, as if conscious that it was charged
with eventful destinies, and business of serious
import, dawned solemnly beneath a vast canopy
of clouds, which shrouded the Welsh mountains
in gloom. December winds were chanting their
melancholy dirge over the death of the year
and the departing glories of the Stuarts; all
seemed in fitting mood to realise the dreary
prospects of the loyalists.

The solitary scene without, all the varied
landscape buried in a drizzling, cheerless, freez-
ing fog,—all warned our little party to press
near the cheerful blaze of the old oak which had
for a hundred summers afforded shade.

Recalling to mind the great object of Wrightwell's visit, and the weighty measures they had
to despatch before the fate of loyal Catholics
in England was sealed, and fixed perhaps, for
ever, the hospitable lord of the mansion, after

the first friendly greeting of the morning, and a
social light meal, was the first to resume the
subject of their anxiety.

" All night," says he, " I have pondered over
our plans and the machinations of the deluded
schemers, who are watching our case and under-
mining our arrangements. Would not a golden
key open the door of Master Maysfiend's understanding and close the eyes of Cheat-the-Gallows, and disarm them of their poisoned ar-
rows?"

" Yes," replied the honest notary ; "but not
of their hidden low cunning. In the midnight
depth of their villany they would repair their
meshes and gloat over their fresh demand for a
much larger sum, or for a still higher reward for
their iniquity—depose before a Protestant ma-
gistrate that they had rejected other proposals."

" And thus it is," cried young Strickland, im-
petuously, "that the noble, the loyal, the true
are crushed under the feet of false-hearted
cowards, black-spotted toadies and sycophants,
who cringe and bow ; or fawning dogs, whom a
gentleman spurns with loathing from his feet.
Thus triumph the feeble and the false ; the
treacherous and the base."

" True, young gentleman," said the old notary, whose long experience of mankind had
taught him to read on the tablet of the countenance, and in the tones of the voice, the volumes
which they covered. " Let any thoughtful man

read the page of history, where too many events like these are recorded, and then doubt, if he can, of that future state of rewards and punishments, where all will be made equal — where patient endurance and humility will be crowned with glory, and exulting villany be cast down to hell."

Candour induces us to admit that, however far the notary may have been looking into the blessings or the miseries of Eternity, the Colonel's thoughts were at this crisis, hovering on this lower world, and particularly on that portion of it in which his own interests were immediately involved. "Alack! who, from one day to another can foresee to whose hands his broad acres and goodly gear may fall?" ejaculated the proprietor. "An hereditary Catholic and loyalist like myself, has small chance to preserve his substance from the grasp of the disloyal, the second edition of the shaveling,—' Praise God Barebones.' When I am gone from this place of my ancestors, dear Wrightwell, it is to your protection, so far as in you lies, I shall bequeath the care of Plowden, imploring you to preserve it for those who may be restored to England, and saved from the perilous chances of these evil days. Oh! that we could circumvent the possibility of anything which may impede this happy alliance, which will cement and strengthen the ancient bonds of friendship between two Catholic families who adhere to the Faith. He who would overmaster Fortune, must grasp her

roughly and instantly, that she escape him not.
Why not at once, Master Wrightwell, confide
the estates to trustees, and leave the event to
Heaven?"

" Because," said the other, " we must do our
duty first."

" You jest with me, my old friend," cried the
Colonel ; " are we not both endeavouring to do
our duty?"

" Yes, but we must not do the work in haste,
and repent at leisure," rejoined the other.

" Better, perhaps," added the dispassionate
adviser gravely, " defer these measures till the
darkness of the times shall have cleared away."

" But, suppose," retorted the gallant Colonel,
" if in lieu of clearing, they darken, even to the
utter extinction of loyalty in the land, must my
family be ruined for want of active precaution?
I am anxious that no convulsion of the state
may so severely separate us as to divide my
eldest daughter and him to whom she has long
been endeared, and is now engaged."

Strickland blushed like a maiden.

" They are young, yet," said the notary,
" years must elapse ere they abide together in
wedlock."

At this moment Horseman, and several stable-
boys exercising the stud, fortunately passed the
window, and the cornet left the room to inspect
the splendid animals, and thus escaped the
following conversation.

"But let those years be a time of happy assurance that their destinies and fortunes are secured by the provident and affectionate foresight of their parents." The elder gentlemen, not even noticing Strickland's exit, continued their discourse.

"The complete accomplishment of your purpose under present circumstances," urged the notary, "surpasses our powers. To attempt it might ruin those whom you would shed your blood to save. Had I been simply your professional adviser, and not the old friend of your family, I would watch and work all night, and undertake that my clerks should all day and all night engross the deed of conveyance, or the instrument of trust; but as matters *are*, such preparations, which cannot be executed without the concurrence of Protestants, would only court the invasion of your rights. Besides, I trust you know me to be an exception to your category of lawyers. Let me then speak openly. There are, sir, many causes at this crisis which must inevitably disturb the right exercise of your judgment, physical as well as moral. Your reason under other circumstances, or even in the heat of battle, would be an excellent guide of conduct, and would hold its unshaken throne. Your heart and its affectionate feelings have their own reasons for action, which your intellect cannot apprehend. The will creates your belief in the success of a project, which my disinterested judgment tells me is impracticable or dangerous. The heart's action is safe or dangerous according to the aspect in which you regard it. Your will, which inclines to an impracticable measure, turns away your mind from that which you cannot contemplate with pleasure; and thus your mind, moving with the will, only holds to that which the will approves, and forms its judgments by what it sees and desires; but unless the understanding can establish the judgment on an unshaken foundation, or on strong probability, a rebellious rabble of doubts and fears from time to time will dispute her decisions, and make us sorry when we shall have done that which we cannot undo. Your view of your own case is not seen through the medium of a pure, colourless light. It flows in upon you through painted windows, tinging the future with a brilliancy which is rather the picture of your anticipations than the real result of your efforts based on matter of fact."

" Your reasoning," cried the colonel, " may be geometrically convincing to scientific logicians, but I must confess my inability to comprehend your meaning."

" Our object," rejoined the other, " is the same, but the means of attaining it different. You view it in a light which reveals to me no evidence which my judgment can accept. You cannot, with such enormous overwhelming interests at stake, see all the probabilities of

their sacrifice or redemption conbined in one
view. Action at any hazard is what you contemplate."

" Certainly, my dear old friend," answered
the colonel, mildly; " but surely we are losing
time ?"

The notary, who still wished the energetic
officer to desist from any step which might prejudice and divert his mind, asked leave to ex-
plain his meaning more explicitly. " In our
present position, indignant as we are at the in-
justice of the invader, our estimate of his future
conduct, and of our own best method to influence
it, or avert the calamities it may entail upon
our children, cannot be impartial. Different
eyes see things differently. For instance, our
gallant youth sees them through a glowing,
coloured light—the vision of hope, tinctured by
the feelings of his heart. He looks out through
the beautiful window of the present, into the
future which it affects. Let our young friend
look out of the painted window through the
medium of his bright anticipations of the end,
and the aim, and the prize of his life. Of all
passions, love forms the most beautiful rainbow,
and colours everything; it outshines every
colourless probability—nay, more, I would not
give much for that love which is not as unman-
ageable as a wild two-year-old—as extravagant
as a spendthrift. It soars above proprieties; it
moves about—not always in perfect good taste—

under all pressing emergencies. What husband or wife—what youth or maiden in love—what mother—but says a thousand foolish things in the way of endearment, which the speaker would be sorry for indifferent strangers to hear; yet they were not, at the time of saying them, un-welcome to those to whom such words of tender-ness were addressed. But then, unfortunately they find their way into the journals of the day, and present but a sorry dish when served up cold for the public table. So it is with our own uncontrolled feelings. When made the motive of our action, when they are fresh from the heart, they seem grateful to those identified with us, and to ourselves; but when reduced to a system, on which we would erect an edifice founded on those thoughts that glow and words which burn, the structure may be demolished by an enemy, or even by an indifferent person, in mere sport; it becomes airy as the baseless vision of a dream, as desecrated and ridiculous as love letters published in a newspaper, or read aloud by a sneering lawyer in a court of justice."

" I suppose," said Plowden, " we cannot see things with your eyes, Master Wrightwell ?"

" No," retorted that sagacious lawyer, " nor do you now yourselves see them with the same eyes that you will see them in the retrospect."

" I see them with a father's eyes," cried the colonel, " with which I desire to behold my fair

domain of Plowden again and again ; and which
I would reserve for my children's children at any
price, save the faith for which my fathers sacrificed their worldly glories to the King of kings."

" God forbid," cried the considerate notary,
" that even your perseverance in the faith in
which you believe should reduce you to extreme
poverty ; for poverty is indeed the solution of
many hundred weaknesses—I mean destitution.
When hunger gnaws the entrails, conscience
sleeps, or connives at whatever may appease
such agony ; and during that slumber may be
seen apostasies from honour, fidelity, and friendship, which rouse the indignation of those who
have been deserted, especially when friends
dearer than themselves are involved. Before we
condemn such deserters, let us consider whether
they may not have struggled, and even hoped
against hope ; whether they may not have hun-
gered and thirsted through attachment to the
cause that afflicts them. Let us ask ourselves what we would have done to escape the
nipping frosts of winter and the bitter pangs of
famine, to save our little ones. Let not the
rich, who cannot if he would, know what poverty
means, say, ' This writer has sold himself; that
traitor is a base and venal wretch.' Not so fast.
It was not the *man*, but his *poverty*, that sold
him. What could he do when his wife and
children were looking up to him for the bread
which he had not for himself? Poverty, sir,

passes over the soul like a blight over the fertile
fields, and blasts the flowers of the mind, kills
energy, and murders hope ; prostrates the intellect, weighed down by the oppressed body. It
dries up all the springs of genius, and it makes
a man grovel in the dust. Why? Because he
cannot stand upright, he cannot bear his brow
aloft, when the mansion of his spirit is levelled
with the dust."

" On the other hand," said the Colonel, "if I
may presume to put in a word, which I have had
from those older than myself,—I would say
abundance weighs down the corn stalk ; the fair
fruit tree's branches break under their heavy
weight ; and at the very best, opulence, at times,
becomes the forerunner of poverty. Affluence
renders a man soft and effeminate, and induces
habits of indulgence fatal to health and true
enjoyment."

" True," said the lawyer, " a competency—
neither riches nor poverty, might realise our
chief good ; and yet, there is, after all, no
external circumstance which can master the
man whose treasure is in Heaven. If a poor
fellow can, especially when young, only take
breath under his vine or his fig-tree, and renew
his strength, let it be exhausted ever so much,
he may gird his loins anew and follow more
prosperously, and even overtake the traveller
toiling up Fortune's steep ascent, whose head,
like yonder rocky heights, seems to touch the

clouds, which the setting sun gilds and purples."

"In the meantime," said the Colonel, thoughtfully, "we had surely better secure ourselves against the calamities which we may still be able to avert. To protect ourselves and all we love from the destitution of poverty is a duty. In many a campaign," continued the officer, "I have enjoyed the welcome drink of the little limpid spring, that bubbled through some meadow, or trickled from some friendly rock. There, after the fevered heat of battle, I have slaked my thirst, and gathered cooling berries from the neighbouring copse, to allay the pangs of hunger. But then it was hope, which in a waking dream transferred me from the scene of privation and trial to the land and home of my happiness. The languor which oppressed me was chased away by bright visions of Plowden. I beheld my wife and children coming out of their favourite abode, to welcome and to bless me. Scarcely could the roar of the cannon on the battle-field recall me from this reverie. But now what have I left?"

"Hope, sir," said Wrightwell; "this hope was to Cæsar the empire of the world;—to you, it is the next best thing to your estates; which, if alienated for a night, may be regained in the morning."

"Not if once confiscated by the usurper, or transferred to his minions," said the Colonel, sorrowfully. " But I defer to your judgment and bow to God's will. Yet, I fear the unauthorised usurper, who robs his uncle of his happiness and his crown, will not spare us. I know that God has been pleased to institute the chief magistracy, and transmit it down through one family ; to communicate to it a portion of his power, without however designating those who were to fulfil it, except on extraordinary occasions. God himself raised Saul and David to the throne, but he has not done so to any king of a later date : for there is not at present on the earth a royal house whose origin may not be traced either to election or conquest. Every government then is of divine right, in this sense, that it is agreeable to the designs of the Supreme Ruler, that there should be governors and subjects. Though the history of the house of Stuart is but of yesterday in England, and a few centuries in Scotland, yet it is sanctioned by Heaven—on its justice I would rely."

" On the whole, modern magistracy, with the exception of its religious influence, has not, I apprehend, much degenerated," rejoined Wright-well, "and even from an invader, who may in spite of our loyal efforts be acknowledged and crowned in England, justice may indirectly be obtained. We must bide our time and leave the rest to Heaven. ' He that believeth, will not make haste,' " added the senior, gravely ; " we must abandon the project, and put in an adage which is

M 2

trite, but as true as it is trite. 'Man proposes, but God disposes.' Perjury, I fear, is not just now uncommon in courts of justice. Many of the witnesses would be produced against your most responsible tenant or friend, to whom you may be inclined to convey the estates, in order to secure them. Only to understand the Welsh language, would facilitate the designs of the opponent; for I have known witnesses understanding English, to feign ignorance of its meaning, in order to gain time in the process of translation, to shape and mould their answers according to the interest they wish to serve. To swear that any Protestant who had not vilified a Catholic, was himself papist, would be deemed a profitable duty. In a case similar to yours, a juryman once asked his English neighbour, what was the nature of an action, in which he, the juryman, had given his verdict.

"Nothing can be more difficult than to obtain, at this crisis, satisfactory evidence in courts of justice. *Prima facie*, there is a case. Three counts against you—Firstly, you are a papist; secondly, a loyalist; thirdly, not merely a soldier of fortune, but a landed proprietor. The magistrates, being at once in this moment of infatuation the prosecutors and the judges, would find little difficulty in deciding in favour of the party for whom the firm of Cheat-the-Gallows & Co. are concerned.

" The cup of their iniquities is' well-nigh full;

their hour of retribution is at hand. The blow which they, through their degraded tools aim at us will recoil upon themselves. But in the meantime, the sting which they leave in us, though it be their death, may be our ruin."

" Injured justice will once more assert her Majesty," said the host. " I would sooner face the lion than the hissing, loathsome snake. I can meet the open enemy hand to hand, amid the bloody strife of war and deadly clash of arms, yet feel serene, surrounded by the dying and the dead. But the loathsome, crawling, subtle reptile sickens me by his filthy coils. His fangs prey secretly into the manly heart which never quailed before a mortal foe."

How far the gallant colonel would have wasted his indignation upon the slow dastardly scoundrelism of the fair-faced toadies and their odious tool of dirty work, we know not, for the neighing of a horse arrested his attention, and diverted his thoughts from a subject so unworthy of his noble nature and attracted his eye to a sight which deeply affected him. Both he and his guest moved to the window and beheld a beautiful Spanish jennet trotting round Strickland neighing in a manner expressive of recognition and delight. The sagacious animal, on hearing the well-known voice of his rider's equestrian companion, had, under an instinctive impulse, broken out from a loose box to claim acquaintance with our hero.

This beautiful creature, who had so safely and
so often carried Mary Plowden by the side of
young Strickland, as well mounted as herself,
was treated by all the inmates of Plowden as a
privileged favourite, and every member of the
family had always admired it, and made it a pet
for Mary's sake. The steed was as hardy as he
was noble, and he had just arrived by easy
stages with Harry Horseman, the distinguished
groom, the evening of the preceding day. If
'love me, love my dog,' be a good adage, love me,
love my horse, is not less just. Strickland had
often caressed the animal and patted him on the
neck, when recommending him to the groom's
care at Whitehall. On the present occasion,
perceiving that the sagacious animal at a distance had recognised him, he stepped gladly to
meet the greetings of the jennet, who called to
him in a soft, gentle neighing. The creature
came nearer and nearer to the Cornet, stood
still, and gave him a pleading look of anxiety
for his late rider, at least so Strickland thought.
As plainly as looks and his language could
speak, the steed said, " I too, have lost her."
And then the poor animal gently laid his head
upon young Strickland's bosom. Struck by the
gestures and singular behaviour of the jennet,
which Strickland had no idea of seeing at the
moment, he was moved by the recollections of
her of whom he never ceased to think; and,
overwhelmed by the tenderness of the animal

expressed in the mute eloquence of sacred
Nature's universal language, our hero for a
moment lost his self-possession, and, clasping
his arms round the neck of his lover's favourite
animal, lifted up that voice which was so soon
to command in battle, and wept aloud ; but no
human being witnessed the extent of his amiable
weakness.

"By my faith, brave gentleman," said the
notary, as he resumed his place by the fire, "the
beasts are more loyal-hearted and true than our
fellow creatures, when we differ from their views."

"Exactly so," rejoined the Colonel. "I must
tell thee, notary, in thine ear, that never in my
life was temptation so strong upon me as that
which prompted me to beat out the skulking old
hypocrite's brains, provided I could have reconciled it with my honour to spill the puddle blood
of such vermin as Cheat-the-gallows, Maysfiend,
and Bilson. But the mild influence of the
touching scene which I have beheld has banished
the fancy which passed through my head, and
mastered the influence."

"God's grace alone," said the pious old
notary, "can enable us to resist such temptation,
natural to the human heart."

"Whatever be the passing feelings of resentment which urge me to execute the law by my
own hand, I will not yield to it till it is consistent
with our safety, and more particularly with that
of the king in fair fight."

"Abide thy time," said the other. "If fight thou must at length, as it seems likely, I pray God thou mayest meet an honourable antagonist, and find fair quarters if the combat goes against thee. The spawn of Satan—of the foul fiends' grandmother, whom thou wottest of—will croak out their own lives in venom, and be killed in the spite which will burst them in their own native slime."

While thus they chatted on, without any great object immediately before them; and the great world, its mighty interests, even the Revolution itself, as a natural event seemed forgotten by them; the butler announced the arrival of Mr. Bilson, and his particular request for an interview with the Colonel.

To describe the rush of mingled sensations that came crowding upon the indignant cavalier were impossible; for even Bilson's colleagues in legal iniquity were but children compared to him. Indeed, than Titus Oates himself, he was only less enviably distinguished for lack of opportunity.

His intellectual resources and tortuous baseness were the gifts through which he compensated for low birth and plebeian origin, by calumniating and plotting against the well born and the honourable. Plowden's usually calm features grew sterner and darker, his lips became more compressed, while he courteously but decidedly declined the honour of any personal conference with the learned Bilson.

To spare his friend the Colonel further an-
noyance, Wrightwell left the room, to rebuke the
man's audacity, and take care that he should not
obtrude himself into the presence of the gentleman, who still considered that his house was his
castle.   The imperturbable notary's great dread
was, that should the diabolical accuser invade
the officer's privacy, he would throw him body and
bones, neck and heels, out of the window, and
thereby afford the cunning clique what they most
earnestly desired.   Before, however, the good,
grave man could pass out of one door, in came
the visitor, sans cérémonie, at the other.

" Good morning, Colonel Plowden," says he ;
" I rejoice to find you here at this glad time ; a
right merry Christmas to you and yours, and
many returns of it in your own happy home, in
this mansion here !   I have come from Shrewsbury to celebrate a midnight mass, as I know
your own chaplain is not here."

" Thanks, thank you from my heart, Father
Wilson," responded the other ; " your entrance
has relieved us from a misapprehension.   It
was Bilson, not Wilson, that was announced."

" And Wilson sounds so dreadfully like Bilson,
especially when the W has not its own sound,
such as the Yorkshire folk give it in ' whole '
and ' who,' " remarked the priest, " that this is
not the first time my name has been confounded
with that of the accuser.   The cowardly ruffian,
however, will not for the future have any advan-

tage from turning my W into B, for so long has
he been at home in scenes of outrage and
fraud that he has in vain armed himself in a
triple coat of brass. Not satisfied with aspersing
the reputation of Catholics, he has absconded
with £50,000 of a good Protestant, his client,
who expected by his aid to succeed to a Catholic
estate. Not having courage to face the gallows,
he has taken ship to America, but if report be
true, overcome by his fears he leaped overboard
into the Channel."

"Poor, miserable man," said the Colonel.
"Not a moment for conversion or repentance !"

"It is, indeed, I know," said Wrightwell, "a
sad aggravation of all your vexations to hear
even of this man's suicide."

"Such men are always cowards," said the
priest. "They neither fear God, nor regard
man, until the pit yawns at their feet. They
plunge into destruction with their eyes closed."

Strickland, who had sometime returned, and
been duly introduced to Father Wilson, who
was well-known to the notary, related Horseman's story of himself, to the Colonel and his
friends, of which the confusion of the names
of Wilson and Bilson reminded him. It so
happened that soon after the scene, which in
the second volume we described near London
Bridge, Tom Killigrew having discovered with
great glee, the gentle groom's personification
of his mistress, came down to him, sparkling in

his scabious velvet dress, and advised him to
resume his own true character and garb, or at
least, to don man's attire as soon as possible,
even condescending to point out a shop where
he could suit himself. He tried on several
ready-made and second-hand suits, and at last,
by a curious coincidence, purchased the only one
that fitted him, formerly worn by a gentleman
of the very same name, who, having done something to render a disguise desirable, exchanged
his elegant country dress for a carter's blouse
and under-garments, and went on his way.
Horseman's figure and general appearance precisely corresponding with the former wearer of
the clothes, exposed him to many perils, and
actually identified him so unpleasantly with the
disguised fugitive, that the poor groom was cap-
tured, tried, and by the merest chance discharged.
Twice had he been arrested on his road from
London to Plowden; and frequently suspected
and delayed. " I am happy," said the Colonel,
" that he has arrived in time for Christmas—
he generally serves mass, and is in every respect
an excellent Catholic, and gifted with many ingenious resources in such times as these ; he had
always been the life of those plays and theatrical
entertainments, which on great festivals are
tolerated by the Church."

Revelry, and innocent mirth, and domestic
reunions, and affectionate salutations of family
endearments had, Christmas after Christmas,

from time immemorial, called up the merry
echoes of old Plowden. The evening now had
set in with storms which evinced a passionate
sort of pleasure in throwing a gloom over
Christmas. They were " no soft dissolving
tears," but regular wailings, in a perfect out-
burst of woe ; wailings in accents wild and
melancholy all through the wintry Heaven. No
joyful light—no peaceful home, upon the infant
Saviour's cradle, on that day smiled ; but sadly
the weather harmonized with the feelings of the
husband, tne father and the loyalist : separated
from his wife, his children, and his king. Almost
a lonely dweller in the ancestral abode, which
so long had on Christmas been a residence of
sweet domestic joy. Alas ! what man is there
beyond the noon-day of life, even under brighter
skies and happier circumstances than those
which tinged the prospects of Colonel Plowden,
on the Christmas of 1688, who has not felt
that the dreamy future of his youth, which
promised everything, has comparatively performed nothing. In the lives of most men,
hope fulfilled, is another word for disappointment.
When from Christmas-day we look backwards
and forwards, and cast down our eyes on the
present, along the past we see a vista of cypresses
and tombs, beneath which sleep in darkness the
companions of our youth, and the dear friends
of our advanced age ; such friends as we have
loved at Christmas we miss. We can never

again find their like on earth. Age, cruel experience of a heartless world, forbid us to form again such congenial, open-hearted, and confiding attachments. Such the retrospect, perhaps, of the best of us middle-aged men at Christmas-tide. The present, even in the bosom of our family, is a sunbeam which owes all its bliss to Him whose birth we celebrate. The future from such a stage in our life appears but a mirage in the desert, which takes its colouring and its beauty from that sun which never sets, and where faith and hope are lost in deathless and unchanging love. The human heart languishes and longs for a communion and a social joy which earth cannot realise ; and, therefore, to many of us Christmas brings sadness, and we know not precisely why.

Strickland, whose unaffected love of nature was only equalled by his fortitude, ventured to say that Christmas, even when clothed in clouds, had still bright living things, contrasted with the general gloom outside. " Look," cried he, with all the native delight of an unsophisticated child. " Look at that sweet little robin, with its scarlet plumage and soft confiding eye. He has gratefully pecked up the crumbs on the window sill, and is now singing his Christmas carol."

" Yes," said Father Wilson, " and you see the bright evergreens in which he takes shelter form an equally bright contrast to the leafless, dark, mournful trees around them."

"It is plain," observed the Colonel, "that what the robin is among birds the evergreens are among trees."

"And yet," remarked the man of law, "methinks to a moody temper evergreens on such a day as this seem like strangers exulting over the rest of the trees in their destitution. Yon fir tree, like the haughty foreigner, triumphs over the sylvan decay. The robin redbreast however must, with all his poetical associations, be dear to us, and welcome to the crumbs which fall from our table, and yet, there seems something invidious in the very music of his sweet, low song."

"Still," said the priest, "in that plaintive cadence there is a voice which says the year 'is not dead, but sleepeth.'" This and much more he said. "And all this leafless and unclouded scene shall flush into variety again."

"Long, long before that natural restoration," sighed the Lord of Plowden, "will a great change have passed over Britain, and though the coming change can to the Catholic be no indication that the term of the dominion of the Church is approaching in England, she is the living among the dead. The sacred robin sadly chants his everlasting hymn through every tempest, and through every change, as sings the Church her deathless song."

"And every change, my dear sir," said the priest, "has its mercies, if not its rejoicings;

the worst evil which can befall us, for it includes in itself many others, is that uneasiness which the mind conceives on account of some involuntary evil. If we suffer ourselves to grow impatient, so far from removing, we only augment our calamity; it sinks us under overwhelming sadness; so that, losing both courage and strength, we deem our sad state irremediable. Inquietude is the greatest evil, sin excepted, that can befal the soul. For as at this moment seditions and evil commotions lay waste the state within, and render it incapable of resisting its enemies from without; so our hearts, when uneasy and disturbed, have no power to preserve the virtues which they have acquired, or to resist the enemy of our souls and bodies. When our hearts are taken with a desire to escape from some evil, or to retain some good, and we struggle impatiently to be free, we are like birds in a net, which, by fluttering and beating themselves violently, instead of making good their escape, do but more completely entangle themselves in the fatal meshes. We cling to what may hurt us."

"I had observed to Master Wrightwell before you arrived, Father Wilson," said the Colonel, "that I am only inclined to such prudent steps as would alleviate or avert the calamity which we fear."

"Certainly," replied the priest, "calmly and orderly to adopt such means as may be best suited to your admirable purpose is not less your duty than our desire.· I do not mean that we are to be negligent or indifferent; but that, in order to succeed, we must be serene and collected. If the calamity never come, then are all our fears worse than vain; if it overtake us, quietness and resignation will enable us to bear the worst, and for which, Advent is calculated to prepare us. The soul that beholds the beauty of that holy poverty which surrounded Him, whose birth we celebrate, holds all earthly possessions by a pure dependence on the will of God; and is freed from the captivity of this world. What though the bodily absence of our friends, who in better times rejoiced together with us round the family hearth, and knelt with us before the same altar, and there partook with us at the same time of the Bread of Life on Christmas morning, be now severed from us by the intervening sea? — what though some of them may have passed out of the flesh? to us Catholics they are present in the communion of saints—so that neither life, nor death, nor distance, nor time can separate us from those we love."

Should the discerning reader object that the tone of this conversation is too serious for the occasion, let him remember that, apart from all intercourse with the outward world, the speakers required a Christian heroism to meet the troubles which they could not prevent. That exile and its crosses were terrible barriers, opposed to their strong will; that to storm, or assail, or in some way defeat the enemy, appeared to him a duty which religion and its influence could only regulate and control. A well of pure thoughts flowed over and found vent in words which calmed down the most fevered crisis of a loving father's anxieties. Confiding hearts involved in one and the same destiny, unlocked their treasures, and thus the hours of this remarkable Christmas Eve were drawn out in grave and thoughtful conversation.

In an oratory, or little chapel, on a steep ascent, amid the deep seclusion of cypresses and spreading cedars, the Colonel purposed that the priest should celebrate the midnight Mass. But the lawyer and the priest, dissuaded him from any exhibition of the faith, which might attract hostile attention, and incur unnecessary danger.

On the altar of the little chapel within the mansion, there the Holy Sacrifice of the midnight Mass was offered; and as the pious father ascended the stairs, he quietly, to his little domestic congregation, said, " At such a solemn hour as this, let us in Spirit accompany the Blessed Virgin and the other pious women going up to Mount Calvary, to be present at the death of Our Lord. Behold! with an eye of faith, your Redeemer carrying his cross before you, to be sacrificed thereon for your sins; and bewail those sins as the causes of all the sufferings on which he entered about this hour—when he became a 'man of sorrows and acquainted with grief.' "

Impressed with such holy recollections, after Mass, the members of the household and the · guests retired to rest, but not before they realised the blessings of that winter morning on which the MIGHTY GOD, "THE PRINCE OF PEACE," "THE LORD FROM HEAVEN," *made Man*, was born and cradled in a manger.

CHAPTER XL.

The fall of waters and the song of birds,
And hills that echo to the distant herds,
Are luxuries, excelling all the glare
The world can boast, and her chief favourites share.

Cowper.

A MORE dreary scene than Christmas morning presented at the foot of the snow-mantled mountains could scarcely be witnessed. In a large and old-fashioned library, with a projecting window to the east, through which a feeble ray of sun was struggling, Strickland found a small breakfast table laid, beside a broad fire-place, in which blazed merrily logs of oak wood. The aspect of comfort in everything within contrasted cheerfully with the outside. On another table lay scattered the latest of those political pamphlets which the distracted state of the nation evoked; many of them written in gall, and tinctured with sarcasm. The greater number were a defence of the position which James had assigned to Catholics, and the cutting attacks on a party who forbade that liberty to a Papist which it claimed for itself and all other sects. There were also Pin-

N 2

daric verses by Prior, and lampoons by Wy-
cherley. Tom Duffrey's songs, "Phillida, Phillida," or, "To horse, brave boys; to New-
market—to horse!" Also "Dryden's Settle."
The Colonel soon joined him, offering him all
the glad gratulations of the day. In another
instant the lawyer and Mr. Wilson entered, and
all sat down to a sumptuous breakfast, which,
after the early Mass, they thoroughly enjoyed.

Along many a shaded walk and winding path
might be seen dimly from the window the few scattered worshippers timidly returning from the little
chapel already mentioned to their sequestered
homes of Plowden. The partridges and pheasants
feeling no fear, came up to the windows for the
crumbs from the table, which the family had
been in the habit of giving them. It was while
raising his head to look at these beautiful birds,
that a picture caught Strickland's eye, which he
had not before discovered. The picture in
shadow, between two windows, was that of a
lovely girl of about twelve years old, bearing a
basket of corn, and surrounded by birds of
varied plumage and different sorts. Water
fowls there were from the lake, and domestic
poultry also, while flights of pigeons were
winging their way from all quarters to her feet.
We need scarcely say, from what we know of
her tastes and habits, that this fair, graceful
child was Mary Plowden. The real living birds
were present; but she, whose delight it had

been to feed them, was an exile in a foreign
land. Strickland gazed on the pheasants; but
he thought on her, and escaped observation.

The lord of the mansion. was evidently a
passionate lover of sport, but never would he
suffer a single shot to be fired within the
hospitable precincts to which the feathered company were invited.

These seem small things in a book, but they are
charming when seen on the spot, completing a
home scene which bespeaks tranquillity and repose.

The weather still continuing so uninviting
to go abroad, the party after breakfast naturally
talked about the coming events of the revolution,
which had indeed cast its shadow before it.
To avoid any religious topic which could give
pain to Wrightwell was the studied purpose of
Colonel Plowden, who recommended him to the
books by which they were surrounded—some
Catholic, some Protestant, and others of a
neutral character. The first volume which he
took from the shelf was one of Stillingfleet, Dean
of St. Paul's, who had by his "Irenicum,"
written against the doctrine of Apostolical Succession, and against the theory of the divine
institution of the hierarchical order. The man of
law declared his inability to see on what grounds
such dignitaries of the Establishment claimed
the property of the ancient church, even granting
it to be corrupted. He next was highly entertained with the "Hind and Panther," of

Dryden, especially where he describes Burnet
in the character of the Buzzard, whom the
Doves or Anglican clergy had elected for their
king. But after some quiet reading the notary
declared boldly to his client, that it was altogether on a misconception of a matter of fact
that Dryden exclaims,

> " How answering to its end a church is made,
> Whose power is but to counsel and persuade !
> A solid rock on which secure she stands :
> Eternal house not built with human hands !
> A sure defence against the infernal gate,
> A patent, during pleasure of the state."

" I know," says the honest man, " our church
has been called an ' Act of Parliament Church,'
by Dissenters as well as Roman Catholics. The
sarcasm, however, implied in the ' Hind and
Panther,' is rather unhappy in its application
to a church whose prelates, ages before the
mission of Augustine, had sat in the Council
of Ariminum."

" Was that before the communion of the
Church of England with Rome and her spiritual
jurisdiction ?" asked Strickland.

" Before popery was heard of," said the
notary. " So far, however, as Dryden alludes to
dissenters, he is correct ; but it is scarcely
courteous to ridicule the Church which he has
deserted. He has treated her as the Pagans of
old treated their children. It is too bad in an
Apostate to dress up the Church which he has
abandoned in the skin of a wild beast, and then

exhibit her baited and sacrificed to the public amusement."

Strickland said he was not aware the Romans made a butcher's holiday by fighting Protestants with wild beasts.

" The scarlet of Rome," said the notary, " to my eye, is not worse than the drab of the Quaker or the costume of the Calvinist;—the German cloak which covers the wolf.

> " Never was so deformed a beast of grace,
> .... But his rough crest he rears;
> And pricks up his predestinating ears. "

" The nation recognises every conceivable shade of religious opinion, I admit," said the candid speaker. " But the subject of my regret is the conflicting doctrines which the clergy of the reformed Church hold among themselves; and yet, as a body of men it was agreed by their enemies that the English clergy were the best men of the day;—and that hundreds of them would sooner resign their preferment than swear allegiance to the usurper." Just at this stage of the conversation, the clouds lifted, and the sun shed a ray of cheerfulness on that winter day.

The Colonel, accompanied by the notary, visited many of his poor neighbours and retainers on the estate; relieving the distressed and encouraging those who dreaded ejectment or persecution.

The holy priest, according to the request of the domestic chaplain, who by this time had reached St. Germains, ministered to the sick, confirmed the wavering, and cautioned them against the blandishments or threats of the heretic.

" What will it profit you," said he, "if you gain the whole world and lose your own soul ! Be strong in the faith. Persevere to the end. Pray that your faith fail not in the evil day."— He gave them his blessing and recommended them to God and to the saints.

As for Strickland, he passed the time in the favourite haunts of his loved one ; wrote a long letter to her full of his agreeable surprise, and full of Plowden—of her palfrey and her feathered friends. Thus the party passed the day till evening, when they prepared for the dinner hour.

They again met after their respective occupations in a withdrawing-room, the walls of which were covered with pictures of great price, the very frames objects of wonder and admiration. One of the most conspicuous was that of the great Louis XIV. himself. A miniature of William of Orange placed over the chimney-piece as captain-general of the army and admiral of the fleet, the great champion of his own country before his refusal and subsequent acceptance of the Princess Mary, attracted general attention.

" It is the only portrait of the Dutch captain I ever saw," said the notary, "which impresses on me the dead certainty of a likeness. That stony, resolute, stern, heavy, and, were it not for his eyes, stolid expression, is drawn to the life. The qualities by which he soars on his lofty aspirations to the throne of his poor uncle, are scarcely obvious to any but a very experienced spectator."

"Whatever may be the talents of the invader," rejoined Strickland, "even charity can scarcely be indulgent to a character whose power is deceit, and whose insincerity is success."

"Not only as a Protestant, but as a Cavalier and a Tory, I own that were it not for William's hypocrisy I could esteem him. He has, perhaps, the whole of those subtle calculations of the firm of Maysfiend, Cheat-the-Gallows, and Bilson combined and centred in himself, but he has more—he has that grandeur of genius and undeviating consistency of purpose which achieve the summit of ambition," retorted the notary.

"Sir," said the host, with an unwonted warmth, "you astonish us by your profound knowledge of the man, so correctly do you judge him. No one, perhaps, ever so steeled his own breast against the natural instincts of humanity, and no one so cunningly covetous of glory was ever so successful. No one, I think, ever rose to such a height through such treacherous acts, that must seem nearly to all but himself worthy of remorse."

"He is destitute," says the priest, "of all that

sympathy and communion of feeling, which can render the summit of his wishes worth the painful ascent. He is, in truth, one of the most unhappy and anxious of mortals; he has no one dear enough to him to share his usurped glories or divide his difficulties. Already the dawn, which seems so enviable and so bright, is overcast, and many signs in the horizon portend a short, dark, and stormy day."

" Very natural," retorted the lawyer, playfully, " that the clergy and the army, who are only to be distinguished as ' black coats and red coats,' the curses of the nation, should complain."

" Wait," cried Strickland, with enthusiasm, " until next Christmas. Ay! only wait a month, and England will have relapsed from her hot fit to her cold fit; and the discontent will not be confined to the ' black coats and red coats.' However this may prove, I wish the fruit of the Orange tree were hung on its own bough."

At this part of the conversation, the old favourite butler entering announced dinner. The Colonel was one of the most accomplished hosts that ever dispensed the honours of a table. Whatever reserve he maintained at other times, here he was free, open, and as courteous as he was cordial. His manner, perhaps, the most difficult to acquire, was the happy union of thorough good breeding and friendly ease. Well qualified, however, as he was to meet every emergency of social entertainment, he showed on

the present occasion far less animation and tact
than was his wont; so great was his anxiety to
avoid the great topic of the day, which occupied
his thoughts so deeply, without betraying the
effort which it cost him.   To forget every subject of regret and enjoy the Christmas evening,
and to make himself agreeable to his little party
was his object, and it was attained ; for he soon
emerged from the gloom of his own dreary
musings, and became one of the pleasantest of
the company.

Soon the pleasing influence of good cheer and
unstudied conversation banished care and made
the present happy.   Father Wilson, against
whom the Colonel had always a joke about Bilson, was no judge of the triumphs of the cuisine,
or the precise aroma and flavour of wines : he
mixed up his Madeira, Bourdeaux, and Burgundy
together in a fashion which would at other tables
have sadly deteriorated him in the estimation of
the bon vivants ; yet he was more quaint and
original than vulgar.   The wine was duly appreciated, however, by all, and went freely round.
Claret, which had a flavour that courted criticism,
began to inspire the pleasant party with that fine
flow of lively remarks and sprightly notions,
which at least to Mr. Wilson were far more
agreeable than the usual table talk on the science
of gastronomy.

"What splendid action that horse has you
hunted last week," said Strickland.

" That's the style of thing they are so mad after in Hyde Park," said the notary : " high action, and as fast as high."

" The jennet Andalusia," is the most beautiful animal I ever had," said the Colonel ; " and, Wrightwell, let her be cared for, at any rate, for she is a treasure."

" But of all the performers I ever beheld," said Strickland, " Young Clare's Irish Faugh-a-ballagh takes the lead. The horse and the rider have but one will. They go at anything, and pass every man in the field. Both will soon be in their native country, and are as impetuous as the king is irresolute."

This remark most unintentionally carried their thoughts to the approaching war in Ireland, which must call the Colonel from his family almost as soon as he could see them settled at St. Germains.

" So, Colonel," said Mr. Wilson, when the dinner was removed, " you are going to France, and thence with the king to Ireland."

This was rather a sore subject ; for the valiant officer's anticipations of the personal command of James, against William's rough hosts, were by no means joyous. Besides, he could not but feel indignant at the recollection that treachery in officers of the highest rank, and the king's indecision, had already disgraced their short campaign, which had ingloriously decided the probable fate of James. " Forty-

five regiments," exclaimed he, as he struck his
hand upon the table, "as regular an army as
ever marched to battle under the royal standard
of England, have retreated precipitately before
an invader, and submitted to him without a
struggle."

"Yes," says Mr. Wilson, who was more
earnest than happy in his remarks; "the
clowns who, armed with pitchforks, and mounted
on cart-horses, had straggled in the train of
Lovelace and Delamere, have borne a greater
part in the revolution than those splendid household troops, whose plumed hats, embroidered
coats, and curvetting chargers, the Londoners
had so often seen with admiration in Hyde Park."
Though this was really not meant to be a taunt,
even the senior officer felt a rising rush of
military furor, which he could with difficulty
control. Nothing but Strickland's veneration
for the office of the holy and well-intentioned
priest could restrain his anger.

The notary, however, threw oil upon the
troubled waters, observing, that he had always
been taught that the very highest duty of a
soldier was obedience to orders, and that it must
have required a more noble courage and self-
denying fortitude in Craven and his officers to
yield to the king's command than to fight and
smash the Dutch guards.

"To abandon the dear, sweet country, with
its healthy pleasures, for the town, and especially

the court, that great focus of intrigue, falsehood, hollow joys, and real sorrows, must be to a man of your tastes a mortification and matter for regret," said the priest to the Colonel.

" There you are right; but St. Germains, I fancy, will be more like a family."

" Of this large and varied family," remarked Wrightwell, "the greatest domestic privilege will be to quarrel, to any excess, without restraint or redress."

" Do you know that my residence here for a month would wed me to country life, so far, that I should wonder why the mighty and the affluent leave their sweet homes and the beauties of nature, and voluntarily expose themselves in the frail vessel of the court, to a sea of temptation and peril. The tide of fortune still rolls onward, and from time to time leaves me safe upon the land which I love. In this once happy spot I long enjoyed the innocence and fresh buoyancy of my children, gladly turning away from the tortuous paths and scheming designs of men's plotting rivalry. How delightful is it then, my friends," cried the Colonel, with ardour, " to relax into the fearless natural gaiety of infant minds and unconcealed thoughts ! In our walks, round many a tree, the little ones used to hide themselves, or run away from me, or give me chase."

" Indeed, sir," said the priest, " you have had a life of more than man's usual share of happiness."

" And will resume it again," cried the notary.

" From children only I fear we have the innocence of joyful hearts ; the fresh outpouring of a guileless and confiding nature. In the paradise of a home like this, with the opening flowers of your domestic Eden flourishing around you, those little ones, the favourites of Heaven, who are but a little lower than the angels, are your pledge of future happiness, beneath the protecting mantle of maternal fondness," said the priest.

The isolated father was affected, but spoke not ; nor was Strickland indifferent to the picture.

" The man hardened by the world and involved in its strifes," said the notary, " as well as the proud soldier, is never so unselfish and amiable as when unbending his stiff, cold, stern nature before the charms of a child. It is thus that we parents for a sunny moment fling away our ambition, and become children among children. How wonderfully does the sinless spirit of the child, who is a child indeed, shed its sweet influence over the subtle workings of the taxed mind of man, soothing its conflicts, and hushing all its petty discords to rest ! "

" Of all the advantages to parents," said the priest, " perhaps the greatest is the power of Christian self-control. Nay, even a kind of instinctive shame checks the indulgence of violent passion or impulse before them, whether it be anger or grief, or the expression of folly.

The eyes of young children are too new upon
earth to be allowed as yet to look upon evil.
Their ears too open to hallowed words to be
filled with sinful language. Their dress is a
robe of snow white innocence, fresh from the
waters of baptism, and must be unsullied by the
stain of sinful example. The truly loving parent
will curb his temper of mind in the presence
of his child; and even to the worldly father
his children are a restraint, for he permits not
his little ones to witness the result which they
cannot understand."

Such was the conversation in which the host
took no great part, for everything told him too
plainly he was no longer in the bosom of a
happy home. His mansion was no longer his
castle, or his hearth a sanctuary, where no
malice could assail him. And never before,
perhaps, did the separation of Strickland from
his dear friends seem so devoid of happiness.

Notwithstanding their intention to revel only
in light and amusing conversation, they went
from one thing to another, till they glided into
reality. The men, in spite of one or two unhappy remarks of Mr. Wilson, were well pleased
with each other, and conversation flowed above
and beyond the ordinary surface of table talk.
The very sight of everything around him reminded Colonel Plowden of past happiness.
There was the window-seat where his daughter
Mary loved to look on the green hills, sloping

down to that dark stream where curling eddies marked the leaping trout.

Here was Mrs. Plowden's favourite boudoir; it breathed of her presence, it spoke of her absence. The chair she sat on last Christmas day was there. Immersed in gloomy thoughts in the early morning, he had wandered from room to room, and recollections of bygone pleasures and forebodings of a dubious future rose involuntarily to his mind, so that he had no heart for mirth. A silence now ensued which fortunately was suddenly broken by nothing more fatal to the conviviality of the party than the announcement made by the butler of " tobacco and lights in the smoking room."

For fifty years this old butler had been in various capacities a servant in the Plowden family, and his reverence for his present master went on increasing with every year. In his eyes the Colonel was the perfection of the Cavaliers—the flower of the family; nor could he bring himself to believe in a Protestant country such another Catholic could be found. He gave him credit for every good quality of which even a Catholic was capable. He was identified with the family; their country was his country; their home was his home; he called all that was theirs his; and loved the children as if he were their grandfather. Never in a servant was there a more faithful expression of the hospitality which pervaded the house

than the manner of Thomas Goodman towards
strangers.   Indeed there is nothing which
declares to us of the present day the character
of the master so correctly as the tone and
bearing of domestic servants to us, as visitors,
especially if we be strangers.

Thomas Goodman, too, understood and even
anticipated the wishes and habits of the master,
and made his arrangements according to the
tastes of the guests whom the host desired to
entertain.   He had therefore, believing the
pleasures of the pipe were suited to the occasion, prepared a small-panelled, lofty room,
usually dedicated to this soothing pastime.   A
china bowl of mulled wine, redolent of orange
and limes, filled the room with a fragrance only
equalled by that of the aromatic weed, which
he supplied together with long pipes in the
fashion of the day.

To this agreeable, well-warmed apartment the
party repaired.   There was at the time we speak
of—and it has increased every day since—a habit
of smoking, which neither good breeding nor
social intercourse forbade.   To young Strickland
only the custom was new.   He cast his eyes
over the table and through the room, and wondered as much as if he had been ushered into
the divan of the Royal Turk.   Here, though
the conversation was free and unrestrained, he
felt all the awkwardness of his position as a
non-smoker.   He sat down pipeless, and won-

dered, in silence, what influence the fumes of tobacco could have on human nature.

" In my first campaign," said the Colonel, " and subsequently in our marches against the Duke of Monmouth, there was no reward or encouragement proved a better allurement towards the good behaviour of the men, than the prospect of a pipe of good tobacco. There is really nothing new in the practice of smoking. The pipe is an old institution, though the herb consumed was different from what is called the ' base and barbarous weed,' which we received as well as potatoes and chocolate from America."

" I believe," said the notary, " the tobacco plant and its perfumes had made the current of the Globe before the potato had crossed the Irish Channel."

" The valuable art, perhaps," observed the priest, " is only an improvement upon the barbarous Thracian fashion of puffing from pipes marjoram fumes after dinner."

" Tobacco," said the Colonel, " is truly a universal conqueror; it invades India, Persia, China, Japan." Then, perceiving that Strickland declined the weed, he assured him that to raise a cloud on his own account was his best defence. In a moment the curling perfumes were eddying in circles from his long pipe, in wreaths about his head, and mingling with the pervading cloud of incense. The soothing influence was so agreeable, that even the novice

o 2

quite enjoyed it, and declared, as an apology for his hesitation and delay, that he had always been cautioned by "counterblasts" against a whiff of tobacco.

"When James I. of England counterblasted against the smoke of London, and fogs of London, he declared that Beelzebub was smoking a pipe," said the notary, quaffing a draught of the nectar beside him. "He showed his royal weakness as plainly as he evinced his vanity, in taking to himself the sermon, with the text, 'James, the servant of God;' for even the manservant and the maid-servant, the soldier and the sailor, and the swain who drove his team a-field, rejoiced in the curling clouds, fragrant with the aroma of American weed. Men smoked, still smoke, and will for ever smoke."

If the uninitiated gentleman felt uncomfortable, he certainly manifested no unfavourable symptoms which were sufficient to interrupt the flow of conversation, which, after this little prelude to the entertainment, took its course in channels as agreeable as they were various and dissimilar, and ran through all the topics of hunting, horses, racing, farming ancient and modern ; from the Georgics of Virgil, down to the last book of Farriery, often mingled with a tone of playful raillery that raised a laugh now and then, which was pleasantly re-echoed.

The disturbances, however, of which there had been rumours, from the more southern parts of the country, were too alarming and advancing to be passed over in silence. The safety of the party might be endangered by lingering too long in the abode of a Catholic royalist. The uncertainty of the rumours and constant interception of letters perplexed them. The Colonel made no comment whatever on the danger ; but resolved in his own mind, before the party retired to rest, to make arrangements on the following day for the departure of himself and his guests to their respective destinations. To break this to them was a delicate and arduous task. He was just entering upon it courteously, with all that mild Christian eloquence of which he was master, and whose suavity is persuasion : all were listening with profound attention, when the tramp of many horses and the clang of arms were heard distinctly coming through the frosty night air along the public road with which the avenue was connected. A suspicion of the truth flashed upon the Colonel's mind : he listened with eagerness, and was soon confirmed in his worst suspicion.

The nearer approach of the horsemen, and the regularity of their pace, made it but too evident that they were disciplined troops, not such as daily flocked to join the motley bands to await the command of Schomberg, but the well-trained troops of some officer deserting from the royal standard, en route for the north of Ireland. Fears of personal danger were strangers to the heart of a Plowden or a Strickland. Their concern was for the cause which they espoused.

The Colonel was in some agitation; his well-known loyalty and his religion invited an assault. He felt that he was but ill prepared to defend his house against an attack, to which he believed it would be exposed. Defended only by a garrison of two soldiers, a man of law, who eschewed violence, and a priest less martial than Bishop Compton or Parson Walker, he hastened to the conclusion that stratagery would be better than warfare.

Simply in the civil dress which they had on at the moment, having first consigned his reverence to the hiding-place, which had not been occupied since the days of Red-nosed Noll, and letting the lawyer shift for himself, the two officers proceeded towards the troopers, to hold, if practicable, a parley with the commander, when presently, in the light of the moon, which was now high and full in the heavens, they perceived a single horseman cantering up the avenue, apparently charged with some message from his commanding officer. It might be to demand the surrender of the mansion. They were ascending a rising ground from which the mounted officer threw a letter over the inner lodge gate, and retiring immediately, they saw him rejoin the troop, which had formed, up near the first lodge, but now peaceably continued their course along the road.

They picked up the missile in some doubt as to its import. No sooner had they returned into the house, than the Colonel opened the letter. It was brief, plain, but written in a strange hand. It ran thus : " Colonel Plowden is solemnly assured of the safety of himself and his family, and notwithstanding any report or suspicion to the contrary, and in spite of any alarm which circumstances may suggest, not a member of his household, or a creature belonging to him will be molested, nor in the present state of affairs shall the slightest injury be done on the estate of Plowden. *For the hands of the Honourable Colonel Plowden*, from one who is grateful for his good offices."

This friendly intimation from the enemy changed the intention of Colonel Plowden, who had resolved, as we have already seen, to leave Plowden the next day, till the event of the impending storm should be decided—an event not less important in its aspect and results than the Norman Conquest. Encouraged by this assurance, he laid aside, at least for a few days, this precaution. He restored confidence to his friends, and playfully pulled Father Wilson out of his den. He had better grounded conjectures than he told his guests, of the quarter from which the pledge of his security had come ; and nothing less than a feeling of honour could have imposed silence on a man of his ingenuous and open disposition.

Little more than a month had passed since
Major-General Kirke had been arrested by Lord
Feversham, on suspicion; but the king, believing his assertions of innocence, and possibly,
under the generous advice of Plowden and Powis,
ordered him to be set at liberty.   Subsequently,
a detachment, which was thought to be sufficient
for the relief of Londonderry, was despatched
for Liverpool, under the command of Kirke.
Kirke's troops, by a slight détour, *en route* to
Liverpool, passsd by Plowden, probably long in
advance of the Major himself.   He had ordered
his confidential officer to march through Shropshire, and entrusted to him the letter already
mentioned.

Wrightwell's congratulations on the agreeable
surprise were as heartfelt as they were graceful ;
the joy produced by the happy termination of
their alarm was great in proportion to their
previous anxiety.   The very mirth which the
party now felt was the strongest evidence of the
apprehension from which they were relieved.

" We may yet weather out the storm," said
the notary.

" I would give more for the guarantee of the
laconic note from military quarters than your en-
dorsed sheepskin," observed the liberated priest.

" I would sooner trust to our own good
swords than to either," was the Colonel's martial answer.

Overjoyed at the great event of the evening,

and full of the scene through which they had passed that Christmas-day, they all retired for the night, or rather for the morning.

Though our young hero laid down in bed he could not sleep ; a strange sensation of excitement and mysterious apprehension—an anxious and unwonted notion of something undefined— a confusion of sorrows and joys came over him ; and at every noise he arose and looked out of the window and up the avenue, which was silent and still.

The hovering clouds of wreathed tobacco smoke seemed to roll darkly around his bed, and through his half-closed eyes he saw figures, wild, fantastic, and unsightly. The reflections of the day—the influence of the night's adventure, which denied him the fair opportunity of measuring his strength with some hostile challenge—all sat brooding like a nightmare upon his bosom ; nor could he dismiss from his thoughts the vicissitudes of his young life, and his unexpected introduction to Plowden Hall. The devices of Maysfiend and Co., to sell themselves to the bad spirit for the filthy lucre of fraud, made a frightful impression on his mind. The great day which he had passed was especially a day of good will. He recalled to his memory the divine legacy of peace, to chase away unhallowed fancies ; but still, like birds of evil wing, they rise to mar his prayer to God for a spirit of forgiveness. He tried to intercede

for the worst of the worst. At last he fell int
the region between sleeping and waking; but at
daybreak he was buried in a sleep perturbed,
but deep as death: and as he slept, he dreamt.
Indeed, so long and heavy was his sleep, that
he was only aroused from it at a late hour by
the report of a gun.

At the very first break of day Colonel Plowden
was stirring and busy with his steward about
the many things to be done and to be
avoided during his anticipated long absence.
The preparations for his journey and the provisions for his escort occupied great part of the
early morning. He inspected his stables, and
gave a friendly word to his troop. He also
investigated the avenue and reconnoitred the
premises as soon as the day advanced into
light, and satisfied himself that the hostile body
of horse had passed on and only left their traces
behind. Although it was scarcely later than his
usual breakfast hour his impatience at the prolonged stillness within and about the house
began te disturb him. He walked hastily from
one object of interest to another, employing his
thoughts by a hundred details of business, while
he muttered to himself, "Will the people never
show themselves?" It was in this mood, as he
paced up and down a walk, that caught the first
rays of the sun, that Strickland met him. After
their friendly greetings, the Colonel asked his
guest how he could sleep so soundly at such a time

while he had been engaged so long out of doors ?
He asked him what influence the smoking and
the nocturnal expedition had on his repose.
After some hesitation, the young officer acknowledged that his rest was not improved by the
exploits of the evening; but rather disturbed
with visions of the night, and in compliance
with his host's desire he told his dream :—

" A haze passed over my sight. The accents
of a well-known voice once more awoke the
sweetest echoes of the mansion. The warm
gales of spring once more breathed on the
earth ; it soon put on a garb of green in field
and in forest ; and in the midst, sweet opening
flowers, or blossoms of Plowden, were breathing
back again a fragrance to Heaven. Aloft in the
air the lark was carolling ; the shrubberies and
the woods were vocal with melody ; tobacco
plantations sprang up on the distant bank of the
Severn and fringed the river. My eye feasted
on the prospect and my ear drank in the de-
licious music. I was in imagination restored to
those we love. But a sudden sound broke in
upon my gay and buoyant train of thought. It
was the voice of the departing year, which
drowned the song of spring and whirled about
the falling leaf. It spoke of the end of all
things ; it bore a sad prophecy of our busy
projects which agitated my heart — projects
which bore the hopes that would fade away and
leave me desolate. As such thoughts passed

through my mind, a rushing mighty wind swept over the scene, completing the work of winter. There lay mingled the pride of the forest—the majestic oak, and the humble apple-tree. All that remained of the once gay, red, bursting blossoms of the apple-tree had fallen into one unsightly mass of decay. The great Leveller had reduced them to a state of equality; both the oak and the apple-tree lay prostrate side by side. Methought I saw, in each of the oaks now hollow inside, an ancient druid, and on the outside the worshipper to whom he ministered. Also in the decayed and rotten cavity, at the heart of the apple-trees, were the little souls of the firm of Maysfiend and Co., who there worshipped themselves, and enticed the worshipper of the apple-juice to swear black was white. The witnesses having imbibed the necessary potion, which trickled from the ancient trunks, were cross-examined by the judge, before whom we were all placed. They proved satisfactorily to the jury, who themselves loved apple-juice, that we were guilty to all the charges brought against us, viz., first of all, of popery; secondly, of disloyalty to King William ; thirdly, of cutting down and otherwise wantonly destroying the generous apple-trees, which had from time immemorial refreshed, by their invigorating apple wine or cider, the poor labourer, and cheered him through his daily labours. A fine of 10,000 pounds, or the confiscation of

the estates—the recantation of the Faith, or
the full restitution of the apple trees in
that beautiful state of preservation which the
evidence established, was the verdict against us.
The crimes of which we were convicted were so
dangerous to the state and so fatal to the comforts of the poor that no security would be
accepted and no time would be allowed for the
growth of the lamented trees. While you and
our legal friend were deliberating on the best
plan to defeat the designs of the idols enshrined
in the hearts of the apple trees, little Mary, for
she appeared but a child, ran into the mansion
from the lawn, where she was playing with her
sisters. In a moment she returned with a little
carved box, in which there were many seeds
which glittered like gold. She took from it with
her fair hand some grains, and sprinkled them
on the dry earth. Instantly the grass began to
move as in waves, and after a few moments
bright rose bushes started from the ground and
budded all at once into sweetness and bloom.
Another of the girls took a little of the dust,
and scattered it in like manner, while lilies,
mingling with carnations and variegated pinks,
pushed up into sight. So each of the playmates
sowed from the seed-box a different kind of seed
and various flowers accordingly sprang up, each
after its kind, until the beautiful promise of
Spring ripened into the lovely perfection of
Summer once more. The oaks had by magic

started from the acorn into Majesty. 'Now,'
says Mary, 'we may look for something even
still more to the purpose.' She dropped some
apple pips from her box—orchards sprang up
around her : succeeding the dead trees new
flowers of the blossoming apple-trees with
their red bursting buds, blushed into freshness
and life. The sun resumed his sway in the
heavens, and the buds and blossoms come
joyfully forth. The blossoms grew into fruit ;
the fruit ripened into mellowed beauty, and re-
deemed us from the penalties of renouncing the
Faith or resigning the estates. Yet within the
apple was a wicked kernel, which had pushed
off and cast away the fair flower dress, and ever
since had been painfully waxing into harvest for
cider. An apple-tree, thought I, is pretty
enough, and yet in beauty nothing equal to the
blossom.

" The images of the little souls in hollow
apple-trees haunted me and grinned grimly at
me ; their faces were in my dream. The
tobacco with its broad beautiful leaf, on the
banks of the river, grew into a cloud of awful
smoke, through which blazed merrily the flashes
from the guns of the Orangeman's army. The
noise of the firing awoke me ; but still I am
certain there was real firing in the night not far
from Plowden."

" Yes," observed the Colonel ; " the gamekeeper shot a weazel, which has been making

bloody havoc among the poultry and game. Nothing more serious, I assure you, my brave guardsman: but here comes old Goodman to call us to Mass."

CHAPTER XLI.

"This fellow's wise enough to play the fool;
And, to do that well, craves a kind of wit:
He must observe their mood on whom he jests,
The quality of persons and the time;
And, like the haggard, check at every feather
That comes before his eye. This is practice."

Shakespeare.

AFTER their morning's devotions, in which, no
doubt, with the daily sacrifice, they offered a
thanksgiving for God's special protection, and a
petition for a continuance of His mercies, our
party sat down to breakfast; but notwithstanding
all their efforts to be cheerful, and even gay, the
meal did not pass as joyfully as the dinner and
evening entertainment of the previous day.   The
alarm caused by the nocturnal march and halt
of the troops had subsided into sorrowful regrets.
The fact that the two officers were destined so
soon to fight hand to hand the very men with
whom they had long been associated, and whose
victories or defeats had been identified with their
own, cast a gloom over their feelings and their
prospects.   To oppose their countrymen in the
deadly crash of arms—to charge the squadrons
who had often supported them, and desperately

to tear that very standard from a brother warrior's hands—that standard for which the Colonel with those associates had so often fought and bled, and defended together at the risk of their lives —to recognise his former friends now in the ranks of the enemy.

The eventful day of parting, too, was now so near at hand as to exclude every other thought from the mind, though other topics were attempted in conversation. The Colonel was naturally cumbered about many things, but the good part which he was anxious to choose rose above their pressure. According to the faith which he held, the consolations, the sacrament of the altar sustained him. The divine prelude to that sacred drama, the 42nd Psalm, especially the touching remonstrance, rose to his heart: "Deus, Deus meus ; quare tristis es, anima mea, et quare conturbas me ?" The answer, "Spera in Deo, quoniam adhuc confitebor illi, salutare vultus mei, et Deus meus," consoled him.

If, indeed, sorrow had invaded the heart of Strickland, few traces of grief were impressed upon his manly, handsome face. The young man approached the priest and the lawyer with an easy smile, holding out a hand to each, and greeting them with all that joyous feeling which the voice of health and youth can best express. Still, some allusion, even, to an indifferent matter; some chance observation; even the entrance of a servant for orders or instructions;

the tramp of horses in the court-yard, would bring back seditious thoughts and rebellious wishes, and unfold the circumstances of the sad reality, and place them right in view.

Breakfast was over, and yet no one moved; a heavy dreary day had again set in, and a heavier reverie seemed to have settled on all except Wrightwell. He read what was passing in the mind of his client and his young friend, and by way of diversion, rather than serious discussion, said, " While you were at Mass, I interested myself in that service, for I stumbled upon the Council of Trent, read through the most important of its sessions, and have come to the conclusion that our elastic and expansive Thirty-nine Articles are ductile enough to admit of the whole doctrine, and thereby include us all in one net."

" Odds fish!" cried the Colonel, " what a group we should be; neither fish, flesh, nor fowl. Your idolatrous worship of the Virgin goes beyond Scripture, and even the Council of Trent."

" I believe," continued the priest, " that you cannot honour or love the Blessed Virgin too much, if you love and honour Our Lord a great deal more."

In vain, for some time, the company sought to catch the Colonel's eye; but it was bent downwards. At last he looked up, and said, " I am determined, since the destroying Angel seems to have passed, to remain here for a few weeks longer, and hope to enjoy your company until I am summoned to France. I have often wondered," continued he, " at the prayer of the condemned for a reprieve of a few days, or even a few hours; but I realise the feeling perfectly now; for I could give a large sum for even a fortnight within these walls, surrounded by my own people. You will watch over my interests in the place, I know," said he, turning to the notary. " If the world goes fairly with me, we shall probably, in a few years, meet again. If not, calamities will be alleviated by the sense that we have done our best. At all events, your own consciousness of the service you are rendering a family who trust all to you, and whose ancestors confided much to your ancestors, will be your reward."

The next moment horses were at the door for the Colonel, his steward, and the lawyer, who mounted to take a survey of the outlying estates, and to make the best arrangements in their power for the comfort of the tenant, and the interests of the landlord, so far as he could presume upon the restoration of James, or on the justice of William.

Strickland, with the gamekeeper, took his gun, and in the distant preserves enjoyed a capital day's sport; while the priest paid visits to the sick and afflicted, ministering out of the bounty of Colonel Plowden to their wants, and

P 2

fortifying them against the fiery trial to which their faith might be so soon exposed. The occupations and pleasures of the day over, the party met again at dinner, and enjoyed the cordiality and social intercourse which the courtesy, kind feeling, and cultivated taste of the host effectually promoted.

There was much in the very seclusion of Mr. Wilson's life which gave the charm of originality to his remarks.

The notary, abounding in resources of many various kinds, but especially in extraordinary law cases of the period, was a companion and a guest of whom not even the most fastidious could soon weary. At one time he would vividly relate romantic incidents in the civil wars, which he or his friends had witnessed ; at another, he would give a complete and graphic picture of Raglan Castle, and its associations. How the fugitive Charles, was right royally treated there by the wealthy and munificent Marquis of Worcester. How Thomas Swift, incumbent of the neighbouring parish of Goodrich, turned his estates into money, and bringing it to Raglan, desired the noble governor, with whom he was personally acquainted, to conduct him to King Charles. " I am only come," said Swift, " to give my coat to the King ; " and in taking it off, the Marquis pleasantly observed, " the coat. I fear, is of little worth." " Why, then," said he, " take my waistcoat also," which, on being ripped up, was found to contain three hundred broad gold pieces.

"This clergyman," to my knowledge, said the notary, "was plundered thirty times by the Parliamentary army. Such was the loyalty of the clergy." Thus, evening after evening would he amuse the company. As for Strickland, if he had been disposed to make himself the hero of his own story; he had much to relate. The game which he bagged, and his remarks on the varied country of field and flood, of mountain and valley, which he traversed, afforded many a laugh and joke.

They all had for the time good reason to be content with the world.

Seldom, indeed, was the party increased; for the politics and religion of the neighbouring squires and their sons would scarcely allow them to pass an evening with such staunch loyalists, without some very unhappy, if not dangerous differences. Their notion, by no means a secret, was, that such a landed proprietor as Plowden could at any time command an enviable position. The Colonel would rejoin, when such observations were addressed to him, "I might barter my faith and my principles for my domain."

Of the life they so agreeably led, one day was exactly like another. We may easily believe with what regret to all, the hour was approaching which must be their last at Plowden. At length, after the lapse of about two months of labour and recreation, that hour arrived.

A packet, sealed in deep mourning, by a special messenger reached the hands of Colonel Plowden. It was a letter, in the king's own handwriting, requiring his faithful servant's immediate attendance on his Majesty at St. Germains.

It was the decease of his niece the Queen of Spain which had plunged the Court of St. Germains into that deep mourning which needlessly alarmed the Colonel and his guests.

James, it appeared by the communication, was already preparing himself for his departure for Ireland, which has been before recorded in these pages. He had offered up prayers for the soul of the late queen his mother at the nunnery of Chaillot, who had founded that convent. To the fallen queen the sympathy of the nuns was very precious in her adversity; and, together with "her three Angeliques" and Marie Paula, there was, it appeared, a probability of including Marie Plowden one day among the professed. The holy and happy home of the queen was the abode where her young friend would dwell. Like Ruth to Naomi, she was in the mind to say to the queen, "Intreat me not to leave thee, or to return from following after thee; for whither thou goest, I will go, and where thou lodgest, I will lodge; thy people shall be my people, and thy God my God." So much the father had inadvertently let transpire as he read the letter.

A throng of contending feelings seemed to pass across the young soldier's brow ; but there was not a moment for words, even if he could command them.

The horses stood saddled, and ready for the departure of the Colonel and his escort through London and Dover, and for Strickland's northern course. The notary and the clergyman each fell back upon his own province to brave the coming trial.

Strickland, attended by Harry Horseman, was well mounted and clearing the road at a rapid rate in the direction of Chester, but not by the most usual route.

Strickland calculated that by short cuts, and avoiding unnecessary delays, he might reach Sizergh before the final departure of Sir Thomas from that favourite residence for France. He was anxious if possible to consult with his uncle as to what measures he should at once take to insure his meeting with Dundee, in Scotland, in case the commander's orders should not find him.

It was on the third evening of the journey that the young hero and his follower, Horseman, at the conclusion of a hard day's journey, found their resting-place in a small roadside inn beyond Lancaster. No one came at the first, no one came at the second call, to attend to the two travellers, and yet the house was well lighted up, and there was a babel of chattering inside.

After a third call in Horseman's most im-

posing style, the burly landlord at length made
his jolly appearance.

"Ye be a cut above my poor house, which
be'nt fit for such grand quality, said the host;
"and besides, the keeping-room and the back-
parlour are already occupied by some military
officers, who take too much upon themselves by
half; but they are on the strong side; I care
not which side they are, so long as they pay
their reckoning."

Fortunately for Strickland, he was in plain
clothes, as his military accoutrements were
awaiting his arrival at Edinburgh. He was not
therefore under the necessity of making himself
known.

"We be but plain folks, landlord," said
Horseman, changing his silken silvery voice and
accent to that of a rough rustic, and scratching
his head at the same time; "we are making the
best of our way northwards to meet some highland drovers, who have the charge of a herd of
black cattle for us. Any hole or corner, or a
bed in the settle will answer our purpose for the
night."

"There are black sheep as well as black
cattle about, now-a-days, and the sheep dog is a
wolf," said the facetious host. "But if ye be
honest fellows and unable to go on, I must e'en
take ye in; but ye must put up with the company, and take heart of grace to help me to
entertain them."

" That's the thing for me," says Horseman ;
" I am used to waiting on gentle folks ; and my
mate here can sit down with them."

The object of master and man was to find out
the character and commission of the guests, and
to avoid being recognised. They exchanged
cloaks before the landlord could return with a
light. The bar into which they were at first
inducted was so arranged that the inmates could
see persons in the public room, but not be
seen.

This situation, while they were waiting the
further pleasure of the landlord, without any
light but that which glanced through the shutter
from the room in which were the guests, enabled
them to hear the conversation between those
gentlemen which interested Strickland.

" Now the coast is clear, tell us what news
from St. James's ? Does William allow
' rabbling ' the parsons and the churches by
the Cameronians ? "

" By no means, Corporal Hackman ; but
King William, for such he is, has no troops
north of the Tweed, and cannot prevent dis-
orders."

" As thy soul liveth, Master Sawyer, and sure
as thou art stout and godly, the Lord's chosen
will smite the remnant of prelatists and papists
high and bare, and leave them neither root nor
branch."

These two worthies continued their dialogue

together, evidently a Cavalier and an old Anabaptist soldier of Cromwell's time.

"Fear not, my old Cavalier, you shall be drunk, swagger, and swear, and fight over your battles again."

"You be d—d. You and the saints may wear high crowned hats, collared bands, loose coats and long tucks over them, and leather boots to boot; sing your psalms, fall on and beat us to the devil, if ever we give you a chance again."

"In the day that we stood for the cause—the cause of the Lord—the enemy was discomfited, and lo! they fell before the sword, even the carnal weapons of Israel. The hosts did flee before us, and our goodly fellows put their hand to the spoil."

"By the Lord Harry, thou art but a snivelling psalm-singing puppy, for thou hast not even a stoup of Bordeaux to make glad the heart of man."

"Tell me thy commission, and if it be for the good of the Lord's people, I will even drink a little wine then for my stomach's sake, and as a pledge of friendship. But is not that packet before thee addressed to that tyrant Dundee, whose sword is as drunk with the blood of the saints as was ever Cavalier in his cups?"

"Thou art as curious to learn my business, as thou art, god-fearing friend, to tell me thine," said the Cavalier, with a whining sniffle.

" I would be up and doing a little business on my own account among the rabblers," said the zealous corporal.

" We are then both in the same boat, and our voyage is much the same—the cause of the liberator and of our noble selves."

Before the last speaker could receive a rejoinder, the landlord returned to the bar. He had all this time been preparing a supper for four in a second room, which the Gospel-Christian and the converted Cavalier had secured for themselves; but they acquiesced in the proposed admission of the strangers to the same table.

This was, as it happened, just the thing for Strickland; for, having heard and seen so much, he desired to see more. How such emissaries could be charged with a despatch to Dundee seemed to him a mystery.

" Leave it to me, sir, to unravel," whispered Horseman, following the host to the supper-table. " They are schemers; separate them by a manœuvre, if possible. I am up to a wrinkle."

The room was cold, and Strickland still kept on the servant's coat, and let the accomplished Horseman play the first fiddle. He had frequently, for the amusement of the servants, and even the children, taken the part of an old Roundhead officer, in one of Shadwell's plays, and could act the puritan admirably; he was at once hand and glove with the Cameronian, for such he was in principle. The most important thing which Strickland had about him was the letter of instructions from Dundee and Balcarres, which he was careful to keep concealed.

" May I perish," said the traitorous Cavalier, " among so many intriguers, but we are scarcely safe with strangers."

" But we have seen enough of the God-fearing youth here to be at home with him. He is a gifted youth, and hath exquisite talents for a preacher of the word."

Notwithstanding the canting whine of the devil, who could quote Scripture for his purpose, Strickland soon perceived from his manner of quaffing off sundry tankards of old October that the man was a seasoned vessel, on whom strong drink made but a very slight impression. As for the apostate Cavalier, his appearance and complexion showed at a glance that he must have had many a hard wrestle with Bacchus, who had brought the blood to his face—the blood of the grape it might be ; still the jolly god had suffused his face with a perpetual blush.

While the Cromwellian was in godly conversation with Horseman, the Cavalier pressed Strickland to try a fresh bottle of wine, strongly recommending it to his notice, and begged of him to pass it to the good youth, his comrade, helping himself at the same time out of another bottle.

Horseman suspected that stupefaction was in the drink, and this suspicion was first awakened by his own secret observation of what had passed in the public room between the landlord and his guests, whom, through the opening in the shutter, he perceived were in close conversation in a whisper, which did not reach his ear. The only words which he could catch were, " despatches for king James." From what he saw it was clear that the guests not only admitted, but desired the company of Strickland and himself. It was under this impression that he affected to taste the wine, then observing, in a careless manner, that it was their habit to see their horses fed, and if the gentlemen would excuse them, they would repair to the stable, and then make an evening of it. The men, as if suspicious of some design, accompanied them as if to perform the same office, when Horseman managed to let the light fall as they entered the stable, ran back to relight it, and changed Strickland's full glass and his own for the bumpers which were opposite the seats of the strangers.

On his return he invited them all to have a hot joram with the landlord, to which the party readily assented. Here Horseman made himself so agreeable, and acted his part so well, that his new acquaintances, availing themselves of his society and the generosity of Strickland, and encouraged by the landlord, whose opinion

of the last comers was highly exalted by the
potations and their profits. Mulled wine,
regardless of expense, absorbed them and they
absorbed it. The landlord plied them well, and
Horseman, if the truth must be told, sang
something like a psalm, according to the
metrical version of the puritans :

> "Those that were stout of heart are spoil'd,
> They slept their sleep outright ;
> And none of them their hands did find
> That were the men of might.

Harry returned arm and arm with the Baptist.
They resumed their seats in the parlour.

"Here's a health to the godly," says Horseman, "in a bumper. Who says nay?" putting
his glass to his lips, and saying to Strickland,
" Off with it, it won't hurt you."

" Who says nay let him be sconced," says
one and all, and off each man drank his glass ;
and in less than an hour the reprobate Cavalier
and his God-fearing friend, feeling unusually
heavy, tumbled into bed, and were soon buried
in an irresistible slumber, which threatened to
last for ever. To all intents, so far as consciousness went, they were dead. The expert Harry,
therefore, deliberately abstracted from the old
Cavalier's pocket the packet, also a letter from
the inside coat of the Calvinist, addressed to
Lord George Melville, a Whig and a Presby-
terian, who had been convicted of high-treason
by James, but sent from London to Edinburgh

by William, a few hours after the prince's arrival. It had reference to the rabbling adventures, but seemed to recommend less violence, and courted the influence of Melville's second son, David. It was enough to show the diabolical cruelty of the godly towards the priests of Baal and to the established clergy. The bearer was recommended for his zeal to Colonel Cleland, the most bitter enemy of Dundee.

The packet, purported to come from Melfort, threatening death and destruction, and the vengeance of King James on all the seditious and disloyal.

It appeared, by the contents, that similar instructions purporting to be the expression of the king's mind, had also, by other hands, been forwarded to Lord Balcarres, as well as to the gallant Viscount. To intercept this, Strickland conceived, would only awake suspicions which might defeat the very object he had in view,— the safety of the commander. The private instructions cautioned the bearer not to let the packet out of his hands till he reached Edinburgh. The nature of the contents, so alien alike to the policy and the mild intentions of James, struck the youth, and he conceived the despatch might be a ruse, and that it was intended to fall into the enemies' hands, so as treacherously to endanger the life of Dundee. After mature reflection, therefore, contrary to the usual contrivance of men in his position, our hero restored both papers to their proper places, and resolved, in order to apprise Dundee of their contents, to hasten with all speed to Edinburgh, even before the expected directions could reach him at Sizergh Castle; leaving Horseman behind him at the inn, to entertain and divert the sleepers on their awaking, from the immediate continuance of their journey to Scotland.

The groom had orders, as soon as the desired object could be accomplished, to follow his master to a spot which was carefully marked down in his new route for the shores of Cumberland, just opposite the Scotch coast of Galloway.

It was not, however, for some days, that the attendant could get rid of his Cavalier and Roundhead companions, who persisted in accompanying him on his way to meet the herd of Scotch cattle, and fall in with his companion in advance. Even Horseman could not outwit them. They had become cautious and wary. If he rode fast, they did so too, and managed, on the long run, to overtake him; till at length, making himself master of the bearings of Nicol forest, a district of Cumberland lying close to the Scottish borders, he gave them the slip, and came up with his master, whom he had traced along the road before he turned into the dark woods; but not before he had engaged a ship to convey themselves and their horses across to Scotland. The sails were hoisted, the little vessel went gaily through the Frith of Solway, and soon touched North Britain.

They immediately continued their journey inland, but had not proceeded far when they found to their inconvenience and peril that the country was so troubled and excited that they could with difficulty make good their way through the dreary Lothians.

Lord George Melville's son, the Earl of Leven, had just been the bearer of a letter from the new King William, otherwise the Prince of Orange, to the convention of the Estates. This communication had, through the influence of the Whigs, precedence, and was read before the despatch which arrived from James at the same time ; the contents of William's letter excited the enemies of James against him, and grieved his friends. Every vote of the Parliament which had been doubtful, when this letter was unsealed was inevitably lost. The sitting closed in great agitation. The Jacobite lords and gentlemen were in a fearful minority. They resolved on a secession, and assembling at Stirling, everything was arranged for the secession ; but the haste of Dundee and the slowness of Athol broke up their plans.

Brave as Dundee was, he seemed, like many other brave men, as anxious to escape the danger of assassination as he was ever ready to face the enemy in open battle ; he knew well that the furious fanatics longed for his blood. His old

troopers, the Satans and the Beelzebubs, who
had shared his victories, were now the companions of his flight. Mackenzie was on his
legs, lamenting the position of the Estates—at
once commanded by the guns of the castle and
menaced by a fanatical rabble—when his lamen-
tations were interrupted by a sentinel, who came
running from the posts near the fortress, saying,
"he had seen Dundee at the head of fifty horse,
on the Stirling road, just under the huge rock on
which the citadel is built." On this news, the
Convention being assembled, they ordered the
doors of the Parliament house to be locked, and
made the Jacobites prisoners. Leven then went
forth and ordered the drums to beat. The Covenanters of Lanarkshire and Ayrshire promptly
obeyed the summons. The force thus assembled had indeed no very military appearance,
but at this crisis was enough to overawe the
diminished adherents of the Stuarts. Troops
were marching towards Edinburgh from various
quarters.

To avoid these parties Strickland and his man
inclined to the Western counties. Indeed,
Edinburgh itself was in a state of anarchy.
There seemed to be no law, and no regular
troops north of the Tweed. One day the travellers joined a company of drovers, another
they diverged from the main road, striking into
paths and unfrequented ways; and thus avoiding
suspicion or any very serious delay, they at last

found themselves on the right bank of the Clyde, and in a fair line for Glasgow rather than Edinburgh. Evening had fallen, when Strickland and his faithful attendant observed a solitary farmhouse in a wild secluded glen. Their horses were tired, and they were benighted in a strange country; right gladly, therefore, did they hasten to the twinkling light arising from some furze that blazed on the hearth; the smoke having no regular vent formed a cloudy canopy over the assembly whom to their astonishment they found within. Here and there a rushlight was stuck to the walls by the tallow. This dusky and uncertain light showed many countenances excited by anger or elated by spiritual pride. It was the din of debate which first saluted the ears of our hero; but it seemed too late in every sense of the word to retreat.

A deep hum of stern voices, murmuring a lamentation about the abomination of desolation in high places, and the captivity of the land, plainly indicated to the way-worn travellers that the inmates were wild Western Whigs and Cameronians. On the entrance of the two young men, they affected to be unconscious of their presence.

Strickland was recognised at once as a Cavalier by the pale-eyed fanatics who glared horridly and shot sullen glances at him. These zealots had distinguished themselves by rabbling, *i.e.* robbing and outraging the established clergy;

Q 2

such were the men into whose hands he had unwittingly fallen. He was making the best of his way out again, when he found two strong men armed with pistols placed in the door-way. In the attempt to pass them, a crucifix escaped from its resting-place in Strickland's bosom, to the horror of the God-fearing covenanters; and it at once seemed to seal his fate. Horseman, whose face and voice were susceptible of all the phases of the puritanical face and voice, perceived his master's peril; turning his head toward the chief speaker when their was a lull, he whined out in the most sanctified tone, and prayed plaintively "that the Almighty would lift up his hand from his people, and not make an end of them in the day of his anger, till the two-edged sword should be drawn from the sheath to drink gore as if it were water; to devour the flesh of the men of Belial; to slay and spare not till the going down of the sun."

"He speaks right," said a sullen voice from behind. "Blow the trumpet in Sion! Spread out a banner against James Graham of Montrose, the man of blood from his youth up." One of the sentinels, who appeared to be one of the drovers with whom on the road Horseman had acted the puritan, whispered him to come out from the Amalekites.

"Have no part or lot in them; touch not the unclean thing; walk not further with this son of perdition; escape for thy life, and tarry not, thou God-fearing youth. Blood crieth for vengeance. The slayer is behind thee."

To comply with the advice to escape was the work of a second. He mounted the best and freshest horse in the stable, where he had left his master's and his own jaded steeds. He galloped off at full speed in the direction of Edinburgh.

The sudden sound of the horse's feet disturbed the devotions of the fanatics, and aroused their instant vengeance. "The blood of this ram, caught in a thicket, shall be a drink offering and a sacrifice ; bind the victim with cords. Art not thou one of those malignants, whose face is as hard as a flint against the hosts of the Lord ?"

"Thou art a rebel to the truth," said a dark-browed man. "Thou art a spawn of prelacy ; the image which thou worshipest betrayeth thee."

"I am proud to say I am a Catholic," cried Strickland ; at the same time he kissed the crucifix devoutly, and audibly repeated a Pater and an Ave.

"Lo! you see he is none of your half mumbling mass-mongers," said one, taking hold of the crucifix, "but a son of the Midianitish woman ; his mouth hath spoken it : seize him at once, and bind him fast."

He was bound and condemned to die, after one night's reflection on the error of his ways, and to give him time to recant and make one of them.

Hour after hour passed on to the fatal moment. Still the holy faith sustained him; still the sense of honour and of truth enabled him to endure, in fervent prayer, the dreadful interval. Every tick of the timepiece, every breath of the sleepers, thrilled on his ears and through every nerve.

The grey dawn was in the sky, when two of the party jumped up and began to make ready their weapons for the slaughter of their victim. They were actually stealthily approaching the table, on which Strickland was bound, when they were arrested by one who seemed the chief of the party. "Hist! I hear a noise." Strickland listened. The trampling of horses, and the commands of an officer were heard. Several shots were fired by the Whigs; but the troopers, with sword in hand, cut them right and left. In five minutes the prisoner was safe outside, and the thoughtful Horseman by his side.

No sooner had the affray which drenched all parties in blood ceased than the groom informed Strickland of the stratagem to which he owed his delivery.

The young man, finding Edinburgh on his arrival terribly distracted, and not knowing where to seek the viscount, attempted in his haste to gain access to the Duke of Gordon in the citadel.

Arrived beneath it and looking up, he perceived an officer from one of the ramparts making a sign to some one below. This officer turned out to be no less a personage than the governor, the Duke of Gordon. The officer below, who, dismounting from his horse, had climbed high enough to be heard, was no other than Viscount Dundee, actually holding verbal conference with the duke as an indifferent soldier on duty. Dundee soon scrambled down the castle mound again to the Stirling road, where Horseman was waiting, and arrested his further progress by an appeal, backed by such credentials as he was able at the moment of his departure from the old farm-house to abstract from Strickland's pockets. He stated plainly, briefly, and forcibly the situation of Cornet Strickland of the Life Guards to the Viscount. Half a dozen troopers were all he could spare, for he had at the moment but about fifty or sixty in the escort of his flight ; giving a word of command to the non-commissioned officer at their head, and bidding him follow Horseman, he galloped off westward as hard as his horse could carry him.

Crowds of stern fanatics filled the High Street, but the soldiers, preceded by Horseman, went by back streets and unfrequented ways to the old farm house, the convocation of the Cameronians.

A squadron of English men-of-war from the

Thames had arrived in the Frith of Forth. On board were the three Scottish regiments which had accompanied William from Holland. This little force was commanded by Andrew Mackay, a Highlander of noble descent.

Some of the Jacobites had retired to their country seats ; others, though they remained in Edinburgh, had passed over to the winning side, or avoided the Parliament house.

Such was the state of Scottish affairs when Strickland and his party passed through Edinburgh in quest of Dundee, who, contrary to Horseman's supposition after his flight from Edinburgh, had retired to his country seat in the valley through which the Glamis descends to the ancient castle of Macbeth. Here our hero at length found him quiet and tranquil. Some of his old soldiers had accompanied him, and formed a sufficient garrison to defend his house against the Presbyterians of the neighbourhood. Here he might, as he informed Strickland, have remained unharmed and secure had not an event, for which he was not answerable, made his enemies implacable, and made him desperate. Had he been aware of what was reserved for him one day earlier he could have escaped great peril before the opportunity of clearing his character had passed away, which the hostile party had been able in his absence to malign.

"An emissary of James, as it appears from the allegations brought against me," said he,

" had crossed from England to Ireland with letters addressed to Balcarres and myself. Also a letter by the hands of a Roundhead rascal, recommended to Cleland, and a despatch to me, purporting to be written by James to me. The messenger managed to be arrested yesterday; was interrogated, and the despatches found. Some of them profess to come from Melfort."

The gallant Viscount recited the contents of the paper, which has already been before the reader, and continued :—

" Hamilton, by virtue of the powers which the estates before their adjournment, confided to him, ordered Balcarres and me to be arrested. Balcarres is in the Tolbooth of Edinburgh, and now that the warrants are out against me in consequence of the intrigue of the enemy, and not the real message of James, I must at once, and for ever, quit this seclusion even before I can mature my plans or muster forces to meet Mackay. I must, therefore, cross the Dee with my brave troops. From what I learn of you, sir," said the Viscount to Strickland, " I am happy to place you on my staff."

Dundee accordingly, accompanied by Strickland, who was attended by Horseman, took up his quarters for a short time in the wild domains of the house of Gordon. There he held some communication with the Macdonalds and

Camerons about rising. For their military character perhaps, he had the contempt of a regular professional soldier; however this might
be, he returned once more to repose in the Lowlands, and remained there till he learned that a
considerable body of troops had been sent to
apprehend him, in consequence of the letters
which Strickland had seen, and which he now
wished he had secured.

The skilful general then betook himself to
the hill country, pushing northward, till with
his small band of horsemen he arrived at the
camp of Keppock, before Inverness.

The new situation in which Dundee was now
placed, the new view of society which was presented to him, naturally suggested new projects
to his enterprising genius. The hundreds of
athletic men, whom he saw in their national order
of battle were here evidently not allies to be
despised. If he could form a great coalition of
clans ; if he could muster under one banner ten
or twelve thousand of these hardy warriors ; if
he could induce them to submit to the restraints
of discipline, what a career might still be before
him !

The head quarters were fixed close to Lochiel's house. A large pile, built entirely of
firwood, and considered in the Highlands as a
superb palace. Lochiel, surrounded by more
than six hundred brave swords, was there to
receive his guests. Mackay, meanwhile, wasted

some weeks in marching and in skirmish-
ing. The first lieutenant-colonel of the Cameronian regiment was Cleland, the implacable
avenger of blood, who had driven Dundee from
the convention. At length, after many movements and military arrangements, Mackay and
Dundee agreed in thinking that the crisis required prompt and strenuous action.

When Dundee arrived at Blair Castle, he
learnt that Mackay's troops were already in the
ravine of Killicrankie. While the Saxon officers
were against hazarding a battle, the Celtic chiefs
were of a different opinion.

" Fight, my lord," said Lochiel, with an
energy that delighted Strickland ; " fight, if you
have only one to three. Our men are in heart,
and their only fear is that the enemy shall
escape." Dundee's countenance brightened.
His young officer of the staff rejoiced. The
enemy had meanwhile made his way up the
pass. The troops were in a valley of no great
extent ; their right was flanked by a rising
ground, the left by the Garry. Wearied with
the morning's march, they threw themselves
upon the grass to take some rest and refreshment. Early the next morning the heights
were covered with bonnets and plaids. Dundee,
attended by Strickland, rode forward for the
purpose of surveying the force with which they
were to contend, and then drew up his own men,
with as much skill as their peculiar character

permitted him to exert. It was desirable to keep the clans; each tribe, therefore, large or small, formed a column, separated from the next column by a wide interval.   .

CHAPTER XLII.

Thus we act, and thus we are,
Or toss'd by hope, or sunk by care,
With endless pain thus man pursues
What, if he gained he could not use :
And t'other fondly hopes to see
What never was, nor e'er shall be.—*Prior.*

To take in one comprehensive view the disposition of his troops, and to form some fair estimate of the strength and situation of the enemy,
was the next business of Dundee, after his decision to come to an immediate engagement.
Accompanied by a few of his staff, including
Strickland, he cautiously ascended, unperceived
by Mackay, the heights commanding a view of
the Garry, and the undulating neighbourhood.

The wild, romantic, terrible, and ever-
changing scene overwhelmed Strickland with a
sense of its grandeur and gorgeous diversity.
The various tints of the tartans and party colours
of the different clansmen ; the eagle-plumed
bonnets of the chiefs, the glittering of the gold
and silver ornaments, in which their persons
sparkled, the broad swords and other bright
armour flashing in the dazzling, glowing, burning

July sun. The distant shout which awoke the wild echoes of the mountain and the forest, multiplied into a myriad of voices, by the sounding rocks, through which they rang and swelled upon the ear. The clang of fire-arms mingled with the exulting notes of the bugle, the distant masses presenting at different movements aspects which contrasted wonderfully with each other : all wore to him a novel, striking, and terrible appearance.

On the right, close to the Garry, were the Mackbeans ; next to them were Cannon and his Irish foot. Then came the Macdonalds of Clanronald, commanded by the guardian of their young prince. On the left were other bands of Macdonalds. At the head of one large battalion towered the stately form of Glengarry, who bore in his hand the royal standard of king James VII. Still further on the left were the cavalry, a small squadron consisting of some Jacobite gentlemen who had fled from the Lowlands to the mountains, and about forty of Dundee's old troopers. Beyond them was Lochiel with his Camerons. On the extreme left the men of Skye were marshalled by Macdonald of Sleat.

In the Highlands, as well as in all countries before war had become a science of wholesale destruction,—the result of long mental labours, personal courage, and bodily powers were the perfection of a leader. Lochiel was especially

renowned for his physical prowess. His clansmen were big with pride, under a leader who,
with his single arm, broke hostile ranks, and
cut down stout warriors. Yet this mighty
slayer of hundreds had the sagacity to see, and
the generosity to remind Dundee that too much
depended on his life to sacrifice it to a barbarous
prejudice. "Your lordship's business," he
cried, " is to issue your commands, and to over-
look everything ; ours is to obey."

" I must establish my character for courage,
and earn the confidence of your Highlanders,"
said the Viscount. " To-day they will see me
in the thickest of the fight. In future battles
I will be more sparing of my life."

Even while he was speaking, Strickland was
astonished at the fire of musketry that was kept
up already on both sides. Now a few Highlanders dropped from their sight. The sun,
however, was low in the west before Dundee
gave the order to prepare for regular action.
His men raised a shout which rent the air and
bellowed through the rocks. The enemy returned
but a feeble cheer.

" We shall do it now," said Lochiel ; " that
is not the shout of men who are going to
win."

He had taken a promise from every Cameron :
a promise to conquer or to die. This chief,
surnamed the Black, was for personal qualities
unrivalled among the Celtic princes, and said to

resemble Louis XIV., but in size was, compared to him, a giant. At eighteen, when a ward in chivalry, under Argyle, he broke loose from the authority of his guardian, and fought bravely for Charles II. He was, therefore, considered by the English as a Cavalier.

It was past seven o'clock when Dundee gave the word. The Highlanders dropped their plaids. The few who were so luxurious as to wear under socks of untanned hide spurned them away. Lochiel charged barefoot at the head of his clan. The whole line advanced firing. The enemy returned the fire, and did much execution. When only small space was left between the armies, the Highlanders suddenly flung away their firelocks, drew their broadswords, and rushed forward with a fearful yell ; the Lowlanders prepared to receive the shock, but this was at that period a long and awkward process, especially in the heat of action, and the soldiers were still fumbling with the muzzles of their guns, and the handles of their bayonets, when the full tide of the Macleans, Macdonalds, and Camerons rushed down. In two minutes the battle was lost and won. Mackay, followed by one trusty servant, spurred bravely through the thickest of the claymores. The general led the few hundred men he could collect, and, placing the river Garry between them and the enemy, he cast an anxious eye around. The energy of the Celtic warriors had spent itself in one furious rush : he had time to deliberate.

So irresistibly tempting at this moment was the booty to men who were impelled to war, as much by the desire of rapine as the love of glory, that it is probable few even of the chiefs were disposed to abandon such a prize, for the sake of James or his three crowns. Dundee himself might at that moment have been unable to persuade his followers to quit the heaps and complete the great work of the day ; and Dundee was no more. At the beginning of the battle he had taken his place in front of his little band of cavalry ; he cheered them on after him and rode forward. The horse hesitated. Dundee turned round, stood up in his stirrups, and, waving his hat, encouraged them to come on. As he lifted his arm his cuirass rose, and exposed the lower part of his left side : a musket ball struck him ; Strickland was fighting manfully by his side, and threw himself between the general and the fiercest of his personal assailants. The general's horse sprang forward and plunged into a cloud of smoke. Strickland, Horseman, and a brave fellow named Johnson, who were close to him, threw themselves at one bound of their chargers after him. The general and his devoted friends were enveloped in the darkness of dust and smoke which hid from both armies the fall of the lion-hearted general in the moment of victory.

"How goes the day?" said Dundee.

"Well for king James," answered Johnson. "I am grieved for your lordship."

"If it is well for him," answered the dying man, "it matters the less for me." Then turning to Strickland, he said, "Brave Englishman, hasten to your commander in chief before the walls of Londonderry, and tell him what you see—my death and his victory." He never spoke again.

The enemy, bursting through the gap which the general's horse and his three defenders had made, pressed heavily upon Strickland. Horseman supported his master, who fought like a lion over the lifeless body of their commander.

At length Hastings's and Leven's men, who bravely fought to the last, while the rest of Mackay's soldiers were flying from the field, closed in upon our hero still defending the body of his general from insult. Horseman flung himself between their broad swords and the brave lover of his young mistress, and was hewn in pieces by overpowering numbers, before the eyes of him whom he preserved, and who had himself for some time spared the life of the brother and nephew of Mackay, who nobly, but in vain, exerted themselves to rally their men. The former, in spite of Strickland's desire to take him a prisoner, was laid dead on the ground by a stroke from a claymore; the nephew, with eight wounds on his body, weltering in his blood, made his way through the turmoil and carnage to his uncle's side, and was now with him in retreat.

About half an hour later Lord Dumferline and some other friends came to the spot. They thought with Strickland that they could still discern some faint remains of life in Dundee. They wrapped the body in two plaids and carried him to the Castle of Blair.

Mackay, who was ignorant of Dundee's fate, pushed across the mountain to the valley of the Tay.

While the Highlanders, proud of their victory, were carousing and revelling at Blair Athol, the lonely situation of Strickland, was enough to try the firmest nerves. He had, however, his choice of horses on the field of battle and for miles around : he mounted one from the Lowlands, which had fled from the first shock of the battle, and was fresh and powerful. Night had set in darkly on the hills; he was in a desert—he had no guide: his friends were victorious, but he had no share in their triumph. He felt bitterly the loss of his faithful attendant Harry Horseman. Still he bore his brow aloft, conscious that though he did not enjoy the day he had helped to win, he had done his duty manfully, particularly to the dying General. His first care was to be sure of the road. A solitary light which twinkled fitfully through the gloom in the last gloaming of the battle-day, guided him to a small hut, almost buried in the crags and birch trees. The inmates spoke no language but Gaelic, and were at first scared by the appearance of an officer in uniform and well armed. He had picked up a few words of their language from the Scotch nobles who were about the English Court, and understood enough to inquire his way. By their directions, and by the help of a pocket map, or rough sketch of the wild country, he found out his way, but not always directly. He rode all night. When day broke, he discovered another riderless horse, fresh and full of mettle ; he mounted him, leaving that on which he had ridden an incredible distance in its place. The light increased his difficulties and dangers. Leven's men were in sight and in good order ; but fortunately the fugitives turned in the direction to rejoin Mackay. Towards the evening of the second day he had more cause for alarm ; for a party of Ramsay's runaway rabble, who fled in all directions, perceiving in the distance a solitary rider, pouring down from the hills surrounded him. They had in their flight flung away their muskets, and were only formidable on account of the situation and their great numbers. Strickland had cut his way through them, leaving many lifeless at his feet, when a fresh party closing round him in the hollow of a mountain were about to overpower him. At the moment, providentially, as he looked for the best

way of escape, he espied a company of herds-
men in plaids, driving cattle from the lowlands.
"Here they are!" cried Strickland, with great
energy. "Stop, you cowards, and you shall
have enough of it!" The ruse succeeded. In
the eyes and the ears of the poltroons the herds-
men and cattle were magnified by their fears into
an army of Celtic warriors, and they fled. Some
of the same regiment, having avoided the battle,
were killed for their coats and shoes, and the
eagle of the mountain fleshed his beak in their
carcases.

On and on the solitary soldier rode south-
ward over bog, moor, streamlet, and mountain.
Thinly inhabited as the country was, the scattered cotters had already heard of the disaster
of Mackay's men. The news of Dundee's
victory, but not of his death, had even out-
stripped the speed of Strickland, and possibly
made the rough places smooth before him.
But as he approached the Lowlands the report
preceded him that Dundee, at the head of the
barbarians, flushed with victory, was coming
down, and in a week would be supreme at Holy-
rood. Strickland was more than once suspected
of being his precursor, and with difficulty could
obtain a handful of oatmeal and a cup of milk
or even water, and a resting at night in some
hovel or hospitable herdsman's hut. It was
drawing towards the evening of the fourth day,
when, completely tired and wayworn, having

touched no food, and having quenched his thirst
only with a draught from a stream, Strickland
heard, as well may be supposed, with joy the
barking of a dog, and looking up he saw a
shaggy sheep dog, which was baying at the
stranger. Following the animal as he ran before
him, he soon heard the bleeting of some sheep
and lambs, and in another moment beheld a
smoke rising in the clear evening mountain air
above the roof of a little cottage, sheltered in
this nook of the hill above him. Poor as was
the habitation, it was a welcome sight to the
weary Cavalier. The barking of the dog brought
the shepherd out. His solitary life had made
him neither indifferent to the rest of mankind
nor morose. He received the young soldier with
a gladdening hospitality.

The shepherd, a farmer—for he seemed to
have great accommodations for herds of cattle—
said he had been well acquainted with Athol
and Blair Castle, the Vale of Garry, and the
Glen of Killicrankie, for that he had frequent
dealings with the herds of the Grampians. He
had heard from them that the false and fickle
Marquis of Athol had forsaken his clansmen.

"Yes," said Strickland, who, by this, perceived that at heart the farmer was a Jacobite;
"while we and all Scotland were waiting in his
domains to see on which side he would array his
numerous retainers, he stole away to England.
His principality left without a head, his fol-

lowers were for the most part induced by the brave Dundee "—here the speaker shed a tear— " to join us against the Williamites."

" I expect a party of the Egyptians, who are making hay while the sun shines, and lightening the Lowlands of stock, for the support of Mackay's half-starved troops," said the shepherd.

Like every man of every age, he remarked that the world was growing worse daily; that even the old gipsy laws, which commanded them to spare in their depredations the property of their friends and protectors, were no longer in force. But they are going from bad to worse, and in these times they drive away a herd of cattle without any regard to the laws of possession, as in peaceful times. He said the men whom he expected were the bairns of the tall, dark, boney, remarkable looking woman who was preparing their supper in an outside barn, the size of the hut. He then led him to a sort of barn, in which, however, it might have been perceived there was plenty of meat, and preparations were being carried on there by the tall woman, whom the farmer called Madge. To the great increase of Strickland's anxiety he observed there were commons for twelve, probably of the same character as that of the gipsy Madge.

All he could learn for certain was that they were on their way from the Cheviot hills, and demanded accommodation as uninvited guests.

The poor farmer, fearing that the night's lodging might cost his unknown visitor any loss of property about him, if not his life, requested that his guest would for the time make him his purse-keeper, at least if he had anything in his possession which he valued highly. The young officer made a virtue of necessity; and, though not without some secret misgiving, he deliberately handed to him a purse of gold to a large amount, divesting himself of every shilling, and some precious emblems of the Faith, one in particular. The farmer returned him a few shillings, saying, an empty purse on a journey would excite suspicion. This arrangement being made, Strickland lay down on a sort of " shakedown," as old Madge called it, of some straw, but, as we may naturally believe, slept not. About midnight the gang, who in their descent had ordered the entertainment, announced their return with various articles of plunder by the bleating of their cattle, which instinctively felt they were near food and rest. The men soon began talking over their various exploits, in language which would have made a less valiant man than our hero tremble. They were not long in discovering the farmer's guest, and demanded of Mother Madge what she had got in yon corner. She, being instructed by the farmer, replied, " A puir body, wi' a tooom purse and a sair heart; ye maun na spier at him for siller; for deil be licket he's e'en gang-ing hame to his father, winsome gudeman, whose hame's on the Eden—the grandson of old Johnnie Faa."

"May be so, Mother Madge," replied one of the banditti; "but we maun rip his pouches a bit."

The life-guardsman soon heard their stifled whispers, and their heavy steps by his bedside, and found they were rummaging his pockets. Finding only a few shillings, they replaced them with scorn. They caroused for some time, and then threw themselves on the fern-covered floor.

So soon as the day dawned the farmer roused his guest, while the revellers of the night were overwhelmed in liquor and sleep. He brought out his horse, which was now fresh and frisky, and guided him for some miles into Ayrshire, without any mention of the treasures in his keeping, till they were on the high road through the Lothians; he then restored the whole of Strickland's property, nor would he accept so much as a single gold piece.

This adventure alone is enough to show how mysteriously attached to the house of Stuart were persons of every class in Great Britain.

"As my father," said the farmer, "cried, in spite of persecution, 'Charlie yet! Charlie yet!' so say I, Jamie yet! Jamie yet! Jamie shall have his own again. His friends shall never want a friend on the banks of the Doone whilst the poor farmer Sandy Macbride Macnaughton

lives." While he spoke he fixed his eyes on
Strickland, "Keep your face towards the sun,
as you will see it in the heavens. Think not of
me," he said, with feeling worthy of a greater
man ; "but care for your own safety. May God
and the Saints be with you." With these words
he turned back towards the Highlands, and Strickland, in dejected mood, pursued his way with
unabated rapidity over open heaths and an unfrequented country, till about two hundred miles
distant from the battle-field of Killicrankie, as
the sun was sinking into the Western waters, he
found himself in Upper Galloway, amid hills
and dales. Passing over a piece of water, which
divides it from Lower Galloway, to a secluded
spot, on an eminence well dotted with wood,
rising above a fertile lawn through which a
rivulet murmured, he beheld a glowing blaze of
crimson. It was the reflected rays of the setting
sun from the window of an ancient cell or chapel,
a dependent on some old abbey, then probably
in ruins. The heights sheltered it from the
north and the east, while the front opening to
the shore looked upon the waters which divide
Scotland from the coasts of Cumberland and
Ulster. This little Gothic building had only
two rooms. It had through the most troublous
times been a safe sanctuary for the Faith. Here
dwelt a monk who had a garden, in which was a
well of healing qualities. During the civil wars,
as the Protestant doctrine invaded the sacred

precincts, the monk lived in close retirement, only administering the Sacraments and celebrating the daily sacrifice in the chapel which joined his dwelling place. The aspect of this abode was pleasantly inviting to a wandering Catholic like Strickland at the close of the day.

As from time to time the populace of Scottish townlands were urged on by their own feelings, or the instigation of the Godly against popish superstition, to destroy ancient shrines and demolish the beautiful temples of the old religion, which had escaped the first burst of the Reformation, such sequestered haunts of the Faith as this little chapel in the recess of Galloway, escaped observation, or were tolerated as necessary evils. Monastic orders were tolerated in the Highlands, and the rites of the Roman Catholic Church observed there, long after the Reformation had swept the *rooks* out of their nests, which were built in the Lowlands. But under the rule of James and Charles the monks of Galloway had nothing to fear.

Father Bennet, the monk, perceiving a young English officer approaching, and taking him as a matter of course for a Jacobite, received him with great courtesy, but not without some alarm ; for the influence of William was already dreaded by Catholics.

No sooner, however, had he recognised him as an hereditary Catholic in the service of James, than he took the right hand of Strickland into his, saying, " Welcome, welcome, my son, to my poor cell. Your company is a consolation in my solitude and privation, which I could not expect."

The dusty traveller, weary, hungry and thirsty as he was, before he rested, or ate, or drank, poured out his soul in confession through the ear of God's ambassador, in the sacrament of penance. Then in the little chapel thanked the Father of Mercy for his protection and guidance to this holy place.

"And now, worthy Englishman," said the priest, " you are prepared for the Blessed Sacrament to-morrow, which will fortify you for life or death : blessed be God !"

"Amen !" answered the traveller, echoing the pious ejaculation of the priest.

Such refreshment as the place afforded was placed on the table; and, after the evening meal, the exciting events in the Highlands and scenes which Strickland had recently witnessed were the engrossing topics of conversation till the hour of longed for rest.

The dawn had scarcely begun to touch the eastern horizon, when the monk offered up the morning sacrifice, which was attended only by a few devout Catholics, who now scared from the Highlands by the Cameronians, fondly lingered round the hermit's cell, in the remote corner of Lower Galloway. His mission, how-ever, extended to such Catholic loyalists as might be passing to and fro in the cause of James.

After a frugal breakfast, the monk and his visitor explored the coast in search of a vessel to convey our young hero to Ireland. They descended into a retiring bosom of the shore of the Frith and talked over the Catholic interests of Great Britain.

"There," says the monk, pointing to a spot not many miles from where they were walking, "Mary, Queen of Scotland, embarked in her flight to Carlisle. Since that unhappy retreat of Mary Stuart, how many storms have swept over the church in Great Britain!

"The retreat of James, or his handful of Irish troops from the north, will probably be as fatal to his interests in Scotland, as was the rash flight of his beautiful and unfortunate great-grandmother."

At that instant a lonely lamb among a flock of goats caught the eye of the monk. "See how gentle is the poor, solitary lamb in the company of the goats; so gentle was our blessed Lord among those who were not of his fold. So ought we to be among those who are outside the church. When in my solitude I repeat my office along the shore on my way to the sick, how many images of the Gospel rise to my memory and my sight! The wildest storms have left us our vessel securely anchored by the cross, and often a rippling wave sings its everlasting song in deep unison with our midnight chant, and whispering breezes from the Saxon shore tell us of the martyrs buried in the Isle of Saints. I pass many a dreary anxious hour with Him who walked upon the water. I see Him in the dead of night; I see Him at the sad grey dawn of cheerless day. He cheers my solitary song, and guides me over the troubled sea; he is ever with me on this solitary strand. How fast do men live in recollection! The events of ordinary years are crowded into hours."

How far the holy man might have gone on in this strain, associating the "outward and visible things of creation" with "the invisible things of the Creator," we know not, if his thoughts which thus gushed into words had not been suddenly broken. They had struck into a path which traversed the shore between rocks and shingle, receding from the beach, but which ran round a space of level sand, when they heard the splash of oars. They hastened towards the little cove whence the sounds reached them, but jutting rocks and a high mound of shingle shut out every glimpse of the landing place. At length, turning round a projecting rock, they perceived a little boat with her sails all lowered, and her oars shipped, lying tranquilly at anchor in a sheltered nook. In a moment they were close to her, but the crew had evidently landed in haste, for their cloaks, provisions, and other necessaries for two or three men, were on board. In ascending the beach by the foot prints which they now traced, they discovered a rough map of the coast, with a rude sketch of the Lakes of Cumberland and Westmoreland, done in pencil mark by the person probably who had lost it. A quotation from Virgil, descriptive of woods and waters, applied to some of the spots dotted down, were written in small text hand.

" This outline," said Strickland, handing it to the monk, " is the work of some voyager, who will sadly feel its loss."

Before the monk could make any reply, or even glance through the sketch, a paper in the same path presented itself to the eye of our hero. " A packet," said he, hastily. Eagerly he picked it up and examined the direction, and with great curiosity inspected the seal, on which there was a coat of arms ; Argent, on a mount an oak tree proper ; over all a fesse sable, charged with three royal crowns.

In the hope of falling in with the owner of the lost treasures, they followed the tracks, which could only be discerned on the sand. This quiet strand, always lonely, seemed now entirely forsaken. Nothing could be a stronger contrast to the swelling purple hills, splendid visions of mountains and meadows, and rivers, than the sequestered scene through which they were wending their way by a different route to the cell. They reached the door of the lonely dwelling, where the first sight which struck them was the appearance of two young men in the garb of sailors. We need scarcely say, that in one of these Strickland at once recognised Mr. Henry Hough, to whom at Whitehall he had been introduced by the Honourable Clare. His costume was of finer material than that of his comrade, who was no other than Hubert Hunter, who signalised himself in liberating the Demi from the cell in Lady Place, with whom he is now associated as a boatman. It was the task of a moment, after the first exclamations of mutual surprise, to ask and to answer a rush of questions. The opposite, or south shore of the Frith, the woods and lakes, and winding ravines, in the bosom of the mountains of Westmorland and Cumberland were the theme of classical Hough's first burst of eloquent and glowing description ; nor was it until he had his hand in the pocket of a light overall which he had on his arm, that he discovered he had lost the valued plan of the lakes to which he was going to refer, with their beautiful margins and glens, amid a sylvan region of enchantment, which he desired to bring before Strickland's eye. The seal, the address, and all were now no longer a mystery. The finder at once handed the re-covered possessions to the owner, who, blushing, seized them with avidity, changed colour, hesi-tated, looked at the sketch, looked at Strick-land's entertainer, cast his eyes on the ground, then on his workmanship, looked abashed, and made a pause, during which the guardsman, with his wonted delicacy and address, presented the boatman to the priest as the Oxford friend of his brother officer, O'Brian Clare, and a staunch loyalist; scarcely had he done so when a third visitor was announced by Hubert, who acted as porter on the occasion.

"Ah! the good Franciscan, Mansuette, from Lorraine," cried the monk of St. Hubert.

"The same," cried Strickland. "The king's late chaplain; I have seen him at Whitehall. Would that the king had been guided by this mild and reverend counsellor!"

"Ay, the worthy clerk did much, very much for us, as an intercessor between Magdalen College and the king. Ay, far more than his rugged temper was capable of appreciating," said Hough, at the same time making a profound obeisance which silently seemed to ask the priest's blessing; yet, as the priest spoke, he almost doubted his own eyes, for the priest was the last man he ever expected to meet again.

The hermit and the friar exchanged affectionate greetings as comrades of earlier and happier days, but glided into that manner acquired by the Catholic clergy, which veils the depth of inward feeling.

"What news?" asked the hermit.

"Cold news from Ireland, and hot work in the Highlands," said the friar. "There I had

still hoped to serve my late master, the mis-
guided king."

Strickland told all he knew, and said the
king's arms were already crowned with success.

" Only as a gleam of sunshine on the hills,"
rejoined the Franciscan ; " the king's troops are
really divested of clannish interest : only a few
hundred soldiers, chiefly Irish, can be depended
on. Cameron is a spirited leader. But the
king's prospects are buried with Dundee. In
my flight from the cruel Highlanders and Cameronians, whom in my ignorance of your language,
I mistook for the Camerons, under Lochiel, I
have been driven to seek refuge in hills, and
rocks, and caves of the earth. Still Heaven is
our witness, how lightly we value ease or life
itself, if we could preserve the purity of the
Church or restore the sovereign and the Faith to
their legitimate supremacy."

" But what has our young friend," asked he,
" to do with the society in which I have the
happiness to meet him ? The sons of St. Mary
Magdalene had some sparkles of grace about
them which I had hoped would grow into the
perfect day, but I had not dared to anticipate so
sudden an event."

Hough blushed, and answered with hesitation.

" My uncle, whom you may remember, thinks
my voyage is *in mediá tutissimus,* or at least,
that I should rest on my oars, to see which way
the wind blows, recommended me to a maiden

aunt in Westmoreland, with an ample supply of money for enjoyment amid the lakes and mountains of Cumberland and Westmoreland, and my assistant, who let you in, has passed from the service of Lord Lovelace to that of a Loyalist."

" But who, my friend, advised you to court danger on the north side of the Tweed ?" said the monk.

The complexion of the unsophisticated B.A., for such he had become, changed from pale to red, while he hastily replied :

" The advice comes from one whom I value, and courtesies have passed between us of late. But the difference of religion severs us, at least as far as she is concerned. The benefit of your counsel, reverend Sirs," said the Oxford man, holding down his head and blushing more deeply than ever, " might remove the impediment."

" Not unless we knew the lady's own mind," answered the Franciscan.

" To learn that," said the B. A., who was certain there was nothing of which he or his correspondent need be ashamed, " you may read her letter."

" In concert only with all our party, provided that they and you are willing they should share your confidence," replied the Franciscan. All bowed their assent, in which Hough himself fully concurred.

Monsieur Mansuette opened the letter, and

read aloud the following lines, or at least their meaning, in the language of the day :—

"For the hands of Mr. HENRY HOUGH, B.A.,
St. Mary Magdalen College, Oxford.

"MY DEAR FRIEND,—You will think my letter tardy; but *so* many things have filled my hands and my thoughts the last three months, that I have not had room for even *you*. In Ireland, I have lately joined a holy sisterhood, who are disposed to receive me into their community. Thanks for the books which you sent me, which I have read with great care, referring to the early ages, to which you invite my attention. The result of my study is to confirm my conviction, that what you have been taught to call popish errors and novel doctrines, and Romish superstitions, were held in all ages of the Church, and that therefore she must have been guilty of popery from first to last. Indeed, my dear friend, I cannot find any period of history when England was not, up to the time of the new light which beamed from Anne Boleyn's eyes on the religion of our forefathers, in communion with Rome. No party of any age, but the little detachment to which you belong, calls your little establishment *Catholic*. Nor would you in any spot of the world, at home or abroad, ask your way to the Catholic church, when you desired to find your way to your own. The reply would direct you to the Popish chapel, or the

Mass-house. You will see much to amuse you in Bossuet's works, which you scarcely mention.

"In visiting Catholic countries, of every clime and aspect, you will see all varieties of the human species, differing in politics, language, and character, all at the same time harmonized and grouped into one single family, kneeling before one and the same altar ; all receiving the same Bread of Life, consecrated in the same language, and the same unchanging words of the Unchangeable ; all believing in the one simple, plain, and literal meaning. You may see every colour, every outward contrast blended together ; the representatives of every nation on earth in one and the same Communion, within the same walls; whereas, in your 'Pure and Apostolical Branch,' in one and the same parish—nay, more, a handful of men, women, and children, all in the same costume, all perhaps closely connected by the ties of nature, of the same politics, split up into different sects ; divided against each other, divided against themselves; divided in everything but their undivided hatred to Rome. They own no supreme head on earth. Each a headless body, without a centre of union or a dogma. But all this you can observe for yourself ; only leave your insular notions behind in England.

"By all means, as you are bent upon diverting your mind, and waiting to see your way more clearly amid the beautiful scenery of West-

moreland and Cumberland, extend your tour to
Scotland, or at least to the Western Isles,
the hallowed retreats of the ancient faith—
the creed of your fathers and my fathers. When
you have a little reasoning at your disposal,
you can weigh these things; but humility,
self-quelling grace, and a sincere desire for the
truth can alone aid your search.   Than Mr.
St. Aubyn you cannot have a more sincere and
able instructor.   I feel the loss of his company
and counsel more than any other privation.
He has leave of absence from his Majesty, and
is at this moment, I believe, in close attendance
on the wounded, the sick, and the dying under
the walls of Londonderry.   As for my own
address, my movements are so entirely at the
service of others, and will be so absolutely
governed by circumstances, that I cannot correctly give it you, or fix any time or place for
the meeting you are good enough to desire.   I
owe you my temporal life; I would give it back
for your eternal life.   But the imaginary being,
the water nymph whom you have so fancifully
pourtrayed, you would never recognise in the
little sister of mercy, whom even our maid, Di
Vine, cannot tolerate.   I am now going to scold
you for asking me to give you that which is not
mine to give.   No, 'tis not my heart, though
that, too, is given to another, 'tis not that I
mean ; but a lock of my hair, which you might
purchase for less than *half* the world from

Mistress Molloy, forenent the chapel of the king's poor Dublin Palace, once the riding-house of Henry Cromwell, unless, indeed, the spoil is already divided among the damsels of the Irish court. I am really glad you did not witness the affecting ceremony, and yet you would, it appears, have afforded me more than the purchaser, who only gave me four guineas for the gold sheaves which she treasured as though each hair were worth the whole price. There is not a gleaning of the harvest—not a relic of the departed Lily—none to mourn her severed locks! For your devotion and affection I am grateful. But you compliment the fine plumage of the bird rather than the bird herself; you seem to value the head more than the heart. The hair is already converted into a set of surgical instruments and medicaments for the poor sufferers whom I am called to attend. But to be serious, should the beautiful ornament which you so kindly desire sprout into a fresh growth on the head of the youthful vestal again before she becomes the bride of Heaven, I shall send you

> The loveliest curl that ever will wave
> O'er her whom you ventured to save.

Your recollections of *Lily Penderel* are by no means flattering to *sister Martha;* for perfect statue-like beauty in which your fancy paints her is never the shrine of deep feeling or intellect. Mind is seldom or ever found in beauty, but is hostile to it; imprinting from the very dawn of reason a prophecy of wrinkles, and in our teens giving those hints of rugged furrows about the eyes and mouth, which time and wakeful reflection impress legibly upon our countenance. Our poetry, or our own heart's deep sorrows, unrecorded on paper, are printed in cypher on our face.

" Besides, those virtues which you would ascribe to me are more worthy of Venus, or some heathen goddess, than of a Christian woman, and yet you are not far wrong in your estimate of us; for pure childlike innocence and spotless beauty are plants of Paradise, and their seeds have seldom flourished into perfection beyond the hallowed banks of Eden's streams. Yet here and there may such a flower be found arrayed in baptismal purity, more lovely than Solomon in all his glory.

" I wish you could see the Irishwomen tending the sick, consoling the dying, even laying out and helping to bury the dead. Many of the sisters, whom I envy, have become victims to their charity : their places are filled up by others equally heroic. As for the Irish priests, they sacrifice their lives freely. They dread no infection; they have no wives or families to whom they carry it; they bestow their all on God in the persons of the poor, the sick, and the prisoner.

External beauty in the eye of the world is

truly a beautiful, nay, an enviable thing, and draws upon itself admiration. Now, such are the fair daughters of Erin, our Sisters of Mercy, above other women, for kindness and gentleness. The young and the old, the wise and the foolish, feel the influence of personal charms, and too often sigh for their gifts. It is, however, the mere tinsel of the casket, but skin deep; and so is the opinion which values it for its own sake. The ugly child, or even the ugly dog, is generally treated coldly or cruelly, while the pet spaniel, or the spoiled, beautiful child, is caressed, feasted, and fondled. But remember, my philosopher and friend, that in the eye of parental affection, the ugly child, unlovely to the world, is dearest; the faithful cur devoted to his master, to that master is not ugly, but admirable. But I know you will quote scripture against me, as you always do. Long hair is the glory of the woman; not if it ties her to the world, at enmity with God, or hangs her in a tree, like the beautiful captain of old. Your classics will have taught you that air and exercise are the best cosmetics; these you will find to perfection in your proposed tour. In the meantime, we will pray that you may richly enjoy that beauty and bliss which never fade—which the world cannot give nor take away; which bloom in grace, and bear their fruits in glory. But I must desist from this strain.

"My estimable uncle, Mr. Morton, has fallen

back upon his country life at Morton Manor.
He will be your true friend. My Lord Lovelace
stormed terribly at the flight of the ungrateful
Papist girl, of whom he desired to make a
'pretty Puritan.' His lordship will be re-es-
tablished in Hurley; but I am beyond his grasp,
or the influence of the Prince. You ask my
prayers—you have them. But rather ask for
the intercession of the Divine Mother of your
God and my God, your Saviour and my Saviour.
Ask the Blessed Virgin to be a mother to us.
Only pray the pious prayer which the Gospel
sanctions : ' Since thy adorable Son has been
pleased to call us all His brethren, and to recommend us all to Thee in the person of His beloved
disciple, &c.,' John xix. 26. She will then represent to the Eternal Father, in your behalf, the
merits, death, and passion of her Son. Cherish the
memorials, my heart's best gift, for the sake of
Him and her whom they represent. That we
may one day meet in one fold, under one Shepherd, is the daily prayer of your sincere friend,—
LILY PENDEREL."

Having read this letter with the most marked
attention, and the deepest interest to the rest
of the company, Mr. Mansuette himself, as well
as the hearers, except him whom it most concerned, agreed that their differing faiths was not
the *only* obstacle to the union of the corre-
spondents. All parties, however, were vastly
relieved from discussion on such a delicate

question by the entrance of Hubert, who reminded Hough that the tide and the wind
were fair for the Western Isles, and no time
should be lost. Neither wind nor tide could
tear the graduate from the faithful few whom
happy accident had thrown so opportunely in
his way. He placed the "Wild Wave" at
the service of the party. In less than half an
hour Strickland, Mansuette, under the conduct
of Hough and Hubert, were on board the vessel,
bound for Ireland, waving signals of adieu to
their new entertainer, as, still lingering on the
solitary strand of Gallowoy, the hospitable
monk watched the little vessel, till it faded into
a mere speck, like a gull in the distance, then
returned again to his holy duties, his chapel,
and his cell.

CHAPTER XLIII.

Come, and compare
Columns and idol-dwellings, Gothic or Greek,
With Nature's realms of worship, Earth and Air.—*Byron.*

For me the mean thatch'd hut is pleasant,
If Mercy there can find
An entrance to the wretched peasant,
The lowliest of his kind.—*The Sister of Mercy.*

OUR party now felt happy and secure from the scouring parties, who would in all directions be on the look out for the victorious, though dispersed loyalists. The gradual change of evening into night was coming down upon the blended scenery of land and water, into the tranquil twilight. The wind too, which had been gradually falling, went down with the sun. Nothing more for the time could be done by sailing, and the boat was now only gently heaved up and down on the slight swells which sighed along the slowly receding shores. For hours there was scarcely a cap full of wind ; but at length, what sailors call a cat's paw began to play upon the water, indicating a gale rising landwards from the North East, but still the " Wild Wave " was able to lie steadily on her course. Her sails were filled, and she merrily swept through the water.

"At this rate," cried Hough, looking at the chart of the coast, "we cannot make the Fair Headland unless we can gain two or three points. There are ugly rocks, and a reef North by West of the Mull," continued Hough. "My hand and eye are quick enough at the helm, but the canvas requires a practised hand."

"Reverend Father," adds the Isis sailor, "take the rudder and keep her a point to the wind at once: there is a regular sneezer brewing and we shall have it in a jiffey. I myself must trim the sails."

Scarcely had this change been made when Hubert cried to his master, "Sir, his Reverence keeps her well in hand, looking to windward like a jolly sea dog."

Strickland was the first to observe that the wind was shifting another point to the East. "If," says he, hastily to Hough, "you were in the right course before, you will now find it necessary to beat up a bit in order to weather the Mull of Cantire; you cannot make the Fair Foreland of Ireland."

"We may make the Irish coast and have a point to spare; but we want a helmsman whose vocation is to preserve the living rather than to prepare the dying," observed Hough in an under tone. "I would steer, but I must be on the look out ahead."

"Were I myself certain of the bearing I would take the helm," said Strickland, who was no stranger to sailing on an open sea. Things were growing worse and worse.

"We are in for it," cried the soldier.

"Shall I take the helm?" cried Hubert, "you can command, master, and I can at least obey."

No sooner had the huntsman succeeded the clergyman in the post of honour, than Hough, who was better up in the nautical orders than the practical working of a ship, sang out, "stand by there!"

"Ay, ay, sir," responded Hubert, with the air of a blue jacket. Before another word could be uttered, a squall broke heavily over the "Wild Wave," and she was all but on her beam ends.

The Oxford man, though a stranger to fear, was also a stranger to such a sea. He pressed Strickland to take charge of the "Wave," which was now wilder than ever.

"Luff, man, luff for your life—quick," was the officer's prompt direction.

"Ay, ay, sir, with a will," was the seaman-like rejoinder; but the very reverse was done. Whether Hubert was flurried, or whether, what is more likely, he did not exactly know what "luffing" signified, he put the helm hard up. In swinging away from the squall, as if she could not help it, she caught the full force of the gale. She lay down so helplessly over the

water, that all seemed lost, when a jerk, and a
crash like a shot were heard. The " Wild
Wave " had righted. Strickland took the helm
and made easy way under reduced canvas.

" You seem over-cautious," said Hough ;
" surely we are not in danger ? "

" Not danger in a craft like a cockle-shell,"
said Strickland, " at the mercy of the wind, and
actually driving before it into the Atlantic
Ocean ; with the coast of Newfoundland for the
nearest breakwater ? "

" What business have we with the ocean in
our passage to the north of Ireland ? " enquired
the father.

" None if we can avoid it," was the calm answer of Strickland, " our last chance in the present state of the wind and tide is to run her on
one of the islands to the south-west : if we fail
in this, we must drift out to sea."

It was dark ; the melancholy splash on their
lee warned them of land or rocks almost under
their bow. Lights were the next moment visible.
The " Wave " still was flying before the wind.
She could scarcely scud fast enough out of its
way. Sea after sea washed over her. It was a
dreadful moment. The Atlantic, or some dark
strange coast seemed her destiny ; but hope was
alive in the hearts of the tempest-tossed
mariners. Though their physical energies were
greatly exhausted ; yet their deathless faith in the
help and guidance of God, urged them, worn

down as they were, to that active exertion, which in the worst emergency gives the mind relief.

With all the canvas they could safely manage, and oars out, they got her clear of the Isle of Mull, for such it proved, though they fancied it was Iona.

"We may yet," cried Strickland, perceiving the mistake, " drift off Isla."

"We cannot be so far West," observed the priest, as calmly as if he were saying his office.

" There is no chance at any rate, while there is stitch of sail," cried Hough, who began to be alive to his real situation. He had more than once been capsized under sail in the Thames. Partly pulling, and partly drifting they continued their voyage, their little " Wave " at the mercy of the larger waves, which heaved her on their backs.   Nothing, indeed, in the history of miraculous escapes was ever more narrow than that of the little crew, whom chance, or rather Providence had brought together.   From the stupor of exhaustion, they were aroused by Hubert's cry, " A ship ahoy!"   Lights appeared ahead.

" She is bearing down upon us," roared Hough, with all the voice he had left.

" Or," said the priest, mildly, " we are bearing down upon the lights, which appear to me to be stationary."

Strickland shot off one of his pistols, but no reply; then the other—a pause—a musket report —another, and then a blaze shot clearly up before them. They pulled with their remaining strength. They were evidently in sight of succour; but the "Wave" was barely above the water, and could not last another hour.

"'Tis the Isle of Iona," said the Franciscan. " Thanks be to God, to St. Colme, and all the holy monks."

And never, indeed, did God seem more merciful, or his saints more propitious; for the ejaculation was scarcely out of his mouth, when the little boat was left high and dry by a wave on the safe beach.

The fact was, the islanders had expected another party of loyalists, connected with Cannon's Irish army, and fired the musket shots as signals. They served, however, as a reply to the report of the pistols, which was carried on the wind. The lights blazed for the guidance of the party whom they expected, but proved a safe direction for the "Wave." They were hospitably received by the islanders, who entertained them till the worthy little "Wave" was repaired and refitted. Refreshed by a comfortable night's rest, they were early in the morning visited by a priest of the Isles, who heartily congratulated them on their escape from the perils of the deep. The tides, he said, were so violent to the west of Mull that nothing but a miracle of mercy could have saved them. He accompanied them to the ruins of two ancient monasteries, and to the church famous as a

burial place of the kings of Scotland, of whom
no less than forty-eight are there interred. But
chiefly it delighted him to point out to the
strangers the cell of St. Colme, the Apostle
of the Picts, of whom he related more legends
than would interest the reader.

"From this cell," added the enthusiastic
clergyman, "the island, according to Bede,
was called Y-columb-kill."

As early as possible they resumed their course
to the most northern point of Ireland, if possible
to make Dunluce.

After much beating and tacking about in
various directions, partly to escape the rocky
reefs and little islands which studded the sea,
which was yet by no means settled, and partly
to gain some better landing than the uncertain
little bays which indented the coast offered, a
savage variety of rugged crags and fearful precipices lay before them. Under other circumstances the vast structure, which nature had
thrown up as a barrier against the wide wild
sea, would have been an object of admiration.
There was, it is true, a calm lull of the
storm, but it was as treacherous as it was
calm. But it allowed the voyagers to contemplate the scene. Perhaps, in the whole
world, there is scarcely a spot so remarkable
for sublime, picturesque beauty as the northern
coast of Ireland presents to the view, especially
from the sea : an undulating surface extends

for miles. Dreary desolation reigns above the fantastic and gigantic heights. Scarcely had our party contemplated the scene, and ascertained from the holy priest, by a little chart which he carried about with him, that they were somewhere just off the North-West of the county of Antrim, and in an opening of the Atlantic, when vast masses of clouds arose heavily over the heights and hung gloomily from these towering aviaries of the western ocean; and in less than an hour after, the plaintive and soft swell which first greeted their approach became louder. The waves began to rise, and heave, and beat themselves against the iron-bound coast, with deep booming like that of artillery. Every gust threatened to dash the adventurers on the rocks both east and west. The sails were all taken down, and even the mast laid along the boat; they made some way, and had less to fear from the fury of the wind, though the wild waves echoing through a thousand caves, resounded with a hoarse and hollow roar.

Strickland and Hough bent manfully and steadily on their oars : the white water curled at the prow and dashed over the little vessel. They attempted to follow in the wake of a boat gathering seaweed, though the natives left two miles between them.

There arose to the south a promiscuous regularity—a sort of uniformity of confusion, developing at every bound of their boat too much diversity to be comprehended. A considerable way along the coast, the cliffs rose in some parts from two to three hundred fathoms above the level of the sea.

"It is the Giant's Causeway that frowns at us ahead," said the priest. "See the breakers how they leap in mountains of foam; they are striking on the hidden rocks, which the giants are said to have founded, as a causeway between Ireland and Scotland."

The boat's head was right towards the coast near which they observed pillars, some thirty feet high, some more even, and of two feet or more in diameter; above these pillars different strata of black stone, rising in some places to the tops of the cliffs, and some even towering above them like chimneys. At a distance of a hundred and fifty yards from this stupendous cliff, which towered above the water, inclining a little to the east, they espied a path rising out of the water. By this they must escape from their perilous position or perish. The young men's ardour for the adventure seemed to increase with their danger. The "Wave" no longer answered the helm, but madly plunged from side to side, and was rushing into the mouth of a yawning cavern, then was driven raging back again by main force. They could see and hear the boiling surf as it bubbled within; it raved beneath the rock with the voice of thunder, while from the dripping cliffs overhead, the spray came down like a torrent, in which the returning waves were broken. To reverse the oars was the work of a moment, but all in vain : the hungry cave roared for its prey, and as it did so, slowly sucked the craft and her crew towards its mouth. Many a prayer was offered up for mercy, beyond rather than at this side death.

"Let us swim for it," cried the priest, "if we can ; spring across the whirlpool, we may yet be saved."

The next moment the three men were buffeting the waves just beyond the eddying current of the whirlpool. For a long time Strickland, who was the most practised swimmer, and the strongest of the party, supported the priest, and for an incredible time, the three men continued side by side ; while Hubert, who was as active as a cat, stuck to the boat, till she actually ran her head into the mouth of the cavern, when springing up some feet above her, he clung to a sharp projecting fragment of the rock which jutted out almost horizontally towards the sea ; and there he hung over the boiling abyss, into which as Hough's eye rested on him for the last time, he seemed to fall.

To do Hough justice he breasted the waves manfully, and released Strickland of his reverend burden. Nor was it till the priest had unconsciously dragged him under the water

more than once, that he, in defence of his
own life, shook him off. The poor Franciscan
went down heavily, and the dark waters closed
over him, as they swept round a sharp point.

Strickland's grief for his lost friend was heart-
rending, and his agony was increased at seeing
the comrade, who had rescued him from the
perils of Scotland, sinking before his eyes. He
swam to his assistance and supported him to a
little boat which lay at her moorings. With
extreme difficulty he got him into it. No sooner
was this done and the excitement of the struggle
over, than Strickland's anguish for his lost
friend burst all restraint, and he broke into a
torrent of tears. " Oh ! that I had perished
with him ! Oh ! that I had never left him while
there was breath in my body !" Uttering such
expressions Strickland flung himself, in a paroxysm of grief, in the bottom of the boat ;
silently, but against his judgment, blaming
Hough for severing himself from the priest.
The young men were still at the mercy of the
tide, which fortunately did more for them than
their united efforts could have done when the
gale was at its height. Encouraged by the gradual
approach of the little punt which Strickland
had so opportunely secured, towards the acces-
sible portion of the platform where they had at
first endeavoured to land, they aroused themselves and plied the little paddles vigorously.
The rapid but correct eye of Strickland soon

ascertained that the path soon after leaving the platform of rock, on which they were in another moment standing, had originally passed upwards along a steep ledge, but that the constant surging of the tides, or the giving way of the under strata, or some other cause had rendered it slippery and precipitous. There was, however, no help for it. Strickland pressed forward to bear the brunt of the dangers before Hough, who was much more exhausted, came up to share it. At length they appeared to be at the brink of a gulf. A hazy mist hung over it concealing its breadth and depth. Both the young men stood uncertain how to proceed. Strickland was anxiously endeavouring to discover some mode of continuing their ascent, and Hough was proposing that they should return to the boat, when, looking round, they beheld the punt out at sea ; so there was no escape by water.

The whole surface of the stern crags and frightful precipices was as bare as the skeletons of some huge antideluvian monsters, except here and there where the sea-pink, or stunted shrub, grew from a crevice in the rocks. The pathway seemed to sink down into the abyss ; and could only lead to destruction.

" May our Blessed Lady be near us and pray for us now, and in the hour of our death," cried Strickland, devoutly making the sign of the cross.

" The Lord deliver us !" ejaculated the other.

Descending from the spot on which he stood,

by the bough of a stunted ash tree, which thrust itself out of the cleft of a rock, the young soldier was enabled to gain, though at a great risk, a narrow ledge at the lowest brink of the precipice over the gulf, by creeping along which he hoped to pass to a spot from which he could leap to the other side of the abyss, and bring assistance from the nearest habitation to Hough. He succeeded as if by a miracle.

The ledge which supported him, however, became more narrow at every step, till he was obliged to crawl along the giddy precipice, almost invisible to Hough, who accused himself of cowardice in not partaking the fate of his comrade. Strickland restrained his imagination and directed his steady gaze to some object above or before him. The rocky ridge, indeed, projected awfully over the torrent, which raged backwards and forwards to and from the sea like the rumbling of an earthquake. At length the crag rose so high that it was no easy matter, even to Strickland, to climb over it. He took fresh courage, however, and with less difficulty than he had anticipated, soon found himself to his agreeable surprise on that sublime and wonderful parade above the tops of the rocky columns of equal height, and perfectly at his ease. He paused on this lofty terrace, and glanced at the whole expanse through which he had traversed, but could discover little uniformity of design in the grand edifice of Nature.

His position and fears for the fate of Hough obliged him to suspend his natural curiosity, and urged him along the horizontal stratum which surmounted many a succession of jointed columns. At length a turn from this lofty stage to the south brought him within sight of some Irish furze and patches of vegetation in a hollow of the rocks; a little further on he descried two kids browzing on a slanting surface of wild oats, grass, and other green herbs. At the lower edge of this inclined plain he perceived house-leeks springing out of what the Irish call sods. To Strickland's surprise it was on the roof of a human habitation that the kids were enjoying themselves. The less adventurous dams of these graceful little animals were nibbling at such vegetation as they could pick up among the cliffs which surrounded the hut, which was constructed between two fragments of rock that served as ends, with a thatched or rather turfed roof slanting from a front wall of the same material up to the face of a rock. The wall of turf or sods was scarcely four feet high, the chimney little more than a hole or crevice in the rock.

"What being," cried the wanderer, "can have offended Heaven so far as to be doomed to such an abode? and yet it corresponds with Virgil's description of a shepherd's hut."

By advancing a few steps and making a sharp turn to the right, he gained a full view of the

cabin. He looked, and listened, and approached
the opening, which was intended for a door:
dimly through the smoke which arose from green
fnrze and heath, a female form appeared seated
on a stone within. He could see no one beside
her, but distinctly heard a voice of lamentation
and woe, which partly drowned her soft, sweet,
silvery, English accent, in the deep, rich, Irish
brogue, then not dissimilar to what Strickland
had heard in the Highlands of Scotland.

"Ochone! ochone! ochone! God help us.
Its drownded he was. Sure he lies in the
churchyard of Dunluce with the daisy quilt over
him. Sure 'twas his own father that finished
him intirely—the pulse of my heart, the darling
boy, the life of him who sent him to the bottom.
Ochone! ochone! sorra a day's happiness I
will have on airth. Oh! Mother of Heaven, what
will I do? My boy! my boy! cut down like a
daisy in spring! God be with him : he's gone,
he's gone!"

That the effect of some heavy calamity had
stunned if not deranged the mind of the incoherent
speaker, was all which Strickland could gather.

"It was the ould stock which lopped off his
own branch," cried the miserable man. "Yes,
my lady, it was myself that have been after
losing my iligant boy—the beautiful, the brave,
the gay gorsoon. But the heaviest trouble is
that I should be alive, while the darlint who
would have given twenty lives for the father who

drowned him is gone : and I not able to have a
mass said for his soul ! Oh ! God pardon—Oh!
merciful Father—Oh ! Blessed Virgin, comforter
of the afflicted, pity me! I think I see him
this minute, as he lifted his head on my shouldher
with a look that would melt the rock here. It
was himself that was the fine slip of a boy.
When no one else cared for old Billy Stafford,
sure 'twas he that stood by me."

Though Strickland had heard nothing which
could afford him any assistance to rescue Hough,
he had heard more than enough to remind him of
that young gentleman's treatment of the poor
priest.

It appeared by such disjointed and incoherent
sentences which brought any meaning to the
listener's ear, that the mourner had been the
captain and owner of a smuggling smack, which
had, under the mask of her own special occupation, carried despatches between the loyalists
of the north of Ireland and the south of Scotland.
That the previous month, after a successful
voyage, she was on her return dashed, by a
severe gale from the north-west, against the
rocks over which a heavy sea was breaking
between Port Patrick and Fairhead. That the
old man and his son being washed overboard,
both kept above water together, by the skill of
the father, until the son's strength failing, he
clung with such convulsive grasp to the father
that both went down more than once. To pre-

284 THE LOYALIST'S DAUGHTER.

serve both lives became impossible : the parent in his agony reluctantly kicked away the drowning son, who was involving two lives in his own fate.

Strickland was leaving the hut, which he had not entered, when the gentle and soothing voice of the English lady—for such her accent and voice proclaimed her—recalled his steps. To be brief, the visitor was a Sister of Charity from some neighbouring community, for her sympathy and address seemed familiar to such scenes. She warned the wretched man against the sorrow of the world which worketh death. Her very soul seemed tuned to comfort ; in her sweet plaintive voice,

" Discover your sadness to your director," she said, " your parish priest, and resign your-self to the will of God during the meantime. To preserve your own life was clearly your duty, since its sacrifice could not avail your poor boy. May God have mercy on his soul ! "

" There is," he said, " at this moment no priest nearer to this spot than Coleraine, for the clargy all along the coast are gone to London-derry to administer the last rites of the church to the wounded and the dying."

Strickland could hesitate no longer ; he entered. A stalwart, fine, fresh-coloured old sailor met his view, with naturally large mild eyes, which belied the sternly sorrowful features of his weather-beaten countenance, and from which there now flitted that wild and restless light which indicated a troubled spirit and an unsettled mind. His hair, now approaching to white, streamed down, even at his age, profusely over his shoulders ; his beard and whiskers mingled with it, and were as shaggy and entangled as the briars which grew over the neighbouring crags. He cut short whatever Strickland was going to say, calling out—

" It's the voice of the Sassenach, the son of the stranger. Has the young lady told you to come here, or are you an enemy of King James, and St. Patrick, and the Faith ? "

" I am," said the Cornet, " a Catholic, in the service of King James."

" If so," cried the old man, " maybe your honour, if I may make so bould, would say the ' Hail Mary.' He did so, and by his manner and a crucifix, which he presented to the old man, who devoutly kissed it, fully convinced him that the new visitor was a Catholic and a loyalist, though an Englishman.

Though inwardly tormented by impatience, Strickland saw the necessity of gaining the confidence of the young nun or novice before he could obtain any succour.

The lady, however, was the first to open a conversation between them on the dreadful civil war which was dooming thousands to slaughter under the walls of Derry. The young Englishman discerned in the composure of her

manner and her tranquil self-possession a
countrywoman of the higher classes : beneath
her coarse and humble habit there was a grace
and dignity which the religious dress could not
conceal.

"Kind Sister," said Strickland, in a tone of
mild courtesy, "excuse me, if my haste be
unmannerly, but the necessity for assistance is
instant. My comrade, in our ascent from the
sea, is reduced by hardship, fasting and fatigue,
and is unable to pass the abyss in the huge
mountain rocks which now divide him from me."

"You must, indeed, be a stranger," said the
Sister, with surprise, "if you are ignorant of
our present location, and the rock temples over
which you have passed. This is the Giant's
Causeway." She then told him that mercy was
her mission, and a holy sisterhood her family.
She had with her, she said, medicines, restora-
tives, and such remedies as either wounded or
half-drowned patients needed.

"Only tell me the spot where you left your
friend and I will accompany you." So saying,
she took a rope which dangled from the roof,
and, having received Strickland's information,
preceded him with the graceful speed of a
fawn, until she paused at the edge of the gulf
to which he had directed her.

"There is no one," she cried, "you must be
mistaken in the spot. I have been for some
months in the habit of walking from Coleraine

to the Causeway, and I know the chief walks over the cliffs, but there is no passage here."

Strickland could not be in error, for he marked the spot where at the side he swung himself over. He was inconsolable, declaring in the bitterness of his uncontrollable anguish, that he had in the earlier part of the day lost his venerable friend, a holy priest, and now seemed left alone in the world.

"There is," she said, "a narrower fissure a little higher up, more alarming in its aspect but less dangerous in reality, as it displays all its horrors and wears no mask." She had scarcely finished this observation when before them was the narrower cleft. At the far side, in the shadowy twilight, appeared the figure of a man, which, looming in the evening atmosphere, looked gigantic, but which on closer inspection Strickland believed to be his companion, but paused in silent expectation. The figure advanced with apparent difficulty towards the edge of the chasm, just opposite the Sister of Charity, who uttered a scream, which scared a vulture from its perch on a lofty cliff, and pierced the rocky caves, which multiplied a thousand echoes of the scream. The emotion, whatever it was which thrilled through her frame, found an utterance which startled Strickland, and drew his attention to the object which so violently affected her. The lady suddenly threw back the long dark veil

which concealed her noble and majestic features.

No sooner had the removal of the veil exhibited a glimpse of the lady's face, indistinct
though it must have been, than some mad impulse impelled the young sailor—for such he
seemed to Strickland; he withdrew a few steps
from the brink of the yawning abyss, so narrow
at the top, then taking a short run to the edge
of the chasm, he alighted on the opposite side,
within two yards of the fair lady, whose fear or
sympathies his position and appearance had
so terribly evoked. But the edge, splashed by
the spray, was shelving and slippery, and his feet
slipped from under him. For a moment it appeared to the two helpless and astonished beholders, that he must be dashed to pieces in his
fall; but as he went down he clung to a stunted
shrub, which grew from a crevice of the rock.
There he was, dangling over the boiling depths,
for the side of the fissure to which he clung so
painfully was smooth, and afforded no other hold
for hand or foot than the root of the stunted
ash, not more than two feet from the edge,
which, to the inexpressible horror of Strickland
and his awe-stricken companion, was giving way,
and must complete his destruction. Despair came
over the youth; he could make no further effort;
he hung motionless, his hands convulsed in their
cramped grasp of the yielding branch. Indeed,
how he had sustained his position at all was a

matter of surprise to Strickland and the holy sister. No human strength however, could possibly maintain him for many minutes thus suspended over the awful abyss.

To all appearance his last hour was inevitable. Strickland and the Sister of Charity stood aghast hopelessly gazing with strained features and starting eyeballs at the unhappy youth.

"What can we do?" cried Strickland, in a paroxysm of desperation. "Had I two men, we would cling to each other, and thus bring him up." The young woman, consecrated to charity, showed that holy fortitude, the gift of Heaven, which alone can sustain us. Her cheek was pale as the whitest marble; but her presence of mind was beautiful. She seemed to gain language and decision as the peril which required them increased. With the speed of light and all a woman's dexterity she fastened her handkerchief to the officer's sword belt, joining them to the rope, which was too short, then fastened one end of it firmly round a rough crag for the security of the whole party.

"Take this," she said to Strickland; "hold it so that it cannot escape your hands, and should the weight below be too great for us, the security of the rope to the rock yonder, will aid us all."

Having said this, she leaned over till Strickland feared she must herself fall into the chasm, and sprang forward to hold her back. But before he could do so, she let down the rope.

She saw that now even Hough's hold was already
growing feeble ; his fingers were torn by the
sharp crag, the blood was starting from under
his nails. A shudder visibly passed over her.
He turned his face towards her with a mute
prayer for succour, and seeing the handkerchief,
instinctively grasped it.

This was a moment of inconceivable suspense.
Would the knots resist the tension ? Would the
rope itself bear the burden ? With difficulty he
raised himself. The rope seemed to yield fearfully, as if it would snap asunder—the handkerchief had slipped, but it only made the knot
tighter. His next effort brought him within
reach of possible safety—he had attained the
slippery and rocky brink ; but there he lay
before his fair preserver, exhausted and senseless,
still in danger of the gulf. Strickland eagerly
seizing the rope in one hand, with the other
raised his friend beyond the reach of peril. At
the same time, with a heartfelt but subdued cry
of joy, the beautiful young religious fell fainting
by the side of the rescued sailor, in whom she
evidently felt no common interest.

END OF VOL. III.

J. Swift, Regent Press, 55, King Street, Regent Street, W.

www.ingramcontent.com/pod-product-compliance
Lightning Source LLC
Chambersburg PA
CBHW020855020726
47497CB00005B/1415